"Ladies don't swear," he said piously.

Eleanor jerked out another stick and peeled off a length of sheeting. "Gentlemen don't refer to their—their posteriors in a lady's presence."

"Ah, come on now, El, aren't we beyond all that?"

Her lips twitched as she tried to repress a smile. "Your bruises have turned yellow," she told him. When he tried to look down, she said, "Hold still. I'm not through yet."

She was fast and efficient, reaching around him to grab an end, freeing it and then reaching around him again. When her fingers brushed across his navel, he sucked in his breath.

"Sorry. Did I pinch?"

He closed his eyes. "Ticklish," he said. He didn't specify which body part was itching now.

* * *

Blackstone's Bride
Harlequin Historical #667—August 2003

Bronwyn Williams

BLACKSTONE'S BRIDE

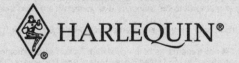

HARLEQUIN®

TORONTO • NEW YORK • LONDON
AMSTERDAM • PARIS • SYDNEY • HAMBURG
STOCKHOLM • ATHENS • TOKYO • MILAN • MADRID
PRAGUE • WARSAW • BUDAPEST • AUCKLAND

ISBN 0-373-29267-8

BLACKSTONE'S BRIDE

Copyright © 2003 by Dixie Browning & Mary Williams

This edition published by arrangement with Harlequin Books S.A.

® and TM are trademarks of the publisher. Trademarks indicated with ® are registered in the United States Patent and Trademark Office, the Canadian Trade Marks Office and in other countries.

Visit us at www.eHarlequin.com

Printed in U.S.A.

Please address questions and book requests to:
Harlequin Reader Service
U.S.: 3010 Walden Ave., P.O. Box 1325, Buffalo, NY 14269
Canadian: P.O. Box 609, Fort Erie, Ont. L2A 5X3

Chapter One

The paneled door closed quietly behind Jedediah Blackstone, shutting out the noise of the lobby just down the hall. Jed had asked for a room on the third floor, but the hotel had already been full when he'd checked in three days earlier. Something to do with politics, this being the state capitol, the clerk had said.

Crossing to the window that looked out on one of Raleigh's busier streets, he cast his mind back over the past few hours. Had he left any loose ends untied? The property had been identified on a large plat on the wall of the land office. The deed had been signed both by him and by the agent representing the railway company, the signatures duly witnessed. The money had been disbursed as he'd requested, the largest portion going directly into his new account at the bank in Asheville, with only enough held out to cover his traveling expenses, which would be minimal, considering the way he intended to travel. And he still had forty acres left over.

For another few days—a week, at best—he could consider himself a rich man. Hardly in the same category as a man like Sam Stanfield, the man who'd had him beaten, branded and run out of Foggy Valley eight years ago for daring to court his daughter—but wealthy enough to keep the bastard from foreclosing on George's farm.

Looking back through the years, Jed had to admit he'd done a damn sight more than court the girl. Not that that had kept Vera from marrying the same sunovabitch who had branded his ass all those years ago.

"Ancient history," he told the pigeon pacing his windowsill. He had too many more important matters to deal with now to waste time crying over spilt milk that had long since soured. Up until George had wired him about the loan Stanfield was about to call, Jed had been in no hurry to sell the property he'd won in a poker game. Hadn't even known exactly where it was at the time, only that it was worthless as farmland, therefore good only for what the past owner had used it for—to try and parlay it into something of value.

But before he could find another big stakes game, he'd heard about the railroad's plans to move farther west, and the same week he'd had a wire from his half brother, George Dulah, describing the mess he was in.

Jed had been in Winston at the time on a meandering trip that would have eventually fetched him up right on the edge of the continent. He'd had a hankering to see the ocean, now that he'd read about it in the encyclopedias. The Atlantic, at least. He had a ways to go before he got to the *P*s.

Instead, he'd headed for Raleigh, where the railroad land office was located. He had taken a room, had himself a bath, dressed the part of a gentleman and set forth to convert the deed he'd won into enough cash money to haul George's ashes out of the fire.

It had occurred to him later that he might have done even better if he'd held out longer, but time was too short. So he'd named a price that was enough to cover the amount of his half brother's loan with any interest Stanfield might tack on, then added enough to cover his own traveling expenses.

When George had first written to him about the drought that had nearly wiped him out, Jed had offered to go back to Foggy Valley and help out on the farm. He'd been flat broke at the time, but he figured another strong back and a pair of willing hands wouldn't come amiss. George had assured him he didn't need help, and that he'd be able to pay off the loan once he got to market with his beef and tobacco.

So Jed had moved on, heading gradually eastward, and continued doing the things he'd enjoyed most: gambling, womanizing and reading encyclopedias. He'd always liked women, ever since he'd discovered them. For reasons that passed all understanding, they seemed to like him, too—a big, rough, uneducated guy who was better known for his skill at cards than any skill on a dance floor.

Before he'd heard from George, he'd been enjoying life, taking it as it came, getting ready to move on to fresh hunting grounds. His half brother had sold his cattle to a drover and come out slightly ahead, but three weeks before the tobacco market opened, his tobacco barn had burned to the ground with the year's crop of burley inside, forcing him to borrow money from the only man in Foggy Valley in a position to help him.

Sam Stanfield. Moneylender, rancher, politician—the man who now owned all the land between Dark Ridge and Notch Ridge. In other words, the entire valley except for the farm that had been in the Dulah family for three generations. According to George, Stanfield was ready to take possession of the Dulah farm, too, unless George could come up with the money to repay the loan, including the wicked rate of interest the old pirate charged.

"Not this time," Jed muttered, dragging his saddlebags out from under the bed. He took off the coat he'd bought especially for the closing in an attempt to look more like a gentleman than a rambling, gambling half-breed bastard with a brand on his behind.

Dressed in Levi's, his old buckskin jacket and his favorite boots, Jed crammed everything else into his saddlebags. As he'd already settled up with the slick-haired kid at the front desk, all that was left was to retrieve his horse from the livery and he'd be on his way.

He would have headed directly for the train station but for one thing. Sam Stanfield's name was not entirely unknown even as far east as Raleigh. Even in the state capitol, Stanfield had friends that kept him informed and Jed wanted his visit to be a surprise. Stanfield had to have known in advance that the railroad was getting ready to make another move, which was why he'd set out several years ago to gain control of as much property in Foggy Valley as he could by driving honest farmers off their land.

George had held out for as long as possible, but when he'd gone hat-in-hand to the bank in Asheville and been turned away, he'd had no recourse but to turn to the man he knew damned well would pull the rug out from under his feet at the first opportunity. The Dulahs might have settled the valley a hundred years before the Stanfields had come carpet-bagging down to the Carolinas, but tradition meant nothing to a man like Sam Stanfield.

Looking back, Jed could see the pattern all too clearly. Like looking at a hand of cards and foreseeing the way it would play out, he'd taken the news about the railroad's westward push through the mountains and added to that the way Stanfield had started finding ways to lay claim to the entire valley.

So far the rails didn't go anywhere near Foggy Valley,

but Jed wasn't going to take a chance that he'd be spotted and word would get back to Stanfield that help was on the way. By now he probably knew about the account Jed had opened in the Asheville bank, knew to the penny how much was in it. The fact that Jed's last name was Blackstone, not Dulah like his half brother's, might buy him some time, but not much.

Jed had a mind to travel the back roads. After eight years of wandering, seeking out card games to support himself, professional ladies for entertainment and public libraries where he could further his education, he was well acquainted with the back roads. In the central part of the state the old wagon trails were slowly being replaced by more modern road, but not back in the hills. There were places there where a man could drop out of sight and not be found for a hundred years.

Eleanor sat on her front porch and watched the sky grow light to the eastward. The only way she knew east from west was that the sun rose in one direction and set in the other. She didn't know what day of the week it was— wasn't even certain it was still April, for that matter. Her calendar was three years old, and daily, or even weekly, newspapers were only a distant dream.

Cradling a bone china cup in her callused hands, she tried to push away the remnants of the nightmare. She knew it by heart now. It never varied. She was trapped like a bird in a cage, being fed morsels of dried corn by people who spoke a foreign language. She would beg to be released—"Open the cage door, please!" she would cry. Might even yell it aloud, there was no one to hear. Sometimes she woke up with a sore throat, as if she'd been shouting for hours.

"Probably snoring," she said. She had to stop talking

to herself. It was no wonder her throat was often sore, the way she rambled on about everything and nothing at all.

The other day she had stood on the back porch and recited the multiplication tables all the way up to the eight-timeses, which was all she could remember. Except for the tens, of course, but that was no challenge.

Her coffee was cold. She hated it black, but they never brought her any cream, rarely even any tinned milk. Only buttermilk, and that was awful in coffee. She set the cup aside, oblivious to the contrast between the fine bone china with its pattern of violets, and the worn hickory boards.

"Three times three is nine, three times four is..."

She thought of the time one of her third grade students had stood before the class and gravely recited, "'Leven times one is 'leven, 'leven times two is toody-two, 'leven times three is threedy-three," and on until Eleanor was red in the face from trying to stifle her laughter.

The entire class was in an uproar. She had barely been able to get herself under control, much less control twenty-three unruly youngsters between the ages of six and nine.

Dear Lord, what she wouldn't give to be back there on the worst day of her brief teaching career, instead of stranded here in the back of beyond, in a cabin on top of a gold mine, a widow, an heiress—and a prisoner.

"I'll have to try again, of course," she whispered to herself, her two laying hens and the big, black-winged birds circling overhead. "Next time they won't be able to stop me."

Shouldering his saddlebags, Jed took one last look around the plush hotel room to make sure he hadn't left anything behind, and then he opened the door. The livery stable was no more than eight blocks away, an easy walk if they hadn't gone and made cement paths all over the damned town. Feet weren't meant to walk on cement, but try telling that to one of these slick, gold-toothpick types that ran the place.

Halfway to the livery, he shed his coat and crammed it into his saddlebag. Hot as blazes, and here it was only April. Too much cement held the heat so that even after dark things didn't cool off enough for a good night's sleep. Time to get back to the mountains. Long past time, Jed told himself half guiltily.

McGee greeted him in his usual manner, by trying to take a chunk out of his shoulder.

"Meanest horse I ever seed," said the boy who had the care and feeding of some dozen animals.

"That's his name. Mean McGee. Call him McGee, though. Hurts his feelings if you call him by his full name."

"I ain't calling him nothing," the boy grumbled, pocketing the money Jed handed over. How much of it his employer would ever see was between the boy and whoever had hired him. Jed had a fellow-feeling for any kid who chose to hire himself out instead of stealing to put food in his belly.

Within half an hour he was out of town, headed generally west. Hearing the sound of a distant train whistle, Jed grinned and gigged McGee into a reluctant trot. "That old sumbitch has got a big surprise coming, McGee. Yessir, he'll blow like one of those volcanoes I was telling you about."

He'd skipped ahead to the *V*s and *W*s last time he'd visited the library, knowing that it might be a while before he got to further his education, then leafed through the *Z* book, where he'd stopped to read about a striped horse. Damnedest thing he ever did see, but other than that, there wasn't much of interest in the *Z*s.

They made fairly good time, stopping each night and bedding down in the open. It was cold, but it felt more like home. Over the course of his twenty-five years, Jed figured he had slept out more than he'd slept in. At least sleeping out in the open, away from towns, he didn't have to worry about any *miscreant*—now, there was a fine word for you—creeping in and robbing him blind.

Three days later he stopped to buy cheese and soda biscuits and drink himself a real cup of coffee. He was in an unfamiliar area, but as the crow flies, it looked to be the most direct route to Foggy Valley. "What are the roads like to the southwest of here?" he asked the man behind the counter, who appeared to be roughly a hundred and fifty years old.

The old man shifted a wad of tobacco and spat through the open door, splashing the red clay a foot away from McGee's big, splayed hoof. "Tol'able," he said. "Old wagon road's growed up some. Most folks takes the new road now."

Jed would as soon avoid "most folks." Surprise was his ace in the hole. One of them. If Stanfield knew money was on the way to pay off George's loan, he would think of some way to stop it.

"Where will I find this wagon road? You say it heads generally southwest?"

"West-by-sou'west. Switchbacks aplenty once it gits into Miller territory. Wouldn't go there if I was you. Rough country."

Switchbacks didn't bother him. Neither did rough country. "How much I owe you?"

The old man named a figure that was several times what the goods were worth, and Jed paid without comment. From the looks of the place, he might be the only customer all week. So far, his traveling expenses had amounted to a dish of chicken pie in Salem and the cigar he'd bought to take to George, to celebrate paying off the loan.

This time the nightmare was slightly different. This time Eleanor was buried under tons of earth, unable to claw her way free, unable to scream for help. She waited for the dream to fade, and then she whispered, "I am *not* helpless! I am intelligent, resourceful and…"

Trapped. Still trapped, despite her determination to escape, in a world that lagged a hundred years behind the times, held captive by a people who were obsessed by gold fever. A people who wrote their own laws and lived by them. A soft-spoken people who were distrustful of outsiders, even those who came into the valley by marriage, as Eleanor had.

They were her late husband's family. Cousins to the nth degree, inbred, uneducated, a few of them even vicious, especially after sampling the product of their own illicit distillery.

Once her breathing settled down, she slid out of bed and made her way to the kitchen, where she poured herself a glass of cool buttermilk. Back home in Charlotte—in her other life—it would have been warm cocoa. Turning the glass slowly in her hands, she studied the pattern etched into the sides. It was one of only three left of the set of tumblers she'd brought with her. The matched set of china had suffered even more. Two days spent jouncing in the back of a freight wagon, no matter how carefully packed, was lethal on fine china and crystal.

The silver that had belonged to two generations of her family hadn't even begun the trip. Instead it had been sold by her bridegroom to finance yet another piece of equipment for his damn-blasted gold mine.

His mythical gold mine. No matter how they might

carve up the earth in search of a new vein, the Millers were deluding themselves, Eleanor was convinced of it. Just because sixty years ago, Devin's grandfather had found a lump of pure gold and a vein that looked promising, staked a claim and brought in his entire family to dig it out, that didn't mean there were more riches still waiting to be uncovered. It meant only that the Millers, her late husband among them, were seriously deranged when it came to the subject of gold.

And just as deranged if they thought they could hold her prisoner here until she married one of them, who would then control what they called "Dev's shares." His grandfather's shares—the major portion of their elusive wealth.

A hundred shares of nothing was still nothing, but try and convince the Millers of that. She'd been trapped in this wild, forsaken place ever since Devin had been killed, and she still hadn't managed to convince anyone that letting her go back to Charlotte would not bring the world rushing in to steal their precious gold.

Tomorrow night she would try again. After last night's fiasco, they might not be expecting her to try again so soon.

Later that morning Eleanor looked around the cramped log cabin, taking inventory of what she would be forced to leave behind. There was little left now, certainly nothing she could carry away with her. Devin had sold practically everything of value she possessed, most of it before they'd left Charlotte. He had obviously thought that because she owned her own home and dressed nicely, she must be well-to-do.

Nothing could be further from the truth. She had inherited the house from the elderly cousin who had taken her in after her parents had died, and could barely make ends meet on her meager salary.

But then, Devin hadn't asked, and she certainly hadn't told him how little a schoolteacher earned. The irony was that they had both been taken in. Devin's charm had been no more genuine than her imagined wealth. Not that he hadn't played his role well. Surprisingly well, considering his background. It would never have passed muster if she'd been more experienced. The proverbial old-maid schoolteacher, she'd been naive enough and flattered enough to swallow his line, bait, hook and sinker.

Looking back, she couldn't believe how blind she had been. Not only had she invited a stranger into her home, she had practically begged him to make a fool of her. Loneliness was no excuse, nor was the fact that the day they'd met had been her twenty-fifth birthday and there'd been no one to help her celebrate. Cousin Annie had been dead several months by then. Her friends were all married, some with growing families.

The truth was, she'd been feeling like the last cold biscuit in the basket. Then along came Devin Miller, stepping out of the haberdashery just as she walked by with an armload of books. She had dropped the books; he had helped her pick them up, and almost before she realized what was happening he was courting her with flowers, candy and blatant flattery. And fool that she was, she'd lapped it up like a starving puppy.

Oh, yes, she'd been ripe for the plucking, her only excuse being that no one had ever tried to pluck her before. Which was how she came to be in a situation that nothing in her quiet, uneventful life could have prepared her for. Held captive by a bunch of gold-obsessed men—the women were almost as bad—who were convinced that any day now, they would all be rich as kings and never have to work another day in their misbegotten lives.

A place where women were considered chattels; education was the devil's handiwork, and flatlanders—people from "away"—were looked on with suspicion bordering on paranoia.

Her first attempt to escape after Devin had been killed had failed simply because she hadn't realized at the time that she was a prisoner. Couldn't conceive of such a thing. She'd walked boldly down the crooked path to the settlement at the base of Devin's Hill one morning a few weeks after his death, and asked if anyone was planning a trip to town, and if so, could she please ride with them as she needed to make arrangements to return to her home.

Her polite request had been met with blank stares or averted glances. Finally an old woman everyone called Miss Lucy had explained that as Devin's widow—she'd called it widder-woomern—her home was up on Devin's Hill.

For her second attempt, she'd waited until after dark and left a lamp burning in case anyone was watching. Sparing only a moment to allow her eyes to adjust to the darkness, she had hurried across the small clearing, her goal being to reach one of the outlying farms she'd seen only from a distance. Devin had once told her that they were not his kin, but they'd been allowed to stay anyway, as their families had been there for generations.

Allowed to stay?

At the time, she hadn't understood the ramifications.

Now she did.

Like a thief in the night, she'd moved swiftly, slipping between gardens and outhouses, thankful for the moon that allowed her to avoid knocking over woodpiles or stepping in any unmentionables.

She'd made it past the first three houses, past two leaning sheds and an overgrown cornfield. Only a few miles to go and she would have been safe. Exhilarated to have gotten so far, she'd tried to plan—or as much as a woman could when she had no home, no relatives and no money.

As it turned out, all the planning in the world would have done her no good. Before she'd passed the last house, the one belonging to the Hooters, Varnelle and Alaska, whose mother had been a Miller, Alaska had stepped out from behind the outhouse, a jug of what Devin had called popskull in each hand and a grin on his long, bony face.

"Where you goin', Elly Nora?"

She could hardly say she was going for a stroll, not when she was carrying all her worldly possessions except for her books, her china and crystal and the sofa that Dev had been planning to trade for a Cornish pump when he'd died.

"I'm going home," she'd told him, knowing she wouldn't be. Not this time, at least.

"Now, you don't want to go nowhere. Poor old Dev, he'd be heart-broke, and him not hardly cold in the ground yet."

By then her husband had been dead nearly two months. After the long, hard winter they'd just gone through, he was as cold as he was ever likely to get. "I just want to go home, Alaska. Back to Charlotte."

"We can't let you do that, Elly Nora."

She'd been so crushed with disappointment she hadn't bothered to argue, knowing it would do no good. Alaska had escorted her back to the cabin. Neither of them had said another word.

And then, shortly after her second attempt at escape, what she'd come to think of as the courting parade had begun. Even now, she could hardly believe it, but the bachelors of Dexter's Cut, practically every one of them between the ages of eighteen and fifty, had waited three months to the day after Devin had blown himself up to try their luck with his widow.

She hadn't laughed—it wasn't in her to hurt a man's feelings, not even a Miller. Instead, she had listened to their awkward proposals and then gently declined every one of them, praying she would never reach a point when she would regret it.

Chapter Two

A hand-lettered sign warned against trespassing. Traveling cross-country as he often did, that was one big word Jed had learned to recognize. But roadways were roadways, and while this one was overgrown, the rutted tracks were still visible.

He could hear the sound of rushing water close by. Evidently McGee heard it, too, from the way he picked up his pace. Jed gave the gelding his head and held on to his own hat as the horse broke through a dense laurel slick to emerge on the banks of a shallow creek some ten feet wide.

He could use a break, and this was as good a place as any. He had saved some of the cheese and soda crackers he'd bought earlier that morning—but first a drink. The sight of all that water made him realize how thirsty he was. Dismounting, he slapped McGee on the hindquarters, knowing the horse was going nowhere until he'd drunk his fill. Founder at the trough, if he let him. Damned horse didn't have a grain of sense.

He was on his knees lowering his face to the rippling surface when a sound and a scent made him glance over his shoulder. One look was all it took.

Ah, Jesus, not now.

Guns and whiskey spelled trouble in any language, but in the hands of a mob of dirty, grinning polecats like the five lining up behind him, the odds weren't all that favorable. His best bet was to get to the other side of the creek, but something told him he wasn't going to have a chance. "You fellows want to talk about it?" he asked, his mind reeling out possible excuses for being here.

One man held an old Sharps bear rifle; another one carried a newer Winchester and the tallest carried a spade over his shoulder. That left two men unarmed, which helped even the odds.

But not a whole lot.

"Have at 'em, McGee," Jed whispered, his hands closing over a river rock.

"We wanna talk about it, boys? 'Pears to me we got us a traipser." Winchester grinned, revealing a total of three long, yellow teeth.

A traipser? Would that be a trespasser? Jed wondered.

"I might have got lost and—" That was as far as he got before the shovel caught him on the side of the head. From that point on, things went rapidly downhill. Later, he would dimly recall hearing a lot of hooting and hollering, rifles being fired and a gleeful suggestion that they tan his hide and nail it to the side of the barn as a warning to "traipsers."

His head ringing with pain, he fought back, the fear of death lending him strength. He even managed to get in a few good licks, mostly with his feet, but five against one pretty much settled the outcome. At least they didn't shoot him outright, but that damned spade was almost as lethal. All he could do was roll with the punches, try to protect his vitals and hope the sumbitches would fall down dead drunk before they managed to finish him off.

His boots... "Ah, Jesus, no!" he yelped, feeling his ankle twist in a way it was never meant to twist.

The smell of whiskey was everywhere. If they doused him with the stuff and set him on fire—

He tried to roll toward the creek. Someone kicked him in the ribs, and then the others joined in, cackling and shouting suggestions. On his hands and knees, Jed tried to crawl toward the bushes, but they followed him, kicking and jabbing him with the butt of a rifle.

"Git that there hoss 'fore he gits away!" one of them shouted.

"Hit 'im wi' the shovel ag'in, it won't kill 'im!"

"You git the hoss, them boots is mine!" The voices came from all sides, like buzzards circling over a dying animal.

"I got 'is hat. Gimme yer jug, 'Laska," someone yelled.

"Go git yer own jug, mine's empty."

They seemed to come from a distance now, the voices...but then everything came from a distance. Either they were leaving or his head wasn't working properly. He couldn't see, couldn't hear, but God, he hurt!

For what could have been minutes, could have been days, he lay facedown in the dirt, hurting too much to move even if he could have found the strength. He could still hear the bastards, but the voices came from much farther away now. Unless his ears were playing tricks on him.

He was afraid to lift his head to look around, afraid that damned spade would connect with the side of his head again. Better to play possum until he felt like taking them on.

Oh, yeah...that would be right after Sam Stanfield apologized for any discomfort he'd caused him eight years ago and invited him to take dinner with him and his family at the Bar Double S ranch.

"McGee?" he rasped. God, even his voice hurt.

No answering whinny. If the damned horse would just move in close enough, he might be able to reach a stirrup and haul himself up. In the bottom of one of his saddlebags he had a Colt .45, but it wasn't going to do him much good unless he could get to it before they came back.

"Git that hoss." Had he heard them correctly? McGee would eat them alive if they laid a hand on him. Wouldn't he?

Jed listened some more. Had little choice, lacking the strength to move. From time to time, hearing the sounds of drunken revelry from farther and farther away, he called to McGee, but either the horse had taken off or he was ignoring him.

Or he'd been stolen.

"Hellfire," he muttered. Groaning, he rolled over onto his back and blinked up at the treetops.

The sun had moved. He was maybe twenty-five feet from the creek now, and there was no sign of McGee and his saddlebags. Or of his boots.

Sunovabitch. They'd stolen his boots, Jed thought, fighting the urge to rid his sore gut of the only meal he'd had since yesterday.

Now what? Lie here like a lump of buzzard bait until they came back and finished him off? It wasn't his nature to run from a fight, but five against one, even when the five were drunk as coots, that was just asking for trouble.

Downhill would be easiest. Trouble was, downhill was where the sound of all that hooting and hollering was coming from. The storekeeper had said it was rough country. Like a fool, Jed had thought he meant the condition of the road.

* * *

Varnelle set the basket of supplies on the edge of the porch and turned to go without a single word, despite the fact that Eleanor was standing in the open doorway.

"Varnelle? Do you have to leave? I could make us some tea."

No answer, unless the toss of a mop of red hair could be construed as a reply. Of the entire clan, the shy, peppery Varnelle had always been her favorite. Any sign of friendship had ended when the bachelor parade had begun. "Is it because you're jealous?" she called after the retreating figure, not expecting an answer, not getting one.

Why on earth would such a pretty girl be jealous of a plain woman nearly ten years her senior? It could only be because they considered her an heiress, the sole beneficiary of Devin's unwritten will. Unwritten only because the Millers didn't bother to write their laws, but obeyed some primitive slate of laws all their own.

"Oh, for heaven's sake, this is beyond absurd," she muttered. "If I don't soon get away, I might do something desperate."

Like shoot her way out. She didn't even have that option any longer since the men had gone through the house and shed, claiming everything of Dev's except for his tooth powder. They had taken his guns, his clothes and every bit of mining equipment he owned, most of it bought with the proceeds from the sale of her house and furniture.

She hadn't argued at the time because—well, because one didn't argue at such a time, one simply went through the rituals, a few of them rather bizarre, and quietly made plans for the future.

For all the good her plans had done her.

"Help me, Varnelle," she whispered to the glossy dark rhododendrons. "Come back and tell me what to do. Help me to get away and you can have anything of mine you want, including this cabin.''

Her clothes? Varnelle was short and nicely rounded, while Eleanor was tall and skinny as a walking stick. If anything could be made over to fit her, Eleanor would gladly hand over every stitch she possessed, even the rose-colored silk she'd been married in.

Oh, yes—especially that.

Her books? Varnelle could read and write—just barely. But she had never expressed the least interest in borrowing any of the books Eleanor had brought with her.

They could have found something to talk about, though, Eleanor was sure of it. ''You could tell me how you manage to make your red hair so shiny and smooth,'' she whispered, touching her own hair, which she managed to tame only by ruthless brushing, braiding and pinning it up before the braids could unravel.

''I'm no threat to you, Varnelle,'' she said plaintively, seeing a glimpse of faded pink some five hundred feet below as the younger woman left the laurel slick and hurried past Alaska's cove. ''In my best day, which was too long ago to recall, I was never anywhere near as pretty as you are. Why do you resent me so?''

Dropping down to sit on the edge of the porch, she nibbled a cold biscuit from the basket and wondered idly how close the kinship was between Varnelle and Hector. Hector was easily the best looking of all the Millers now that Devin was dead. He'd been guardedly friendly to her whenever he'd been the one to bring her supplies.

Miss Lucy had explained when Devin had first taken her down the hill to introduce her to his family, that for years she'd been responsible for keeping track of such things in order to prevent inbreeding amongst the clan. The old woman had seemed pleased at the time that Devin had married an outsider, saying that new blood in the clan would make arranging marriages easier in the future.

Come to think of it, she had mentioned Varnelle and Hector at the time. Eleanor remembered thinking that Varnelle was still a child. She was definitely no child now, not the way she had filled out her faded gowns. As for Hector, Devin had once told her that his cousin had gone all the way through the third grade.

My God, Eleanor thought—she had *taught* the third grade.

"One day, when Heck makes his strike," Varnelle had confided back in those early days when she hadn't been quite so resentful, "he's a-gonna marry me and move to Charlotte or maybe even New York, and we're not niver comin' back here n'more."

"Then who would work Heck's share?" Eleanor had asked. The gold shares were vitally important to everyone in Dexter's Cut, whether or not any more gold was ever found.

"They's plenty that would for a cut."

Share and share alike, that was the Millers. Hound dogs and chickens, moonshine and occasionally even women, but not the gold. At least not with outsiders.

Looking back—an occupation that filled far too much of her time lately—Eleanor marveled at how any woman who had once been considered intelligent could get herself into such a fix. She'd been a whiz at mathematics, good at literature, history and geography, although not quite so good at the sciences. When it came to the subject of men, however, she was no wiser now than she'd ever been. In other words, dumb as a stump.

Rising, she swept up the covered basket that had been left on her front porch in exchange for the empty one she'd set out that morning, and went inside. The house smelled of lye soap. She'd scrubbed the floors and washed the curtains again that morning, more for something to do than for any real need.

Just last week someone had left her a quarter of salty, hickory-smoked ham. She'd been eating on it ever since. Today's piece of fried chicken was a welcome reprieve. Still, no matter how hard she worked, she never felt much like eating. Years from now, she thought, bitterly amused, another generation of Millers would be bringing food baskets to the batty old woman who lived alone on Devin's Hill, leaving them on her porch, dashing back down the hillside, giggling and telling yarns about her.

Probably call her an old witch.

Maybe she would grow a wart on her nose, cultivate a cackling laugh and practice riding her broomstick. Maybe she would send a note down the hill asking for a cat, preferably a black one.

Or maybe she would write a note, put it in a bottle and drop it in the narrow, whitewater creek that churned its way down the mountainside, where it would doubtlessly be panned up by one of the damned Millers downstream, who in turn would guard her closer than ever.

Now she rummaged through the basket again, in case she'd missed some little treat. The last time Heck had brought her supplies she'd been so desperate for someone to talk with that she'd asked him to stay for supper.

"Can't." Crossing his arms over his massive chest, he'd looked her square in the eyes. Not for the first time she noticed that no matter what he was saying, whether he was being friendly or noncommittal, his expression never varied. Blue eyes, clear as a summer sky and just as cool.

"Then let me go home," she pleaded.

"Can't."

He didn't have to explain. By now she knew all the

reasons by heart. She'd heard them often enough. As Miss Lucy had explained, "Chile, they ain't niver gonna let you go. They're all a-wantin' Devin's share and you're a-settin' on it."

"But I offered to give up any claim I might have," Eleanor had explained countless times. "Besides, you keep telling me I don't even have a claim."

The old woman shook her head. "You do and you don't, that's just the way things is. We let you go back to the city, next thing we know they'll be flatlanders a-swarming all over the place, lookin' for old Dexter's gold mine. If they's any gold left, it b'longs to us. My best advice is to take your pick of the men here, hitch up and commence to breedin'."

And so they kept her here. Knowing she wouldn't have any one of them, they all watched over her lest she escape, for if that happened, Alaska had told her, the first single man who saw her would want her.

A fallacious argument if she'd ever heard one. A woman wearing gowns that had been several years out of style three years ago, that were now so faded as to be colorless? A woman whose hair had grown wilder than ever for lack of decent care? A woman valued only for her property— a three-room log cabin perched on top of a hill that was riddled with more holes than a gopher farm?

She was twenty-seven years old, for heaven's sake. Too old to want to attract another man even if by some miracle she could, but far too young to spend the rest of her days in isolation.

In desperation she had offered to deed them all her interest in everything her late husband had once owned. "As a widow, I can certainly do that."

"Might be, but that'd take a lawyer. Once he got a whiff of gold, he'd move in with his fancy papers, and then first thing you know, he'd be a-holdin' his papers agin' us and a-driving us out, just like what happened to the Cherokee.'' It had been Heck who had explained it to her, patient and enigmatic as ever. ''Short o' shootin' him and buryin' the evy-dence, there ain't much we could do 'bout it.''

She'd been playing the same game ever since. Trying to escape, and when that failed again and again, trying to reason with the world's most unreasonable people.

''There has to be a better way,'' she told herself. ''No one can keep a woman prisoner in her own house, not in these modern times. Not here in the United States of America.''

The trouble was, the modern times had never reached Dexter's Cut, much less Devin's Hill.

A bitter laugh escaped her to mingle with the sounds of birds, the soughing of the wind in the trees and the distant yapping of those dratted dogs.

Nice dogs, actually—she'd lured one of them up here a few times for something to do. Something to talk to. He'd even allowed her to scratch behind his long ears. But the dog was free and she wasn't, and so she railed against the dogs, and against her gentle and not so gentle backwoods prison guards.

Devin's Hill, every wild, wooded acre of it, including the creek and the three-room cabin, was still a prison, no matter how lovely the surroundings in the springtime.

No matter how cold and lonely in the winter.

At least she was finally learning to control her anger and resentment, knowing it only made her poor company for herself. But on a day like this, when spring was more than a promise, she was frustrated beyond bearing. Was she fated to grow into an embittered old woman here all alone?

Scratching idly at a poison ivy blister on her wrist—her first of the season—Eleanor sat on the edge of the porch again, her limbs spread apart in a most unladylike fashion, and tried to think of some means of escape she hadn't yet tried. She couldn't think of a single thing. Lacking stimulus, her brain had ceased to function.

Maybe she could bribe them by offering again to hold classes. The last time she'd offered, Miss Lucy, spokeswoman for the clan, had told her the Millers didn't want her teaching them any of her highfaluting notions. Miss Lucy herself taught any who wanted to learn how to make their letters; their parents taught them whatever else they deemed worthy of knowing. All the rest was the devil's handiwork. A more narrow-minded lot she had never met.

It explained a whole lot, to Eleanor's way of thinking.

And now another winter had gone by. Two years since she'd become a bride, five months since she'd become a widow and a prisoner.

It was spring again, and she was so blasted lonesome she could have howled. Beat her fists on the floor, kicked rock walls—anything, if it would have done her a lick of good.

"A lick of good," she whispered. She was even beginning to talk the way they did—a college educated woman.

Some days, she questioned her own sanity. What if by some miracle she did manage to escape? Where would she go? She had no money, no relatives—she certainly would never beg from her friends—but unless she managed to secure a position immediately, she would have no place to live and no way to support herself.

Here, she at least had a roof over her head and enough to eat.

But if she stayed here she would eventually turn into that other woman. The Elly Nora who went barefoot and talked to herself—who whistled back at birds and carried on conversations with chickens. The Elly Nora who'd been known to stand on a stump and loudly recite poetry to keep her brain from drying up like a rattling gourd.

She was just plain lonesome, dammit. And growing just a wee bit strange in the head.

Fighting a sense of hopelessness, she licked her fingers, greasy from eating fried chicken. "Miss Eleanor, your manners are shocking," she said dryly. "Simply shocking."

She shrugged and stared out at the hazy blue ridges in the distance. "Miss Eleanor, you can take your blasted manners and go dance with the devil, for all the good it will do you."

She shook her head. "Talking to yourself, Eleanor?"

"And who else would I talk to? Oh, I do beg your pardon—to whom would I speak, if not myself?"

Lord, she missed the sound of another human voice. Days went by between the briefest exchanges. After nearly half a year of living alone, she would even have welcomed Devin's constant carping again.

From the day a few weeks after they were married when he had rushed in all excited, claiming to have struck a tiny new vein of gold, all pretense of being a loving bride-groom had disappeared. Gone was the handsome, charming young man who had come down from the mountain in search of a rich wife. In his place was a taciturn stranger who came up from his precious mine only when hunger and exhaustion drove him above ground. He even…stunk! No time to bathe, he'd claimed. No time to do more than gobble down whatever food she had cooked and look around for something else of value that he could sell in order to buy more equipment.

She would see his measuring eyes light on the slipper chair that had belonged to her mother, or the little desk where she had once graded papers. Then, in a day or so, one of the Millers would roll up to the front door with a wagon, and Devin would apologize so sweetly.

"It's just an old chair, Elly Nora," he'd said when the slipper chair had disappeared. "A few more months and I'll be able to buy you a whole set of chairs and a table to match. We'll drive right up to the front door of that factory over in Hickory and you can pick out anything you want. If it don't fit, we'll build us another house to hold it all," he promised.

Soon she discovered just how worthless his promises were. Convinced he was only days away from the vein his grandfather had found and then lost, he had worked day and night. Too tired to eat, drink or sleep, he had soon ceased even pretending to be polite to Eleanor.

Eleanor was convinced that his exhaustion had contributed to his death. Hector said he'd miscalculated the length of fuse. For whatever reason, he hadn't made it out of the drift in time. In a single moment, Eleanor had gone from being a disillusioned bride to being a destitute widow.

They needn't worry about her marrying an outsider. Having once been married for her tiny savings account, a small house and a few pieces of old furniture, she would wither up and blow away before she considered marrying another man.

Wiping her fingers on a square of gingham that had been torn from one of her old aprons, she stood in the doorway and tossed the chicken bone outside. "You're welcome, my friends," she said, knowing that sooner or later some creature would come creeping out of the woods to snatch up the bounty.

In the distance, the dog barked again. Someone was firing a rifle. She'd heard several shouts earlier, but couldn't tell what they were yelling about. Drinking again, no doubt. Run a few traps, plant a few rows of corn, pan for hours and dig more holes in the ground—that was the daily life of a Miller of Dexter's Cut. After that, they would take out the jugs of white lightning and celebrate whatever it was such people found to celebrate.

Evidently they were celebrating now. Perhaps someone had actually discovered a few grains of gold, although the noise sounded as if it were coming from higher up on the hill rather than lower down, where most of the panning was done.

Curious, Eleanor sat and watched the shadows lengthen, watched the lightning bugs come out. She listened to the sounds of the dying day, to the bird that always sang just at dusk, whose name she could never remember. To the sound of some small animal thrashing through the underbrush.

Thrashing through the underbrush?

Not her animals. They crept. They clucked and scratched or browsed. They hopped or flew, and a few even slithered. None of them ever thrashed.

Swinging her bare feet, she continued to watch the edge of the laurel slick, searching for whatever had made the odd noise. It sounded almost like...a groan?

And then her eyes widened and she was on her feet. "Oh, my mercy!" Racing toward the edge of the clearing, Eleanor reached out to catch the battered creature that stumbled through the rhododendrons and staggered toward her. A few feet away, she stopped, suddenly wary.

Chapter Three

He wasn't one of the Millers. Eleanor didn't recognize the man as anyone she'd ever seen before. Barely even recognized him as a man, the way he was slumped over, his arms cradling his body as he broke through the laurel slick and lurched shoulders first into the clearing.

She reached him just as he collapsed, nearly carrying them both to the ground. Bracing her feet, she managed to lean her weight against his in a manner that supported them both until she could regain her balance.

"Steady, steady," she murmured. "I've got you now—don't try to move." *Oh, God, oh, God, what do I do now?*

In the dusky light his hair appeared black. Or wet.

Blood? That wasn't water dripping across his face. It was too dark. "Are you hurt?"

Of course he was hurt! This wasn't the waltz they were doing!

"They— I—" Clutching her, he swayed, tried to speak and broke off. He tried again. "Damn," he muttered.

Eleanor replanted her feet and braced herself to support his full weight. "Shh, don't try to talk, just lean on me. Can you walk at all?"

If he collapsed she could probably roll him uphill to the

cabin, but getting him inside would be another matter. Tie him in a quilt and drag him up the steps? Was it physically possible?

It might finish him off. Whatever had happened to him, he didn't look as if he could survive much more punishment. Both his eyes, his mouth…his entire face was battered and swollen beyond belief. Dear Lord, it hurt just to look at him.

"What happened to you?"

"Mm." It was more groan than answer.

"That's all right, you don't have to talk now. Let's just rest a bit."

"Mm!" There was urgency in the single utterance, enough so that she sensed his meaning. He wanted her to…

Hide him? "All right, we'll try to get you inside, but if you have any broken bones, walking isn't going to help," she told him, reduced to stating the obvious. "Lean on my shoulder—steady now. That's it." He was a good half a foot taller than she was, and must outweigh her by fifty pounds. Hard as a rock, but a dead weight. "Don't try to hurry—that's it, one step at a time."

Who on earth could have done this awful thing? One of the Millers? God in heaven, she hoped not, but there was no one else around.

It took almost more strength than she possessed, but eventually they made it as far as the porch, moving two steps forward, falling one step back. "How on earth am I going to get you up the steps and inside?" she wondered aloud.

He held up a shaking hand, silently pleading for time to catch his breath.

Just as well, because she needed time to think. There

was no way she could drag him inside without his cooperation—at least not without aggravating his injuries.

"What to do, what to do?" she murmured, not expecting an answer and getting none. She had managed to help
cousin Annie from her bedroom to the front parlor so that
she could watch the passersby, but by that time her cousin
had weighed barely eighty pounds. This man was built
like…a man.

"Who are you? Who did this terrible thing to you? It
wasn't the work of an animal, I don't see anything that
looks like teeth or claw marks."

Might as well talk to a rock. The poor man was past
answering. It was a wonder he'd managed to get this far.

"Where did you come from?" she asked.

Could he have been coming to help her get away? Had
he somehow heard of her plight and come to help, and
been caught on his way up the hill?

Lord, she didn't want to be responsible for this.

She couldn't even summon help from any of the Millers,
not until she knew who had done this awful thing…and
why. If it had been Alaska, he wouldn't even need a reason, not if he'd been drinking.

"Now," he panted after a few minutes.

"Yes, well—all right—we'll take it slow and easy."
She eased her shoulder under his arm, conscious of the
heat of his body. Aside from the coppery scent of blood,
he smelled of whiskey, but something told her he wasn't
drunk. Could he have come to buy whiskey from Alaska
and got into a fight over the payment?

At the moment it didn't matter. He needed help and until
she knew more, she didn't dare call on anyone to help her
help him. He was wet and shivering. Dirt and dead leaves
were stuck to his clothes, his skin. He was barefoot. One

sock on, one sock missing, which told her he hadn't set out that way.

"Who did this to you?" she asked again as she helped him deal with the last step up onto the porch. Something was wrong with one of his limbs. It was either broken or badly sprained. If it was broken, moving him this way had to be causing irreparable harm, but what else could she do? She certainly couldn't leave him lying outside with night coming on.

From the valley below came the faint sound of more shouting. Someone fired a gun. She had a feeling they weren't hunting. They never shouted when they were hunting. At least, not when they were hunting wild game.

Hurry, hurry, hurry, she urged silently.

They made it through the door, and Eleanor took a deep breath and steered him toward the sofa, one of the few pieces of furniture Devin hadn't sold. "I'm sorry we don't have a doctor, but there's a woman in the village below here who's considered something of a healer."

He caught her hand in a painful grip. Dark eyes glittered through swollen lids.

"What are you trying to tell me?" she whispered. "You want me to go? You don't want me to go?"

He shook his head, his look so urgent that finally she got the message. "You don't want anyone to know you're here."

His response said it all. What was it he feared, that this time they might succeed in killing him? "All right, just rest then for now. I'll do what I can to clean you up, and after that…well, we'll see."

She gave him half an hour to rest before she came at him with a basin and cloth. She needed to know the extent of his injuries. If the man died on her…

He wouldn't. She simply wouldn't allow him to die.

Cleaning him up was embarrassing for her and painful for him. She was no fainting maiden, afraid to look at a man's body, for heaven's sake, it wasn't that. Not entirely. But no matter how gentle she tried to be, there was no way she could discover where and how badly he was hurt without causing him further pain.

"My, you do have an extensive vocabulary, don't you?" she said dryly the third time he let fly with a string of mumbled obscenities. At least he was speaking in words of more than one syllable now.

"Sorry." It was more a groan than an apology.

"Never mind, I've heard worse than that from little boys."

She hadn't, but he didn't need to know it. If she didn't know better she might have thought the twitch of his swollen mouth was a smile.

Later that evening Eleanor lit the parlor lamp. Her guest was still on the sofa, which was not a good fit. As tall as she was, she could barely lie flat on it. The stranger was several inches taller. His neck was bent at an awkward angle that the pillow didn't do much to alleviate.

She eyed the distance between there and the bedroom door, a matter of less than ten feet. The cabin was basically a square, with one side being taken up by what she termed a parlor, the other with a kitchen and a closed-off bedroom.

"We need to move you to the bedroom," she said, standing back to survey the damage now that she'd cleaned him up some. He'd been wearing a buckskin coat, but one of the sleeves had been dangling by a thread, almost as if someone had tried to pull it off.

He looked at her. At least she thought he did. With those swollen eyes, it was impossible to be certain. "Do you think you can move if I support your left side?" It was his left ankle that was swollen. "You could use the broom as a crutch."

He mumbled something and she said, "Is that a yes or a no?"

More mumbling. One hand lifted and she thought he pointed to the window. "Close it? Open it wider?"

More swearing. At least that's what it sounded like. He could barely move his lips.

Hands on her hips, she said, "All right, I'm going to suggest a few things. If I'm right, nod your head." Which would probably hurt, too, but they weren't getting anywhere using words. "You're hot. You want me to open the window."

Was that a nod, or a negative? He barely moved.

She tried again. "You want me to hide you in case whoever did this comes looking for you."

This time there was another stream of curses, followed by a groan. She leaned over and whispered, "Shh, don't try to say any more, I understand."

Oh, yes, she understood. The Millers distrusted all strangers. This man was a stranger, an angry stranger if she were any judge. Who could blame him if this was an indication of their hospitality?

"Never mind, I know you can't talk, but you might as well know it now—sometimes I tend to talk too much. Comes of living alone," she said as she lifted the afghan she'd spread over him when she'd peeled him down to his long underwear. That, too, was wet as if he'd been caught in a downpour—or dunked in the creek—but she hadn't been able to bring herself to strip him completely bare.

"All right then, let's see if you can sit up. It's only a few steps away—right over there where the door is." Torn between wariness and sympathy, she studied her unexpected guest and tried to think of some way to make the transfer easier.

There was simply no way. As gentle as she'd tried to be, he had groaned when she'd peeled his muddy blue jeans down over his bare foot. Hopefully it wasn't broken, but even a sprain could be painful.

She positioned herself on his good side and slid one arm under his, taking most of his weight on her shoulder. He groaned. She grunted. "Don't worry," she managed. "I'm a lot stronger than I look."

Working together they managed to get him onto his feet. Or rather, onto his foot. With her on one side and the broom on the other serving as a crutch, he hobbled toward the back of the cabin.

His body felt unnaturally hot, and she wondered how long he'd been lying out in the woods before he'd found his way to her cabin. If he was already feverish, it could be either lung fever or an infection of one of his wounds. Surely it was too soon for that. But then, she still didn't know the full extent of his injuries. Wouldn't until she got him out of his underwear.

Feeling her face flush, she told herself she would worry about that later. For now, she needed to get him onto the bed before he collapsed. Then she could start by cutting off the tight cuff of his long johns. It had to be constricting circulation, with that swollen ankle.

If he had internal injuries, she could only pray that they were minor. She should have paid more attention to biology as a student, but at the time she couldn't picture a situation where knowing how a frog was constructed would be of any value.

He practically fell across the bed, giving her mere seconds to sweep the covers aside first. Then she had to reposition his heavy limbs until he was lying more or less straight on the feather tick. Her sheets would be wet clean through, but that was the least of her worries.

What on earth was she going to do with him? He was too big to hide under the bed, even if he could crawl under there. There was simply no place else to hide, but if the Millers were to show up—if they were to come inside and discover that she was harboring a strange man…

They couldn't. Chances were they'd been the ones to do this to him, but even if they hadn't, they hated strangers. They would drag him away, and in his present condition, he might not survive their rough handling.

"Think, Eleanor, think!"

He focused a bleary eye on her face, and she said, "Sorry—I told you I tend to talk to myself."

All right, she was thinking. What if he were a fugitive? A bank robber? A train robber? What if the sheriff was after him and had followed him here? In that case, she could be arrested as an accomplice.

On the other hand, if she explained how she'd found him and they took him away, she could insist on going with them. Not even the Millers would risk trying to hold her against her will with a sheriff as witness.

"No. Don't even think about that now," she muttered. Whoever or whatever this man was, he was no threat to anyone in his present condition. He certainly didn't need any lawmen dragging him down the mountain. What he needed was to sleep until he could tell her where he hurt, what to do about it, who did this to him and whether or not they were likely to follow him here.

At the moment, though, she needed to get him up long enough to peel the rest of those wet clothes off his poor battered body. If the parts that were hidden were in as bad shape as the parts that were visible, he might not even survive the night.

And if he died...

"Don't even think about it," she muttered as she turned to her sewing basket to find her scissors.

"Mm?"

"I wasn't talking to you," she said hurriedly, fingering the thick knit of his long johns. "That is, I was, but I don't expect a reply. I think I might have mentioned that I tend to talk to myself occasionally."

This time when he said, "Mm," it was without the questioning inflection. In other words, she translated, "I hear you, woman."

One piece. She would have to cut around the waist and pull them off in both directions. A blindfold might help her modesty, but it wouldn't help get the job done.

"Be still now, don't move," she cautioned, and positioning the scissors, she slit the left leg of his underwear up to his knee, wincing at the way the cuff had cut into his swollen ankle. Between bruises and abrasions, his skin was a lovely golden color, like well-polished maple.

"I'll be as gentle as possible, but we have to get you out of these wet clothes before you catch pneumonia." She cut all the way around just under the knee, then lifted the remnant away. Now all she had to do was get the top part off, then she would worry about what came next.

"Here, let me cover you with this," she said, unfolding the crocheted afghan she had found in Cousin Annie's hope chest after her cousin had died. She had wept gallons at the time, but being the practical woman she was, she'd packed it in her own hope chest, which by then she had thought of as her hopeless chest.

She covered his midsection and began unfastening the bone buttons that led from the hollow of his throat all the way down to...

Wherever. "You look like you were dragged all over

the mountain," she said, seeing that one eye was slightly open.

No reply. He appeared to be fascinated by the unadorned whitewashed walls. The poor man had to be every bit as embarrassed as she was, letting himself be cut out of his underwear by a strange woman.

She continued to chatter to take both their minds off what she was doing. "I thought at first you might have tangled with a bear, but I'm pretty sure there aren't any bear caves around here, at least not any longer. I think the mining must have driven them away."

Accustomed to conversing with herself, she didn't wait for a response. "There, roll over a little bit so I can cut around your waist. I'm just going to cut the top part loose and pull it off first." Leaning over him, she tried to roll him onto his side. She got no farther than halfway when he let out a sharp cry.

"I'm sorry!" He must have internal injuries, and here she'd been lugging him around like a favorite doll.

She waited for him to catch his breath, then eased him onto his back again and reached for her scissors. "I think this will be easier, don't you?" She began to cut. First the right sleeve, then the left, severing it from the body of the garment near the shoulder. There were bruises, but so far as she could tell, nothing was broken. At least nothing visible.

Stepping back, she surveyed the rest of the garment, aware of the beautiful shape of his muscular arms. He wasn't knotty, the way some of the Miller men were—the way even Devin had been. Instead, he was smooth and golden, his forearms reminding her of Michelangelo's statue of David.

Mercy!

"All right, here's what we'll do then," she announced.

General Eleanor, advising the troops of her battle plan. "I'm going to cut away your union suit." She was holding the scissors up in her right hand.

His eyes widened so that she actually caught a glimmer of the darkness behind his poor swollen lids. Obsidian was the term that came to mind. "Mm-mm," he warned.

"Mm-*hm*," she countered. "I'll simply cut it up from the bottom to where it opens down the front, and then pull it out from under you. It has to be done, you know, else you'll catch your death, lying in a wet bed. I'll be as gentle as I possibly can."

With the afghan spread over his middle for modesty as well as warmth, she positioned the scissors. His eyes widened still more, until she could see that his eyes were brown, not black. Topaz, not obsidian. They only looked black because his pupils were enlarged from…pain? Fear?

"I won't hurt you," she said softly, reassuringly. "I would never deliberately hurt anyone." And just as she began to cut away the sodden fabric, the oddest feeling came over her. Staring down at the stranger on her bed, with all his injuries—with his face swollen and discolored—she felt something almost akin to…recognition.

Which was beyond absurd. If she'd ever seen him before in her life, she would have remembered. He wasn't the kind of man, even in his present deplorable condition, that any woman could forget.

"Oh, for heaven's sake," she muttered, embarrassed by her own reaction.

Fortunately, he couldn't see her flaming face. His eyes closed and remained shut until she had cut almost all the way to his groin.

"No."

The single word momentarily stayed her hand. "We

agreed, you can't lie around in wet clothes. I'm going to cut across to the placket and—''

"Madam," he said just as clearly as if his lips weren't swollen like a split melon, "you're not getting anywhere near my privates with those scissors of yours. Leave me be and I'll get undressed.''

"Well for heaven's sake." She laid the scissors down on the table beside the bed. "I wasn't planning to do you any harm, I only wanted to make it easier for you.''

Her face must be steaming by now. She knew as much about a man's anatomy as any other woman who had been married for nearly two years. That is, she knew where it differed from a woman's, and which parts were more sensitive than others. She hadn't planned on getting anywhere near those particular parts, but if he thought he could do better, then let him. At least he was speaking now.

"I'll just go—go and put the kettle on, then. Call me when you're done.''

Chapter Four

He was asleep when she returned, giving her time to study his face. The horrid swelling around his eyes was already discolored, his lips split and swollen. The square jaw bore not only a shallow cleft in the center of his chin, but two cuts and a darkening bruise.

Suddenly, she had a feeling of being watched. His eyes were closed, his breathing even. Living alone had obviously distorted her senses. "Are you awake?" she whispered.

The shadowy beginnings of a beard darkened his face, which would make cleaning him up more difficult, but the twins had taken Devin's shaving things. Besides, after the way he'd reacted to her scissors, she wasn't particularly eager to approach him with a straight razor. "Hello-o," she caroled softly. "You probably should try to stay awake until we're certain that lump on your head is only skin-deep."

Brain damage. My God, what should she do about that? Had he said anything that made sense? Or even anything that didn't make sense? Head injuries were not to be taken lightly.

Damn the Millers! Throwbacks to the Dark Ages, every

last one of them! What did they do when someone was sick or injured, call Miss Lucy to cast a spell?

"Wake up," she snapped. Standing over him, she couldn't help but be aware of his powerful body. He was muscular, both his lower parts and his upper parts—she didn't know about what was in between. Devin, like most of his cousins, had been short-legged, but powerfully built from the waist up, probably as a result of working with pick axes and wheeling barrows full of dirt along narrow underground tunnels.

Or perhaps it was hereditary, she no longer cared. This man was different. His hands, for all the bruised and bleeding knuckles, were without calluses. Square-palmed, long-fingered, with well-kept fingernails. Unlike the Millers, who went barefoot ten months out of the year, his feet were narrow, the arches high, not flat and callused and broad.

"Who are you?" she wondered aloud.

There was no response, not that she'd expected one. Evidently, he had used the last of his store of energy dragging himself up the hill to safety. That alone, she thought as she busied herself filling the kettle and dragging her washtub in off the back porch, was enough to tell her that his presence must be kept secret from those in the valley. He'd come up the hill, not down toward the settlement, when anyone knew that going downhill would have been easier.

His ribs were injured, that much she'd concluded by the way he'd reacted whenever he was forced to move his torso. A broken rib could cause untold internal injuries, which he might already have suffered. After getting him out of his underwear she should have insisted on looking him over for evidence of further injuries, but she hadn't. He had suffered enough for the time being.

Besides, she'd been too embarrassed.

Sooner or later, though, she would have to examine his body. His back, his sides, his—the rest of him. He might even be bleeding internally, in which case, where on earth did one apply a bandage?

She took out her washboard and tossed a sliver of soap into the tub, making a mental note to request more soap the next time her supplies were delivered.

As the kettle began to simmer, she filled the tub half full of cold water, thinking about the first time she had sent down a shopping list, naively thinking someone would be going to the nearest town to shop. She'd ordered three bars of French lilac soap, hard milled so as to last longer, a tin of lilac-scented talc and a stiff new hairbrush, as her own was all but useless.

Two days later one of the twins had ridden up the hill with her order. Three chunks of homemade lye soap and a box of cornstarch. No brush. Not even a new comb.

That had been the beginning of her awakening.

Shoving back a length of tangled curls that had slipped free of the pins, she went through the pockets of his Levi's before dropping them into the tub. They were empty. No surprise there. Whoever had beaten him had obviously robbed him as well. Nevertheless, she felt in the pocket of his faded chambray shirt before tossing it in after his Levi's. Next went his single sock. If his ankle got worse, one might be all he would need, perish the thought.

As for his coat, it could probably be salvaged, but it would never be the same. It was ripped in two places as if it had snagged on something. One of the sleeves had nearly been torn off. It would have to be sponged and dried slowly so the leather wouldn't stiffen before she could even attempt to mend it.

She slid her hand into the outer pockets. Nothing there,

either. Hardly a surprise. It was in the lining that she came across a flat pocket. A money pocket? She knew less than nothing about men's clothes, only that their hosiery needed darning far more often than her own. Cautiously, she slid two fingers inside…and pulled out a folded piece of paper that looked as if it had been through the wars.

The kettle began to rock just then, and laying aside the paper, she finished filling the washtub.

"I don't know when you'll be leaving," she muttered to herself as she swished the soap around to make suds, "but you'll want something to wear. Did I tell you that the Millers—they're my late husband's family. They live in the settlement down below, and the thing is, they don't particularly care for outsiders."

He had already discovered that for himself, she thought, if what she suspected was true.

After a few brisk rubs she left the garments to soak and tiptoed back to the bedroom to see if her guest was still breathing. Whether he was or not, he was going to be a problem. She'd had her next escape all planned. Now it would have to wait, at least until he was on his feet. Then, if he wanted to stay on here, he was welcome to stay, with her blessing. They might even bring him supplies as long as he set the basket on the porch and remained hidden from view.

She told him just that the next time she tiptoed into the bedroom to check on him, neither expecting a response nor getting one. "I'm soaking your clothes. Not your coat—I'll do the best I can with it, but it'll never be the same again, I'm afraid. I'd lend you something of Devin's but his cousins came up right after he was buried and took away all his clothes and his other personal possessions. Devin was my husband, did I tell you? He blew himself up."

She sighed. Talking to a sleeping man was no more productive than talking to herself, but at least she didn't feel quite so foolish. He *might* hear her, even though he couldn't respond.

Standing there staring down at that poor battered face, it struck her all over again that there was a naked stranger in her bed. One who might or might not be a wanted criminal. "Please don't die on me," she begged softly. "I wouldn't know who to notify, or even how. And I could never dig a hole deep enough to bury you in this rocky soil."

She leaned over and peered at his face, searching for some sign that he'd heard her. At least whoever had split his lip hadn't knocked out any of his teeth. He had nice teeth. In fact, his mouth would probably be quite shapely once the swelling went down.

"Hello-oo," she crooned. "Are you in there? Can you hear me?" She took his wrist and found a slow, steady pulse. His hands were filthy, his hair was almost as matted as her own, but he was still alive. Thank God for that much. Carefully, she laid a hand on his chest. He was warm. Not really feverish, just...warm. And hard. His heart was definitely beating.

She lifted her eyes and sighed. "Lord, you're going to have to tell me what to do next, because I've never done this before."

Actually, she had. Not the same, but she had nursed her elderly cousin through her final illness the summer before she'd been married.

Gazing down at the stranger, she felt the oddest tingle throughout her body. Whoever this man was, he most definitely bore no resemblance to cousin Annie. Eleanor waited to see if he would open his eyes. When he didn't, she covered him with a quilt, then tiptoed from the room.

It had to be somewhere near midnight. She was too keyed up to sleep, but perhaps she should lie down for a few minutes.

Jed woke up gasping for air, each breath hurting as if a dozen devils were stabbing him with red-hot pitchforks. Squinting through swollen eyes, he saw lamplight splintering from the woman's pale hair. Her face was in shadow. For a moment he had trouble placing her. His skull had been rattled enough to shake his brain loose, but then he recognized her as the same woman who had dragged him into her house, stripped off his clothes and come after him with a pair of scissors. That had been…yesterday? The day before?

He'd managed to move on his own then. Now, he couldn't move if she set the bed on fire. Opening his mouth, he tried to speak but no words emerged. Lips hurt. Everything hurt, from his hair right down to his toenails.

How the devil could hair hurt?

His did. Felt as if someone had tried to scalp him. For all he knew, they might've succeeded. He attempted to lift a hand to find out, but the effort was too great. Bald wasn't so bad. One of his friends was bald as a pigeon egg. Couldn't think of his name right now, but he could picture him easily enough.

God, he hurt!

Daylight was streaming in through the east windows when next she opened her eyes. She felt as if her bones had been pounded with a hammer. Good thing she hadn't left her poor stranger here, he'd be worse off than ever.

"Coffee, coffee," she muttered, stumbling toward the kitchen. It was then she saw the big, galvanized washtub in the middle of the floor. As a rule she did her laundry on the back stoop, where she could stand on the ground without having to bend over. But if someone had caught her washing men's clothing, she would have had a lot of explaining to do.

Coffee would just have to wait. Before she'd even lifted the garments from the final rinse it occurred to her that she wouldn't be able to hang them outside. Back in Charlotte she had used the attic in rainy weather, but here there was no attic. She would have to dry everything in the kitchen, either that or build up a fire in the fireplace.

While she was trying to decide where to string a line, she thought of the letter. Should she give it to him when he woke up?

If he woke up?

Or should she keep it in case he didn't recover and someone had to be notified. But in that case, how could she get word out? She could hardly ask any of the Millers to mail a letter or send a wire for her. They had refused every time she'd tried to get in contact with any of her friends back in Charlotte.

The more she thought about it, the more convinced she was that it had to have been Alaska and his whiskey-making friends who had done this awful thing. When they had what Devin used to call a skin full, they liked nothing better than to engage in a fistfight with everyone piling on, making enough noise to be heard halfway to the moon. Devin had called it good-natured brawling, but there was nothing good-natured about beating a man half to death.

Now what? she wondered, feeling even more helpless than usual. The natural thing would have been to hurry down the hill and ask for help. Under the circumstances, that was out of the question.

She brought in her clothesline and strung it across the kitchen area, letting the excess line dangle from the nail.

She knew better than to shorten a good clothesline, having learned how hard it was to get a replacement. She had asked over and over for more. Might as well have asked for the moon. They must have thought she wanted to use it to lower herself down the backside of the mountain, a sheer drop of more than two hundred feet.

She turned the Levi's inside out so that the doubled parts—the waist, the seams and pockets—would dry. If he survived, her stranger would need something to wear. If he didn't, he would need burial clothes. Either way, she would have them ready for him, but he'd have to do without underwear. There was no way she could piece together his union suit, even if he gave it up. So far he'd refused to allow her to take the bottom half. For all she knew he might still be wearing it. At this rate, her whole bed would be mildewed. Crazy fool. "Go ahead, die of lung fever, see if I care," she muttered, wringing out his one black sock.

But of course, she did care. It wasn't in her *not* to care.

After baling out the tub, she turned it down on the back stoop and thought about the next problem. Food. Her rations were carefully allotted for a woman living alone. She could hardly ask for more without inviting questions.

She tiptoed into the bedroom to see if he was still breathing. He was. Slowly, evenly, and so far as she could tell, without any sounds that would indicate that a broken rib had punctured his lung. "I don't know who the devil you are," she murmured, "or what you're doing on my mountain, but if you survive you're going to have company when you leave."

In the settlement called Dexter's Cut, Hector paused outside Digger Hooten's cabin, checked his fingernails, finger-combed his shoulder-length hair, and then called through the door. "Digger? You to home?"

The runty redheaded man appeared at the door, eyes narrowed against the bright morning sun. "'Mon in, Heck. Set a spell." Digger was a flatlander who'd married a Miller and produced two children—a daughter, Varnelle, and a son, Alaska, the latter named for the dream he'd always had of heading north in search of gold.

When he'd heard about Dexter's Cut, he'd figured he'd save time and money by filing a claim on Miller land. Couldn't be done. So he'd filed a claim on one of the Miller women instead, which was less trouble in the long run. He'd never found more than a few grains of gold, hardly enough to be worth his time digging. But then, his luck might not have been any better in Alaska, and he was too old now to start over.

It was common knowledge that Heck had never had much use for Alaska, so Digger said, "I reckon you come to see Varnelle. She's over to Miss Lucy's. Gone to get something for my wife's bellyache. Right useful girl, my Varnelle. Pretty, too, if I do say so as shouldn't."

Fortunately, Varnelle took after her mother. Digger was a homely man.

"Nope, I come to see you." Heck sat on the room's only chair while his host settled onto one of two wooden benches. "Nice weather," he added. An educated man, Heck knew when to haul out his company manners.

"Tol'able," the old man responded.

Heck had thought long and hard before approaching Digger, but the buck-nekked truth was, he loved his daughter. "Hear tell you been panning some," he ventured. Most of the locals panned the creek on days when it was too hot to work the fields. That way they didn't have to feel guilty for laying out while their women were firing up a hot stove to cook their dinner.

"Panned some last week. Didn't do no good. Wore m'knees out, but that there gold's done washed all the way down to the river and gone by now. Ever'body knows that."

"Then how come you wasted time pannin'?" This was going to be tricky as a tote sack full of rattlers. Digger wasn't mean like Alaska. What he was, was crafty. It took a right smart man to get around him, and third-grade education or not, Heck wasn't sure he was up to the task.

For Varnelle, though, he was bound to try. "About your daughter," he began when the old man cut him off.

"I seen the way you been lookin' at her, boy. You ain't foolin' me, nosiree."

"Well now, she's a right pretty woman for a redhead." He thought he'd add the qualifier so as not to appear too eager.

"Tell you what I'll do, boy. You ain't the onliest man that's come a-sniffin' at her heels, but you show up with Dev's share of the mine and I'll set you right up there at the top of the list. Can't say fairer'n that."

Heck pursed his lips, laced his fingers across his flat belly and looked thoughtful. "Well now, much as I'd like to oblige, I don't reckon I can do that." He'd expected some kind of a clinker. Old Digger was a greedy man, always had been. "On the other hand, don't reckon any of the others can, either, so that makes us even."

They passed the time of day for a few more minutes, and Heck made a point of mentioning what a blessing an unmarried daughter was to an old man and his woman. "'Course, lacking a husband to keep 'em sweet, a woman'll turn real sour as she gets older. Some of 'em gets downright mean. I don't reckon you'll mind that none, though, seein's she's kin.'' He paused to let the words sink in. "Have to support her, too, but at least she'll be around to see you laid out all nice and proper when the time comes.''

He left a few minutes later, the question he'd come to ask still unanswered. Digger Hooten was not only crafty, he was smart as a whipsnake.

If there was any way in the world Heck could get his hands on Dev's share, he would do it in a minute, yessir, that he would. Trouble was, those shares weren't like pieces of paper a man could slip in and steal. What they were was twenty-five solid acres of the most promising land in the entire settlement, the very same hill where old Dexter had struck pay dirt sixty years ago. The land had been passed down to his grandson, who had died and left it to his widow. The only way a man could lay claim to it now would be to marry Elly Nora.

Heck didn't want to do that on account of he loved Varnelle. Besides, if he married Elly Nora, the property would be his, but he'd have to kill her before he could marry Varnelle. And while he'd done his share of killing, he drew the line at killing a woman.

So he figured he'd just study on it some more. That old hill weren't going nowhere, he told himself, and neither was Elly Nora.

Time passed. Hearing a slight sound, Jed opened one eye and there she was again. The light was different now. More time had passed. How much time? He didn't have time to waste. George was counting on him.

His thoughts came in batches between painful breaths. He could see her face more clearly now. She was older than he'd first thought...if he'd thought at all. Mostly, he'd just felt and wished he could stop feeling. He studied her

some more as she gathered up things from the washstand—
a hairbrush that had seen its best days. An ivory comb and
a towel. It occurred to him that she resembled a picture of
a woman he'd seen in one of the big churches in Raleigh.
Hair like a lumpy halo, face like a saint.

She came over to the bedside then, and he saw the shadows under her eyes. He wanted to offer to give her her
bed back—it was obviously the only bed in the house—
but he lacked the strength to speak. Lacked the strength to
move if she took him up on the offer.

So he watched her through aching eyes and wondered
who she was, what the devil she was doing here, and which
was the best way out of here without running afoul of those
gun-toting, hell-raising pig-swills that had jumped him
down by the creek.

Her shadowy eyelids were fringed with thick, colorless
lashes. With the angle of the light, it was impossible to
tell what color her eyes were. Curiously enough, it mattered. He was right partial to blue-eyed women, always
had been.

Hers weren't blue. But then, they weren't black, either.

He tried to turn over onto his side for a better view.
Jesus, that hurt! Those bastards had kicked his ribs in,
laughing all the while.

At his gasp, the woman leaned closer. "What hurts?"

"Everything," he managed to whisper. He said it with
a grin. At least he grinned on the inside—didn't know if
it made it all the way to the surface. Never let it be said
that Jed Blackstone wasn't a good sport, even when he
was cashing in his chips.

Could those goons that had jumped him have been hired
by Stanfield? Why else would they try to kill a stranger
who'd done nothing more than stop for a drink of water?

He needed answers and he needed them right damn now.

That wasn't all he needed, he suddenly realized. Moving restlessly, he tried to sit up.

A pair of gentle hands pressed him back down. "Shh, you just lie still and rest. Would you like a drink of water?"

"No, dammit, I need to p—"

"Tell me what you need and I'll get it for you. Don't even try to get up yet, I think you might've hurt your ribs."

Tell me something I don't know, he thought, angling his head to get a better look at the woman who had either rescued him or dragged him here to finish him off. At this point, he wasn't certain of anything.

She was tall for a woman—too thin. The kind of hair that looked as if it had never seen a brush. Not exactly pretty, but not what you'd call plain, either.

"Lady, I need to get up and you need to get the hell out," he said clearly, his voice urgent. Even talking hurt. He must've bit his tongue when they'd caught him on the side of the head with that spade.

"Oh," the yellow-haired woman said, her eyes widening. "I'll bring the chamber pot. Can you manage by yourself?"

"What if I can't?" He couldn't move his lips, but he could make himself understood.

She blinked, and then damned if she didn't laugh.

Had he said something funny? If so, it had been purely unintentional, because funny was the last thing he felt.

"I don't think you can make it out to the privy in your condition."

Come to think of it, neither did he, but his bladder was fit to bust. He needed a pot and some privacy.

She gave him both.

"Here. If you need any help, I'll be right outside."

Blushing, she drew a white porcelain chamber pot from under the bed and set it on the table beside him. At the door she paused. "If privacy is what you need I have more than enough to spare," she said with a funny quirk in her voice. "Besides, I need—I need to feed the animals."

Letting him know she wouldn't be lurking outside the door, in other words.

She lingered a moment, adding, "Not that I have any animals, just my two laying hens. Hector—he's one of the Millers—he gave me a puppy for company once, but it followed him right back down the hill."

He squinted at her through his partially open eye, wondering if she was totally witless. Wild color flushed her cheeks and she turned and fled. A moment later he heard the outside door slam.

He managed to relieve himself, feeling as if his head was floating a few feet above his shoulders. His belly felt funny, too, not sick like he'd been drinking bad water, but sore, like he'd been worked over by a gorilla.

Five gorillas was more like it. "Jesus," he gasped, and then flopped back onto the bed and closed his eyes. The slightest movement brought on another pitchfork attack. He was dead certain sure by now that he'd cracked a few ribs. The question was, how many and how cracked? Cracked to the point where the slightest wrong movement could kill him?

Or cracked just enough to make lying perfectly still for the foreseeable future his only option?

At least his head was clearer now. For a while there it had been touch-and-go. He'd actually been afraid they had punched his brains out, but he remembered everything now. Remembered signing the deed and arranging to send most of the money home. Remembered giving McGee a piece of cheese and a soda cracker when they'd stopped by that creek...

What the devil had happened to McGee? He and that miserable old croppy had been together too long to part company now. They had a history together, ever since Jed had saved him from the glue factory. Jed had agreed to feed the biting, kicking, crop-eared old sunfisher and in return, McGee agreed not to bite him, kick him or throw him hard enough to break his neck. So far, for the most part, both had kept their word.

He hoped to hell one of those bastards tried to catch McGee. The last time he'd seen them, they'd been lurching off down the road, one wearing his hat, another one carrying his boots, laughing and cussing a blue streak as they tried to keep from falling on their ugly faces.

If they met again he'd be ready for them, if he had to bind himself up like one of those dead Egyptian kings he'd read about. Given better odds—say three to one instead of five to one—he liked his chances just fine. He wouldn't go looking for a fight, though. Not this time. He had places to go and things to do, and he'd already wasted two days. Or was it three now?

A tap on the door was followed by a soft voice inquiring if he needed assistance. "I'm all right," he said, lying through his teeth. If he still had any teeth. He could feel with his tongue, but that hurt, too. Besides, he wasn't sure he wanted to know. "Sleepy," he added, hoping she would go away. From the way his head felt, he must've made intimate contact with every rock this side of the Eastern Divide.

Sleep. He'd give himself a day. Two, at most, and then he would find his horse and get the hell out of here, with or without his clothes. The lady could go on talking to her chickens from now till they started talking back, it was no skin off his teeth.

If he still had any teeth.

Chapter Five

An hour later Eleanor tapped on the door again. She'd held off as long as she dared, knowing he needed his rest. But what if he weren't resting? What if he had passed out? Or worse…

When no answer was forthcoming, she opened the door and peered inside. He was sound asleep, breathing slowly through his swollen lips, but breathing. Evidently exhausted, he had slept through the night, the following morning and most of the afternoon while she'd waited anxiously to see if he was going to live or die. If only there was some way to tell if a body was bleeding internally.

There probably was, only she was no physician—just a third-grade teacher in a small school on the outskirts of a big city.

He was cleaner. At least his hands and face were cleaner. Now she intended to tackle the rest of him. His scalp, for instance. His hair was caked with dried blood, but when she'd tried to examine an obvious lump to see the extent of the damage, he'd started cursing. And then tried to apologize, which had made her feel even worse.

"I know you hurt," she'd told him earlier when she'd come to collect his ruined underwear to wash it and see if any of it could be used again. "I'll try to be as easy as possible, but I need to look at this place on your head."

Scalp wounds bled copiously, she had read that somewhere, but to determine if his wound was more than scalp deep she was going to have to cut away his hair. That would mean another battle. She hadn't forgotten the last time she'd come at him with a pair of scissors.

"If the rest of you is as filthy as the parts I've already bathed," she told the sleeping man, "your cuts and scratches are probably already infected. With or without your cooperation, sir, I'm going to have to clean you up and put something on your injuries before it's too late."

There, let him think about that.

She'd brought in a basin of warm water, two towels and a chunk of soap. Carefully, she set the basin on the bedside table. She would have to work quickly so as not to tire him further. "You need to get well and get out of here," she muttered under her breath. "Because if it was the Millers who did this to you, and if they follow you here, I'm not sure I can protect you. I'll try, of course, but they won't listen to me, they never do. Hold still now, I'll be as gentle as I can."

Lowering the afghan so that it covered him from his waist to below his knees, she washed his chest and just beneath. He wasn't particularly hairy, but a thin streak of silky black hair circled his flat nipples and dissected his torso, disappearing under the flowered purple cover.

"They took Devin's rifle, did I tell you that? If it were just one man, I might fight him off with a skillet, but if they think you're here, they'll come trooping up my hill like a—like I don't know what. If they're drinking, things could get out of hand. I'm going to have to turn you over now. I'll be as easy as I can."

He gasped during the process, but he didn't resist. She

had sense enough to apply pressure to his shoulder and his hip, in case his ribs were injured. She was pretty certain they were, as there were two fairly deep cuts on his side. A doctor would probably stitch him up, but that was far beyond her skills. If she even dared try she might faint. The best she could do was wash him, smear on some of Miss Lucy's turpentine and bear-grease salve and bind him up.

But first she needed to finish bathing him while the water was still warm. The last thing he needed on top of everything else was to catch a chill.

She managed to slide one arm under his body to shift him so that she could see his full back, but when she tried to turn him toward her he cried out.

"I'm sorry," she said quickly, frozen in a backbreaking position. What now? Finish turning him over or forget about his back? If he had any cuts there they might fester unless she could get to them and treat them. She had already torn a sheet into strips, intending to bind his ribs, but unless he allowed her to move him again, she couldn't even do that much.

"I'm sorry, this has to be done," she said firmly. Steeling herself to ignore his groans, she managed to roll him over onto his stomach. He muttered curses; she mumbled apologies. "Actually, you're not even bleeding here, only bruised. But…" In the process of rolling him over, the afghan had pulled away from his body. Now her gaze swept over his narrow buttocks.

The scar was an old one. It was none of her business, she told herself as she applied a warm, soapy cloth to his shoulders. My God, what on earth…?

She took one more look at the peculiar scar, but except for the parts that needed attention, she avoided looking at his naked body again. One way or another, she vowed silently as she gently cleansed what looked like a knife wound on his thigh, she vowed that whoever had done this cowardly thing would pay for their sins if she had to blow up Devin's hill and every last tunnel that riddled it.

"In fact, it might be just the diversion we need to make our escape," she said thoughtfully.

Facing the wall to hide his embarrassment, Jed frowned. The woman rattled on like a dried gourd in a high wind, but...

Our escape? He knew damned well where he was going, and the last thing he needed was a traveling companion.

"The trouble is," she confided earnestly as she poured liquid fire in his open wounds, "I don't know a blessed thing about dynamite, do you?"

"Dynamite?" He managed to open one eye just as she stepped away from the bed. That was a bit extreme, even for him. All he wanted was to find McGee and get the hell out of here. He'd leave Satan to mete out any punishment due.

He managed to roll onto his back again unassisted, pulling the tapestry throw over his privates. She looked at him worriedly and asked if he was hurting.

"No," he lied. Nowhere except for his ribs, his head, his back and his left ankle. Except for roughly two-thirds of his body, it didn't hurt a bit.

"There, you see? You're getting better already." The smile on her face made her look almost pretty. Not as pretty as Vera, but pretty in a different way.

"Now, I've decided to bind up your ribs in case any of them are broken," she announced. "I have the strips right here, but if you're tired, we can wait a little while until you've had time to rest up from your bath."

"Mm." Meaning, just go away and leave me for the next few years, I've had about all I can take for one day.

She looked as if she wanted to say something. He didn't want to hear it, whatever it was, but as exhausted as he was by the last half hour's activities, he owed her that much. She was trying her best to help him, and she didn't know him from Adam.

"Name," he said. His voice sounded like rusty water poured over gravel. "Jed—Blackstone."

Her face brightened until it was…not exactly pretty, but nice. For the first time he noticed that her eyes were all the colors of the forest—green, brown, gold and gray. She said, "How do you do, Mr. Blackstone, my name is Eleanor Mayne Scarborough. At least, I was a Scarborough before I married Devin Miller."

Ask a simple question, Jed thought, amused in spite of feeling worse than the floor of a cattle car after a five-hundred-mile trip. He hadn't even asked her name… although he didn't mind knowing. If he had to deal with the woman for a day or two longer, it might help to know what to call her.

"Could I ask you a personal question?" Holding the basin on one hip, the towels on the other arm, she tilted her head. "How on earth did you get that odd scar on your, um—posterior? I couldn't help but notice when you were—when I was—that is… Well, it looks just like two snakes, side by side."

He closed his eyes, feeling fresh anger sweep over him from something that had happened eight years before.

"I'm sorry," she whispered. "I don't know what's wrong with me. Well, I do, of course—living here all alone for so long, I've lost every sense of decorum I ever possessed."

He didn't know about decorum—he'd have to look that one up—but she hadn't lost her sense of kindness, Jed thought as he watched the blushing woman scurry away.

If she hadn't been there—if she hadn't been the one to find him, he might not have made it through the night. As it was, he had not only made it, he was going to damn well recover in time to get his money from that Asheville bank and shove it down Sam Stanfield's throat.

Yeah, he was. Just as soon as he could breathe without lightning striking every vital organ in his body. The binding would help, but it would need to be tight to do any good. He was pretty sure his ribs were only cracked, not broken, but he wasn't about to risk any sudden moves.

As for his ankle, it was probably only sprained. He could already move his foot, although it hurt like hell. The truth was, he didn't know anything for sure. With a horse or a cow, he could tell at a glance, but when it came to his own anatomy—not to mention a few other subjects— there were still some crater-size holes in his education. He'd managed to patch up a few of them, but he kept tripping over new ones.

She'd been a schoolteacher. She'd told him that while he'd been pretending to sleep. Taught little kids. Just his luck to fall into the hands of a good-looking woman who could see right through what little polish he'd been able to achieve to the big, dumb oaf underneath.

Not that he was in any condition to take advantage of her, even if he'd wanted to. He'd been too busy since George had wired him about the threatened foreclosure to enjoy his usual pursuits, what with handling all the red tape concerned with any land transfer and making sure the deal was kept secret until he could pay off Stanfield. The land agent had insisted on having a paper record dating back to when God invented dirt. Never in all his days had Jed signed his name on so many documents, most of which he could barely read.

But he'd taken his own sweet time scanning all those

big words in the fine print as if he knew just what each one meant. Scare 'em out of trying to put anything over on him. Every now and then one of the black-suited men would harrumph and spit toward the cuspidor, meaning, "Get on with it, you dumb-head."

But Jed hadn't allowed himself to be rushed. Instead, he had stared at them, lifted one eyebrow and gone back to reading a bunch of meaningless words on the contract. Then he had signed his name—Jedediah O. Blackstone— right above where someone had printed it out in neat black letters. Added a few extra flourishes for good measure.

The *O* stood for nothing. He didn't have a middle name, but that was nobody's business but his own.

"Jed? Are you still awake?"

"Mm," he said. He'd been awake more than he'd been asleep almost from the first, only he'd let her think he was sleeping. Woman could talk the hind leg off a three-legged jackass. He wasn't up to answering any questions, so he'd pretended to be out of it. But now that he'd sized up the situation, he needed some answers. Needed to know the best way off this damned anthill, and what the odds were of running into the same stinking redneck weasels again. If the widow Miller could be believed, there was no way down without wading through the middle of their nest.

"Well," she said, standing beside the bed, so close he could smell her woman's scent. Smell whatever it was she'd been cooking that smelled like vanilla. "I'm making you some bread pudding. It's soft enough so you won't have to chew. And some soup."

He said "Mm" again, because the truth was, he was afraid if he tried to open his mouth, his lips would split wide-open. He hated the taste of blood, he purely did. Tasted it a few too many times in his younger, rowdier days.

"Well," she said again, and stood there, the look of bright expectation slowly fading.

"Thank you," he managed without doing any damage to his swollen mouth. He owed her that much at least. Hell of a lot more, only it would have to wait. First thing he needed to do was get back on his feet, find a way out of here, and settle with Stanfield. He had a long-standing score to settle with that gentleman.

But that would have to wait. First he had to pull George's acorns out of the fire.

"Well," she said for the third time. She was tapping her foot like a feisty rattler, but he didn't think there was any venom in her. "If you're really awake now, we can start getting you well, and then we'll talk about how we're going to get away from here."

Eleanor forced herself not to hover. Once he was awake enough to take a bit of nourishment she could find out more about him. Things such as what he was doing here, where he'd been going, and how long he thought it might be before he could—before they could travel.

As frustrating as it was to have him sleeping away the hours, she had to admit that after months of stupefying boredom, she felt vibrantly alive again. Standing beside the bed, she continued to study the man. She suspected he wasn't always asleep when she looked in on him, but if it suited him to pretend, there wasn't much she could do about it. Both his eyes were closed again. For a minute he'd opened one of them. She thought some of the swelling might be going down, but the color had spread all the way up to his hairline.

"I've come to bind your ribs," she said, watching to see if he reacted. She'd tried before, but he'd groaned and moaned so much she'd offered to wait. "The sooner we get it over with, the sooner you can go back to sleep."

She waited to see if he reacted. There, that was a twitch, she was sure of it. Almost like a wink, only both his eyes were still shut.

He sighed. "I give up," he said. "Do what you have to do."

The only trouble was, he was lying down. She needed him standing, or at least sitting up. Evidently, he knew it, because he rolled over onto one side unassisted, braced himself with his arms, and pushed to a seated position. There was no disguising the fact that he was in pain. She winced for him, but she refused to put it off any longer. "The sooner we get this done, the sooner you can move without its hurting so much."

I hope, she added silently. Taking one end of a strip of sheeting, she held it against his collarbone and said, "Hold this."

It took longer than she'd expected, because she had never done it before. Never done anything even faintly like it. By the third strip she'd learned how to secure the ends until she came to the very last one. After a moment of hesitation, she tucked it under, her fingers pressing into the flesh of his waist. While she'd been wrapping him she had run her hands over his torso, front, sides and back, to see if anything was obviously out of place. She could tell by the way he breathed that he was hurting. She'd apologized until he'd finally told her to just get on with it and leave him in peace.

She had two strips left over. The poor man was exhausted. She helped him down again, pulled the covers up over him and left him to recuperate. Closing the door, all but a crack in case he called out, she leaned against the wall and closed her eyes.

Mercy, she'd forgotten how pleasurable the feel of a man's warm body could be. Had she ever felt that way about Devin's body?

She honestly couldn't remember. Probably not. It had all been so new at the time. It had taken her nearly a year to get over her shyness, and by that time Devin had been more interested in digging for gold than he was in bedding his wife.

Absently stroking the cloth draped over her arm, she marveled at the salacious thoughts that had filled her mind as she'd reached around him again and again, so close she could feel his warm breath on her face. She wasn't the kind of woman to lust after a man, especially not a stranger who was lying helpless in her bed, dependent on her for care and protection.

But she'd thought about him that way, oh yes, she had. Wondered what it would be like to slide her hands down over his chest and move them down over his buttocks....

Shameless. Demented. "That's what comes of being a hermit. A hermitess," she corrected.

"Mm?" Evidently he wasn't yet asleep.

"Nothing," she said through the crack in the door. "But if you're still awake—that is, if you're not too tired—we could have supper. I can have a tray ready in no time at all."

She could? Using what, pray tell? Her larder wasn't exactly brimming. She had used the last of her sugar to make a soft bread pudding, but it was barely a teacup full. Hardly a meal for a grown man. "I'll be back in a little while. Try to get some rest."

As he didn't protest, she hurried away, worrying over what to cook that he could eat. It would have to be something soft. Soup, only soup took time, even if she'd had a good soup bone. Besides, she had learned with cousin Annie that trying to spoon soup into a patient who was lying flat in bed was a messy process, at best.

Less than an hour later she shouldered the door open and tiptoed inside with an enameled tray that had belonged to the mother she barely remembered. "Time to wake up," she caroled softly. "Did I tell you I took care of my cousin? Not that cousin Annie needed binding, but I used to make soft bread pudding for her, too—and soup. All kinds of nutritious soups."

He was awake. He gave her that slitted look, as if he were wondering if he'd landed among the Lilliputians. She set the tray aside, washed and dried her hands, then ran one finger over the pat of butter she'd brought to go on the cornmeal mush. Leaving the bowl and spoon there, she turned to him. "First, we'll see about your lips. This should help."

And before he could protest, she touched his mouth with her buttery forefinger. Gently she moved it over first the top lip, then the full lower. He had nice lips—even with the swelling she could tell that much. The upper one dipped in a nice bow in the center. She hadn't seen his teeth yet, at least not all of them, but from what she'd seen, those were nice, too. Not too small, not too large— not crooked and not even yellow. He obviously didn't dip, didn't chew and might not even smoke cigars.

Gradually she became aware that his eyes were open. Not only that, he was staring at her in a way that made her aware of what she was doing. "Oh. There, that should help," she said, snatching her finger from his mouth.

All business now, she spooned up some of the mush and poked it toward his mouth. It was thick enough not to drip, thin enough to be swallowed without chewing.

He ate silently, his gaze never leaving her face. She

avoided looking back, pretending, instead, to concentrate on feeding him without spilling anything on the bedding. But she couldn't help but notice his powerful shoulders, bare above his chest binding, and the arms with their dusting of dark hair. His hands were as battered as the rest of him, yet she was certain that once healed they would be shapely and well kept. She liked large hands on a man. It made them seem…capable.

Jed Blackstone was as different from Devin as night from day. Dark, where Devin had been blond. Long all over where Devin had been long in the torso, but short in the legs.

Dapper was the word that had first come to mind that day when she'd bumped into Devin on her way home, her arms loaded with books and groceries. She had a feeling this man would never be called dapper, no matter the quality of his clothes. There was something about him, something untamed, for want of a better word.

As she dipped up the last spoonful of the thick yellow mush, seasoned with the last of her precious butter, she wondered what she was going to do about tomorrow's meals. Half her skimpy garden was just beginning to come in, the other half long since played out. She had two laying hens that provided one and sometimes two eggs a day. Several times a week someone from the settlement brought her supplies. A jar of buttermilk, but rarely any butter. Occasionally a bit of ham or fried chicken, and often a few biscuits or a square of corn bread, but mostly it was staples. Flour, salt, cornmeal, lard, beans and coffee, all in amounts carefully calculated for one.

Now she had a man to feed. It was for his sake, she told herself, that she had not only to keep him here, but to keep his presence secret until he was able to fend for himself. Granted, she'd been so desperately lonely that even a man who didn't talk beyond the barest minimum was better than no one at all, but that wasn't the real reason she was so excited she could barely sleep.

Once he was able, he would leave, and whether or not he knew it, she was going with him. All she needed was someone to get her past the settlement. She had tried and tried, but evidently she wasn't doing it right. Direct by nature, she'd never been good at subterfuge.

This man looked as if he knew about subterfuge, never mind that he'd been beaten to within an inch of his life. Brute strength wasn't always enough, not when the woods were filled with Millers. It would take devious planning, something she had never been good at…until now.

"For the time being, you're my secret," she whispered, feeling optimistic for the first time in months.

Chapter Six

Eleanor looked in on her patient only once or twice during the night. Surely no more than half a dozen times, and then only in case he needed something and lacked the strength to call her. Each time, she lingered long enough to make certain he hadn't stopped breathing.

Again, she marveled at how strange it felt to have a man in her bed. Standing over him now, she wondered how old he was. Wondered if he were married, if he'd been running away from something, or toward something. Or someone. Few strangers ever wandered onto Miller land. Those who did never repeated their mistake. The Millers weren't known for their hospitality.

His eyes were closed now, but she could tell by a certain tension that he was awake. His hands, lying outside the covers, were curled into fists. She set the breakfast tray on the bedside table. "Are you awake?" she whispered.

No answer. Mercy, his face was a sight. Two glorious shiners, one the color of raw liver, the other more like wet slate. Had some of the swelling begun to go down?

It was hard to say. His own mother might not recognize him if she saw him now. If he wanted to go on pretending he was asleep, that was just fine with her, but only up to a point. The man had to eat if he were ever going to get well.

"Jed?" She spoke his name and waited.

No reaction. Not so much as a tightening of his poor lips.

"After you finish breakfast I'll make you a poultice for those eyes. I should have done it before, I just didn't..."

Didn't think. Didn't know what to think, more like.

Standing over him, she waited to see if he would respond. "And for your mouth, and that place on the side of your head."

She was whispering. Why was she whispering?

When he managed to open one eye, she beamed. "There, see? You're already feeling better, aren't you? You'll feel even better once you eat some nice cornmeal mush. I drizzled molasses on it." Because she'd used the last of her sugar in his bread pudding, but she saw no reason to tell him that. "I'm going to brew up some willow bark tea. It tastes awful, but it eases the pain. Can you sit up? Here, let me help you."

She leaned over him and slid a hand under his shoulders. "When I lift, wriggle your bottom. I'll scrunch up your pillow and—" Oof! He was heavy! Not quite a dead weight, but not far from it. How on earth had he managed to get this far after he'd been beaten?

For that matter, how had he managed to sit up long enough to let her bind his ribs? "They say it hurts more the second day, but after that, it starts feeling better."

She didn't know what "they" said. Cousin Annie had wakened one morning unable to move or even speak. One whole side of her face drooped, but she was never, so far as anyone could tell, in any pain.

Finally they managed, but not without groans and curses on his part and endless apologies on hers. Finally, picking up the spoon, she started to feed him when he reached out and took it from her. "Do it myself," he said gruffly.

"Of course, if you'd rather."

She didn't know whether to go or stay. Men could be such independent creatures. "Would you like—?"

"Sit. Talk."

That was the last thing she'd expected him to say. She had scarcely stopped talking ever since she'd dragged him home with her. "If you like," she said politely, sitting on the only chair and arranging the skirt of her faded gray muslin around her. "Is there any particular topic you're interested in discussing?"

She told herself it wasn't laughter she saw in his eyes. They were too swollen to see much of anything except for a glint of color so dark it defied the light.

"Millers," he said, and it took a moment for the meaning to register.

"You want to know if they're capable of beating a man half to death?" She pursed her lips and considered all she knew about the people who stood between her and freedom. "Some of them are, I'm afraid. One or two in particular, especially when they're drinking, or if they feel threatened. And some of them do drink a lot. And I suppose you could say they're rather paranoid."

"Paranoid." He repeated the word, appeared to be turning it over in his mind, but said nothing.

Having finished his breakfast, he set the bowl and spoon on the bed beside him just as she reached out to take it. Her fingers brushed his, and she looked at his swollen knuckles and wondered which of the Millers was sporting bruises or black eyes. Alaska would definitely be one of them. Even Devin had been wary of Alaska's temper when he'd been drinking, which was most of the time.

"I told you why they're keeping me here, didn't I?"

He nodded. About to go over the story again, she decided he didn't need to hear how she'd been taken in by a handsome face and a lot of empty flattery.

"They live on hopes and dreams," she said instead. "Every deluded one of them. My husband was the worst of all, probably because his grandfather's first strike was made right here on this very hill. Actually, it was his only strike. I don't think the poor old man ever found another speck of gold, but he kept on trying until the day he died." She sighed, her gaze focusing on the past. "So did Devin. Kept on searching, that is. Until the day he died. Did I tell you that?"

She probably had. Goodness knows, she'd been talking a blue streak.

Jed coughed, winced and swore. She told him that his bindings needed tightening. "I'm not sure I can do it alone."

And he couldn't help her. Short of planting a foot on his side to gain leverage, which was hardly the recommended technique, she couldn't think of a way to bind him any tighter.

"Tourniquet," he said.

"I beg your pardon?"

He grimaced and shook his head. After a few moments passed in silence, Eleanor said, "Let me go see if the willow bark tea has steeped long enough." She stood and reached for the tray.

"Sticks."

Pausing, she sent him a questioning look. She was tempted to beg his pardon again when it dawned on her. "Sticks. Like wringing out laundry. Of course!"

Leaving the dishes in the kitchen, she hurried out to the woodpile and collected several of the smallest sticks of kindling. She wasn't quite sure how to use them in this case, but between them they would find a way.

Propped up on the bed pillow with the rolled quilt behind his back for added support, Jed waited to see how she would go about it. He could think of several ways to achieve the needed results, none of them particularly comfortable, but the results should be worth any momentary discomfort. Before he could think about getting away from here, he had to be able to move freely and to breathe without feeling as if his innards were being punctured.

Eleanor held a stick of pine in her hand and frowned at his chest. "Hmm," she said thoughtfully.

Between them, they worked out a method. She would jam a stick under the top layer of binding and twist until he told her to stop. After securing the end by tucking it under a fold, she would go on to the next, always working from the front.

God help him if he tried to roll over onto his stomach. Even sitting up he could feel the hard ends jabbing him through the padding, but at least he wasn't as apt to kill himself off if he happened to sneeze.

"There now, how does that feel?" she asked, satisfaction evident in the flush of color that stained her cheeks.

He could have told her he felt like a porcupine that had taken to wearing his coat inside out, but he didn't. She was doing the best she could with the resources at hand. He could hardly ask for more than that. "Bring on your willow bark tea," he said. "My mother used to make the stuff. Bitter as gall, but it does the trick."

"Oh. You have a mother," she said, as if awed by the confidence.

He knew she was curious, but she could just live with it. He wasn't about to tell her how his mother had left an uncomfortable situation among her own people, taken up with Loran Dulah, nursed the old man's wife through a lingering illness, looked after their son and then ended up bearing the old man another son and raising both boys until she'd died of lung fever.

His private, personal history didn't concern anyone, not even his half brother, who knew most of it, anyway. All she needed to know was that he would never take advantage of an unprotected woman, even if he were in any condition to do so. Even if he were tempted.

The following day Eleanor circled the cabin in search of wild greens. From time to time she would glance toward the house, half expecting her patient to be standing in the doorway. Now that his ribs were bound and he could halfway see out of one eye, he was chafing at the bit, clearly eager to be on his way. "Stubborn man," she muttered. But then weren't they all?

As if she would even know. She couldn't remember her father. Dreamed she could, but it was probably only her imagination—the tall man who held her up to touch the angel on a Christmas tree, who let her sip from his coffee cup. Who laughed when she giggled hard enough to wet her pants.

Both her parents had died in the influenza epidemic when she was three, and she'd gone to live with her unmarried cousin, Annie Mayne, a schoolteacher in Charlotte. She must have cried every night for years, but if Annie had heard her, she never mentioned it.

Annie had never married. Never even had a suitor, so far as Eleanor knew. As for Eleanor herself, she had once attended a tea with the new minister at their church, but the only other single man she'd known well enough to do more than exchange pleasantries with had been Devin— the man she'd married.

And as it turned out, she hadn't known him at all.

Having gathered a basket of wild mustard, dandelion, lamb's-quarter and cress, Eleanor stopped by the henhouse to collect the eggs. "Thank you, ladies," she said, scooping up grain with one hand and scattering it on the ground. The hens would have a good scratch before the squirrels discovered it. It was the best she could do. If she left them cooped up they'd be easy prey for weasels and raccoons.

Jed insisted on feeding himself again when she took him a boiled egg and what she called pan bread, which was no more than biscuit dough patted into a large flat cake and cooked on top of the stove in a skillet with the lid askew. It wasn't pretty, but it was quick and easy, and she'd dribbled a bit of honey on it. He liked his coffee black and bitter, which was just as well. She was running short of coffee beans, though, so he might have to settle for water.

"The less you move around, the better," she reminded him. "As soon as you finish your breakfast I'll bring you a basin of water for your hands, and then you can sleep some more. Sleep heals," she said earnestly. At least it did if a body was going to heal. It hadn't healed cousin Annie. She had slept and slept and then she'd died.

Without his having to ask, she handed him the chamber pot and then left, closing the door behind her. She would take him the basin and soap when she went to collect the pot. Poor man…it had to be embarrassing. How would she feel if their positions were reversed?

She spent the next half hour in the ragged garden she had halfheartedly planted when Miss Lucy had sent up slips of this and that. She'd had no intention of being here to harvest anything, but if she hadn't seemed interested, they might have asked why, and she'd have had to tell them that it was because she had no intention of spending another summer trapped on their blasted, tunnel-ridden hill.

The morning sun beat down on her shoulders, searing right through the threadbare gown as she swooped down to snatch a green stalk from the ground. She stepped on her hem, heard it rip, and grimaced. Oh, well—the blasted stuff had gone to seed anyway, that which hadn't frozen. As for the dress, it had seen its best days too long ago to remember.

Her trousseau had consisted mostly of the carefully maintained and frequently remodeled dresses she wore to work, most of them of some neutral shade that didn't show dirt. Her two good dresses included a blue sprigged muslin and the rose silk that had served as her wedding gown. By now she'd worn everything to death except for those.

And her hair. What on earth was she going to do about her hair? Cut it off? It might come to that. Her soft-bristled brush was so worn it only skimmed over the surface. Hair like the type she'd been cursed with—curls so tight they defied a comb—needed a good, stiff brush and regular grooming. Instead, she washed it with lye soap and let it dry in the sun, scarcely bothering to look in a mirror, as there was never anyone here to care how she looked.

Tonight she might sweep up her hair and gather it into a knot at the back of her head. She still had half a dozen tortoiseshell pins, although she'd lost most of her supply. It had never occurred to her when she'd first set out from town that she would no longer be able to shop for such simple things as hairpins.

She was on her way to the house when someone called her name. "Elly Nora?"

Wheeling around, she clapped a hand over her heart and nearly dropped her basket. "Oh, it's you, Hector. You startled me. I was expecting—that is, I wasn't expecting you."

She watched her cousin-in-law stride into the clearing, his eyes as blue as morning glories in his lean, tanned face. He really was a handsome man, but he was still a Miller, every bit as hardhearted as the rest of the clan underneath that pleasant manner.

"I been out stumping this morning." He wiped his forehead with a bandana, then stuffed it back in the pocket of his overalls. "Hot work. Thought I'd come up and see how you're getting on. You need anything from town?" Going to the nearest market town was an all-day affair, not to be taken lightly. "I'll be headed out at first light."

She stayed where she was, hoping to draw him away from the house, but he sauntered over to the tiny back stoop and sat, one big bare foot swinging as he filled his pipe with tobacco.

She could have told him she needed hairpins, but more than that, she needed to get rid of him. What if he went inside the house? He seldom did unless it was raining or snowing, but what if this time he decided to come in for a visit?

Or what if Jed wandered outside? Granted, the poor man could barely move, much less get up and walk, but what if he tried to turn over and it hurt and he cried out?

She didn't think Hector had been involved in the beating. More than likely it had been Alaska and his whiskey-making cronies, but then again, she had never seen Hector in a temper. He was certainly strong enough to do serious damage.

"I can't think of anything I need, but thank you for asking." Then she thought to add, "Well, maybe another sack of cornmeal. Mine got weevily." Mercy, she never knew she was so good at lying. "I've been drinking more coffee lately, too—perhaps another pound of coffee beans? And maybe some hairpins and ham or bacon?"

He nodded. "Don't reckon you've heard anything lately?"

Heard anything? Like what? A man crying for help because he'd been attacked by a band of drunken backwoods ruffians? "Well, I thought I heard thunder last night, but it never rained. Ground's as dry as a bone."

He nodded again. Nervously, she went on, gilding the lily as cousin Annie used to say. "The ravens were kicking up a fuss this morning, and to hear those eagles screaming, you'd think they were fighting a war instead of just courting. And whichever dog that is that barks all night—"

"Billy's old coon dog. He treed Miz Lucy's tomcat. Cat come a-shinnying down the tree and lit into him, like to tore him up. You partial to peppermint? I could bring you some candy."

Candy? What ailed the man? Had he decided to follow suit and court her for Dev's shares, the way all the other bachelors had done?

Merciful heavens, not now, she thought frantically. The last thing she needed was another suitor. At first she'd thought the others had been teasing when they had offered her their hand in marriage, twisting the traditional words. But one thing the Millers lacked —among several she could name—was a sense of humor.

"If you want to know what I'd really like—other than to go back to Charlotte, that is—I'd really, really like a newspaper. I don't even care which one, just so I can keep up with what's going on in the world."

Just so she could see if anyone wanted to hire a teacher just as the school year was drawing to a close. Or a tutor, or a housekeeper, or even a shop clerk.

"Well, we ain't at war, if that's what you was worried about. I reckon that there's something. They's a whole bunch of new places being built up along the new railroad lines, and they's fixin' to let some more o' them western territories into the union. If you like licorish better, I could bring you some of that 'stead o' peppermint.''

Smiling stiffly, Eleanor waved away a swarm of gnats attracted by her sweaty skin. The sun felt more like July than April. How could she make him leave? To think of all the times she would have welcomed his company— welcomed any company at all. Now that she couldn't wait for him to go, the stubborn man wouldn't move.

''I went to school,'' he said, looking so proud and shy she felt her resolve begin to melt. ''All the way to the third grade, did Dev tell you?''

''He told me,'' she said gently. My God, how was it possible in this day and age for such pockets of sheer ignorance to exist? The governor ought to be tarred and feathered and run out of Raleigh.

''I think that's commendable, Hector. Have you ever considered going back to school?''

Don't ask questions, you fool—don't invite him to linger! What if he hears something and goes inside?

''Don't need to,'' he said, swinging his foot. It was the only sign that he was at all embarrassed. If he were embarrassed enough, would he leave?

''Of course you need to,'' she said firmly. ''Every man needs to be educated. How else can you hope to keep up with what's going on in the world?''

The foot swinging stopped. He eased off the porch and said, ''You real sure you didn't hear nothing a few nights ago?'' Was it her imagination, or was that suspicion that narrowed his gentian-blue eyes?

Wordlessly, she shook her head. Surely Hector hadn't been a part of it. She had thought better of him…but then, he was a Miller, after all, third-grade education or not.

Moving with maddening deliberation, he knocked the

burning tobacco from his pipe against the sole of his bare foot. "I'll bring you a sack o' meal and some coffee beans," he said. "Maybe some meat. You need some corn for them hens o' your'n?"

She nodded. Anything—anything to get rid of him.

Chapter Seven

How odd, Eleanor thought as she watched the dense laurel thicket swallow him up. In the shy, polite way of the Miller men—most of the Miller men, she corrected—it was almost as if he were courting her. Yet, not once had she caught any sign of real interest in those clear blue eyes. Even the twins, Buster and Abner—two wild young hellions barely out of their teens—had been more convincing. The lure of an older woman, perhaps.

And of course, the lure of all those mythical gold shares.

Catching a final flash of blue on the path below, she breathed a sigh of relief. It had been bad enough before, knowing that she was a prisoner. Now that she had something to hide—some*one* to hide—her situation was even more precarious.

Once inside, she glanced through the bedroom door to see if by any chance Jed had overheard anything. He might have recognized Hector's voice. She hoped not, but still…

He was sleeping. Or pretending to sleep. In any case, she might as well take the opportunity to bathe and change out of her gardening clothes. She had a tendency to crawl from place to place when she was gathering greens.

She bathed quickly, glancing frequently toward the open

bedroom door in case by some miracle Jed should emerge to surprise her. Standing in the middle of the kitchen floor in her drawers and bodice, with a man lying only a few feet away made her feel oddly breathless. Not only daring, but downright wicked.

After donning clean underwear she considered her options. Earlier she had brought most of her personal things out into the living room, hiding her underwear in a box under the sofa and hanging her dresses from pegs on the wall where Devin's and his grandfather's guns used to hang. If Hector had come inside, he would have had to wonder why they weren't in the bedroom.

Now she looked over the paltry selection. Certainly not the rose silk, that was much too fine, but there was really nothing wrong with wearing her blue sprigged muslin. It was certainly modest enough, the high collar made even higher with the row of ecru lace she had added when the seam at the throat had begun to fray. Besides, it was only sensible to save her everyday dresses for housework and gardening.

Her hairbrush was still in the bedroom. She'd forgotten to retrieve it, along with her other pair of shoes. After sniffing the muslin dress to be sure it didn't smell musty, she slipped it over her head, hurriedly fastened the jet buttons, and tiptoed into the bedroom.

He was still there. She hadn't imagined him. It wouldn't have been the first time she had imagined a friend—someone to talk to when loneliness made her fear for her sanity. After endless months of being alone, with only the briefest infrequent visits from people with whom she had nothing in common, she still couldn't believe there was a man in her bed. True, he wasn't much company, but he was a real, live, warm human being. Someone she could talk to without feeling as if she'd slipped too far round the bend.

Eleanor told herself it was good that he was still sleeping. Good that he'd slept clean through the middle of another day and into the afternoon. Sleep was beneficial, and besides, she was having trouble putting together three meals a day for two.

"Do you like my dress?" she murmured, turning to catch her reflection in the small looking glass over the washstand. "I bought it brand-new the year I graduated from college. I added the buttons and lace myself the year after I started teaching. I think they add a rather nice touch, don't you?"

No answer, of course. Not so much as the flicker of an eyelid. The swelling was going down nicely now that she'd made him cold compresses for both eyes, but his poor face was a sight to behold. She hadn't noticed before, but he had nice eyebrows. Dark, silky, just thick enough, with just the right amount of arch.

"I thought first of using pearl buttons. With the blue, you know. But the jet adds just the right touch of formality so that I can wear it for special occasions."

His mouth really didn't twitch, did it? It was only her imagination. She'd been staring at his face, willing him to wake up and talk to her. She was probably just seeing things.

With a sigh, she collected her shoes and her hairbrush and left, thoroughly ashamed of herself. "For heaven's sake, Eleanor, the poor man is ill," she muttered, plopping herself down on the sofa. "He's not a toy, brought here for your amusement. Behave yourself!"

Easier said than done, she thought ruefully. For a mature, respectable woman, she was acting like a shameless hussy, flirting with a poor man who was in no position to defend himself.

With an impatient sigh, she glared at the spool-heeled

high-tops, bought years ago to wear to church. She hadn't worn them since Devin's funeral, but she knew in advance they were going to pinch. For everyday wear, she had her sturdy, flat-heeled, round-toed teaching shoes, but now, like so much else in her life, they were threatening to fall apart.

Sometimes she even went barefoot, something she had never, ever done back in Charlotte. Cousin Annie claimed worms could get into your body through the soles of your feet. For a retired schoolteacher, Annie Mayne had harbored a few peculiar notions, but Eleanor missed her far more than she missed her late husband. If Annie had still been alive, none of this would be happening to her now. She would never have been vulnerable to a man like Devin Miller.

Sliding one bare foot over beside the pointy-toed shoe, she compared the shapes. Her feet had spread, probably from going barefoot in the house. It was plain to see the shoes no longer fit properly, if they ever had.

"Vanity, vanity," she muttered. Tugging on her hose, she crammed her foot into one of the stylish shoes and winced. No doubt about it. She'd be limping before the day was over.

Covering her dress with a clean apron, one she'd made from one of Cousin Annie's kitchen curtains, she tottered into the kitchen, washed the greens and put them on to boil with a pinch of salt. Oh, for a strip of seasoning meat. Adding salt, water and one precious egg to a cup of cornmeal—it wasn't actually weevily, she'd only said that as an excuse to get more—she made corn bread to go with the greens. It wasn't much, but it was the best she could do until more supplies were provided.

At home the evening meal had been called dinner. As much as she'd tried to maintain civilized standards, by no stretch of the imagination could wild greens and corn bread be called "dinner."

Nevertheless, she arranged it on one of her three remaining china plates and folded a linen napkin beside it. All her life she'd been drilled on the importance of maintaining standards. "I've backslid as far as I intend to," she declared to no one in particular as she elbowed the bedroom door open and entered, tray in hand.

My mercy, was that a smile tugging at the corners of his poor battered lips? "I'd better put something on that mouth of yours again. It's healing nicely, but once you start talking and—" She started to say smiling, but in case he denied it, she changed it to eating. "—and trying to eat, you could open the split again."

He actually did smile then. She nearly melted on the spot. He had a beautiful mouth now that most of the swelling had gone down. She couldn't remember the last time anyone had offered her a genuine smile. The Millers weren't much for smiling, not even Devin, once he'd won his objective.

"Pants," he said.

"Your blue jeans? They're clean and dry, just as good as new," she said. "I could help you put them on, but you'd probably be more comfortable the way you are now."

He was wearing only the strips of sheeting on his upper half, the bottom of his long johns with the left leg cut short to accommodate his swollen ankle, which was no longer quite so swollen. She had managed to get the things off him long enough to wash and dry them, but it had been an uphill battle.

Another uphill battle, she amended silently, thinking of the way he had struggled up the path and practically collapsed at her feet.

"I wish I had some news to share," she said brightly, "but not much ever happens up here." Did he know about her visitor? Had he recognized the voice? "It's only wild greens, but I made some corn bread. I hope you like it— I used the last of the butter on it." On your portion, she amended silently. She would eat her share dry. It wouldn't be the first time.

"Fry bread."

"I beg your pardon?" She lifted a fork full of greens, but before it could reach his mouth, he took the fork from her hand. "Well, all right, if you insist, but I don't mind feeding you, not one bit."

If he didn't need her to feed him, he wouldn't need her company, and she didn't want to leave. She tucked a towel under his chin to keep the greens from dripping all over his binding, noticing as she did how fast his beard grew. "I could bring my supper in here and we could dine together?"

Jed took a bite of corn bread and she waited for some indication, either that he liked it, or that he would welcome her company.

"Yes, well...I'll just get my plate and be back in a minute. Did you want pepper vinegar with your greens? I forgot to ask."

"Thank you, no. It's good. Bread's good. Thank you."

Outside the bedroom, she leaned against the white-washed log wall and beamed. He talked whole sentences. He liked her food. He didn't tell her not to come back. "'Oh, frabjous day, callooh, callay, she chortled in her joy,'" she misquoted.

Did he like poetry? Did he like Lewis Carroll? Oh, they had a million things to talk about. She'd been saving up forever!

* * *

While she clattered around in the kitchen, Jed scraped up the last of his greens. He'd give ten dollars for a beef-steak, but not only did he not have ten dollars—they'd stolen his damned saddlebags, with everything inside—his clothes, his gun, his money—but he wasn't sure he could handle anything thick and tough.

Besides, the woman—Eleanor—obviously didn't have any beef. Judging from what he'd seen and heard, she had little of anything. Were her kinfolk trying to starve her?

For a skinny woman, she was shapely enough, but she could have used another five or ten pounds. He liked well-rounded women. Liked all women, he just didn't care to get involved with one. He'd tried that once a long time ago and still bore the marks.

"I'm putting the kettle on for tea," she called out from the kitchen. "Real tea this time, not willow bark."

He said, "Mm."

What the devil was that gibberish she'd been spouting when she'd left to get her supper? Who was Ka-Lou? What was a kalay? He knew what a chortle was, it was a kind of a laugh—a chuckle. He also knew that if he tried it, it would probably kill him.

She came through the door carrying a plate, a fork and a napkin, beaming like the lantern on a caboose. It was all he could see, that smile of hers. What was it about her smile that was so different from other women's smiles?

One thing came to mind right off. Other women usually wanted something from him. Money, for the most part. Fifty cents, a dollar—two dollars. Whatever the going rate was.

He had never quite figured out what it was Vera had wanted from him, back when she'd first started hanging around her father's lineshack where he'd been staying while he worked fence. It sure as the devil hadn't been money, because he hadn't had any. Old Stanfield had been big on promises, but slow to deliver when it came to paying off his hands. By the time he'd left there—been run off, more like—he'd worked two and a half months for the old skinflint, and had yet to see a payday.

Unless he considered sleeping with Stanfield's daughter payment. After the first time, money had been the last thing on his mind.

"Well. I see you've already finished." She sat and started to eat, looking at him expectantly after every forkful, like she expected him to start a conversation.

Jed considered pretending to fall asleep again. If she stayed in the room with him much longer, she was bound to talk. And if she asked him a question, he might feel obliged to answer. That required breathing, and breathing still hurt.

The damned sticks digging into his chest through the rags hurt. His face hurt, his head hurt, and so did his leg. His ankle throbbed like war drums. The skin was as tight as any drum. He knew. He'd twisted around until he could see. Damn near ruined him, too. He'd all but cried himself to sleep and then slept all day.

How long had it been now? Two days? Three? Lying here in bed, trussed up like a damned mummy, he had trouble keeping track.

"Well," she said. She said that a lot. Sort of like, "What shall we talk about now?"

"What shall we talk about?" she said brightly. "I've been thinking, and I believe I know how we can get away once you're well enough to travel."

"Mm?" She didn't need any encouragement to babble away like a mile of white water.

"You see, I've been going about it all wrong. At first I openly asked for a ride to the nearest town. After that, I tried to think of ways to convince them to let me leave, and then I started trying to sneak away.'' She shook her head, poked a forkful of greens between her soft pink lips, tilted her head thoughtfully and said, "Salt."

He didn't say a blessed word. Didn't need to. Some creatures needed a prod to get them started; all she needed was a pair of ears.

Didn't even need that, come to think of it. Half the time while he was asleep, or pretending to be, she was out there all by herself, rattling on about gold and crazy people and somebody called cousin Annie. Talking to her chickens. Talking to a peckerwood that was hammering a hole up under the eaves. Fool woman actually offered him corn to quit drilling.

Might get better results if she'd offer him a few worms.

"—but of course, they have this stupid thing about Devin's shares. I told you about that, didn't I? How my late husband inherited this mythical gold mine from his grandfather, and now I've inherited it from him, and I don't even want it, even if there is any gold left. I'm convinced there's no more than a few grains at best—just enough to tantalize them into thinking they're going to strike it rich any day now. They keep on panning the creek, putting up signs to keep anyone else from daring to come anywhere close. Honestly, you'd think by now—"

"Huh." That was it, then. His offense. Not only had he come close to their holy-water creek, he'd been on his hands and knees getting set to drink his fill.

"I'm sorry. Did you say something?"

Nothing she needed to know. Trying to get a word in edgewise was like trying to split a playing card front from back, not worth the trouble.

"I know, I know—I talk too much. It's a failing I'm working to cure."

Jed had to chuckle at that. Nearly killed him, but he laughed and groaned, and then laughed some more.

Alarmed, she jumped up, set her plate aside and leaned over to try and keep him from hurting himself. Although how she thought throwing her arms around him could help escaped him.

Her hands were all over him, supporting his shoulders, jabbing those twist sticks into his chest as she pressed him back against the pillows. He had three pillows now. Hers, dead Devin's and a third one to replace the rolled-up quilt. Must have plucked her hens and stuffed a pillow slip.

"I'm all right now," he told her reluctantly. Having her hands all over him, her face practically brushing against him—that was kind of nice. Took his mind off the fact that while he was lying in bed being waited on hand and foot, Sam Stanfield could be closing in on George, fixing to drive him and his family out of Foggy Valley with no more than they could carry off in a gunnysack.

"What was funny?" she asked, taking her place in the chair again.

Nothing was funny, not one damned thing. Or rather, you are, he wanted to say, but didn't. She wouldn't understand, and he wasn't up to explaining. Instead, he asked a question of his own. "How did your husband die?"

In other words, did you talk him to death, or did one of the village witch doctors do him in? Or maybe he ran afoul of the same gang of maniacs that nearly put out my lights.

"He blew himself up."

Well, he thought, using her most oft repeated word. Can't get much deader than that. He was mildly curious, but he could do without hearing all the gory details. He was more interested in this plan she claimed to have conceived for getting them safely out of the territory. "Mm," he said thoughtfully.

It was all the encouragement she needed.

"He was blasting right near the adit—that's the entrance to the mine—trying to widen the drift in another direction. Some of the others said his fuse wasn't long enough. Anyway, we buried him sort of in the same place, since that's where most of him was. Hector poured cement over his grave so nobody would dig there. I wrote his name and the date while the cement was still wet. It was the best we could do. It's shady there, of course, so flowers won't grow."

Jed closed his eyes, at a complete loss for something to say. He'd been called glib a time or two—especially when a game turned sour and the other players were a whole lot bigger than he was, not to mention better armed. But in all the learning he'd done since he'd left Foggy Valley, broke, beaten and branded, too dumb to know when he was licked, he had never learned the proper way to deal with a genuine lady.

Especially when he happened to be lying in her bed.

"Looks like rain," he said finally. Let's see what she could do with an opening like that.

"There's not enough grass up here to keep a cow, that's why the only animals I have are my two layers. I can't even raise frying chickens, because I can't grow enough feed and someone would have to cart it up the hill, so it's just easier for them to raise all the meat down in the valley and bring me whatever I need. Well…within limits."

It was a perfectly reasonable response to his own observation, Jed thought, amused. Used about five times as many words as she'd needed to do, but none he'd needed to look up.

"I took a course in economics," she said, trying to hide her bare toes under the hem of her pretty blue frock. She thought he hadn't noticed. He could have told her that even groggy with pain, there was little that escaped him. She'd been wearing pointy-toed shoes when she'd brought in his tray. Left 'em behind when she'd brought in her own.

"That's why I can't boil my hens. You see, it's a matter of interest and principal. My hens are the principal and the eggs they lay are like interest. If I eat the principal, there'll be no more interest, it's as simple as that. That's why it came to me when I was collecting eggs—a way we could both get away with no one noticing. Only first, we have to get you well enough to travel."

Chapter Eight

Maybe, Jed mused, he wasn't as far along as he'd thought. The swelling on his head had gone down, his headache little more than a distant pounding. Evidently, though, he'd managed to shake loose a few important parts under his thick skull. Just when he thought she was making sense…she wasn't.

He closed his eyes and pretended to be sleepy, and after several long moments—moments during which he felt her gaze moving over him, either measuring him for a shroud or trying to gauge whether he'd be more of a help or a hindrance—she left.

He opened his eyes and breathed in the lingering scent of greens, lye soap and some intangible essence that was hers alone.

The next morning—the third day? The fourth? Jed had lost count. He waited until she was hanging her laundry on the line before he tried to get out of bed. It was a slow and painful process, but it had to be done. Lying in bed was making him weaker, not stronger. There was an outhouse about ten yards behind the cabin. He would either make it or he'd die trying.

He damned near died trying. She'd handed him her broom to use as a crutch that first day, so he collected it again on his way out. It helped. Couldn't put much weight on it, but it helped to steady him. The swelling had gone down some on his ankle, but it was still tender.

It was his ribs that bothered him most, though, and there wasn't much he could do about it except walk straight, try not to cough, sneeze or twist, and hope he wasn't doing any permanent damage. Cracks would mend, given enough time.

Which was something he didn't have to spare.

She was still outside when he emerged from the privy. Leaning against the rough plank door, he took stock of his surroundings, never losing sight of the woman on the far side of the clearing. There was a worm fence, four rails high, running across the back of the clearing where there'd been a sizable slide at one time. Recently, from the looks of it. At least, it hadn't stared to grow over yet.

In the edge of the clearing he spotted several bee gums with the tops missing that were overgrown with vines. The old man who'd built the cabin might have tended them, but it didn't look as if anyone had in recent years.

He tried and failed to picture Eleanor raiding a gum for honey.

Hard to picture such a woman living alone here at all, much less doing all that needed doing to survive. In that blue dress she'd worn last night, she'd looked fine enough to grace any parlor, bare feet and all. Pretty as a picture, in fact, with her hair bundled up on top of her head. Started out that way, at least. Hair like that, wild and thick and curly, was never meant to be confined.

He watched as she tossed a handful of corn to her hens. Any minute now she was going to see him standing here and run clucking like one of her chickens, shooing him back into the house.

Levering himself carefully away from the outhouse door, he took a few unsteady steps toward the cabin. With any luck he could make it back before she spotted him.

She stayed outside, messing around in what she probably called a garden. His mother could have showed her a garden. Bess Blackstone had grown the finest vegetables in all Foggy Valley, enough to feed her family and lay away for the winter months.

Another lifetime, he thought sadly. Mostly he didn't think about the past, but from time to time something would remind him. He still carried the letter he'd received from Vera, forwarded by George nearly eight years ago. He'd been rescued by a traveling preacher, who had made him get in touch with his family and tell them where he was. George had forwarded the letter to the preacher's address, and Jed had carried it ever since, to remind him of who he was, of what he had barely escaped, and of how much he had to accomplish.

After about six weeks, he had parted company with the preacher, and as it turned out, he'd ended up accomplishing more than he'd ever dared hope, more from luck than any earnest labors. But he still had one task before him.

Loran Dulah had treated him fairly. He'd been a stern man, a cold man, showing no more affection for his oldest son than he had for the son he'd had with his Cherokee housekeeper. Jed had been seventeen when his father had died. He'd left a will, leaving the farm and all he possessed to his oldest son, with no mention at all of his younger son.

That's when Jed had gone to work for Sam Stanfield. No one in the valley had liked the man, but Stanfield, who'd owned half the valley at the time, had been the only man hiring. He'd begun to increase the size of his herd of blooded cattle, thus the need to run miles of new fencing.

Determined not to let George see how much it hurt to have been overlooked completely by his own father—he didn't care about the property, but dammit, they were blood kin—Jed had hired on with Stanfield.

And met Stanfield's only child, Vera, home for the summer from boarding school.

Eleanor brushed the corn dust from her hands and turned to go back inside. That's when she spotted him, her broom tucked upside down under his arm, hobbling back toward the house. Anger mixed with the urge to rush forward to catch him if he started to fall, but she held back. Putting herself in his place, she would probably have done the same. It had to be galling, having a strange woman helping him with the most intimate tasks.

He reached the back stoop with no trouble. Due to the way the land sloped it was higher than the front entrance. Four steep steps instead of three shallow ones. She waited with mixed emotions, a few that didn't bear close examination, to see what he would do.

When he glanced up and saw her watching him, she merely lifted her eyebrows as if to say, "Well? What's your excuse, other than a total lack of wit?"

He grinned at her. The arrogant, black-blue-and-purple devil *grinned* at her.

And darned if she didn't grin right back.

Shaking her head, she left him to get in as best he could, knowing his pride had to have suffered these past few days. It was bad enough to lose a fight without having to be rescued by a woman. In some ways he reminded her of the little boys she had known in her brief teaching career.

"I can run faster than you can."

"No you can't!"

"I can jump higher than you can."

"Cannot!"

"I can pee farther than you can."

"Boys," she muttered, washing her hands and drying them on a freshly laundered towel that still smelled of sunshine.

It took him nearly five minutes to climb the four stairs and let himself in through the back door. She didn't offer to help. Breathing heavily, he leaned against the doorjamb, watching her as she put a bowl of beans in to soak and refilled the kettle.

"Something to do with chickens," he said, and she blinked at him.

"What about chickens?"

"My escape."

"Our escape," she said, stressing the pronoun.

"My mistake," he said, echoes of that impudent grin lingering on his grizzled, multicolored face. At the rate his beard was growing, that intriguing cleft in his chin would soon be totally hidden.

"You're as bad as I am," she said, flustered for no real reason other than the fact that seeing him vertical instead of horizontal, she was aware of what a splendid creature he must be when he wasn't bruised and swollen and strapped up all the way to his armpits.

"Got your pants on, I see," she said, and felt herself growing warm with embarrassment.

"I did."

And they fit just fine, she thought, noticing the narrow line of skin showing between the top of the denim and the bottom of his bindings. She'd noticed it before—the lovely golden tint of his skin, but seeing it when he was clothed—

from the waist down, at least—was somehow different. As if he were no longer her patient, but her guest. That had to be what brought on this fluttery feeling inside her bodice. Maybe *she* needed binding.

"Sit down before you fall," she said gruffly.

"Can't." The grin was still in place. "Shot my wad."

"Oh, for heaven's sake, here—let me help you back to bed." She moved to position herself under his left arm, first taking the broom from his hand and propping it against the wall. "Say when you're ready."

"Sofa."

"Sofa," she repeated. "You're as bad as I am." She'd be the first to admit her conversations were inclined to be hit-and-miss affairs. When there was only one participant, the rules flew out the window.

She tried to steer him toward the bedroom, but he refused to be steered. He smelled good—like soap. She'd left a bar of soap, a dipper and a basin out by the rain barrel, for cleaning up when she'd been digging in her garden. Evidently he'd taken advantage of it on his way inside.

"All right, the sofa, then," she said, "But just for a little while. After we eat lunch, you'll have to go back to bed. I need you strong and well again if we're going to get away anytime soon."

This time it was tacitly accepted that they would leave together. She could hardly go off and leave him to the mercy of the Millers, unable to fend for himself. She would like to think he wouldn't leave her behind, either, but they had yet to discuss the details of her plan.

"Chickens?" he prompted again once she helped him get settled with his left foot propped on a cushion.

"I'll tell you about it while we eat. I'd better see what I can put together." Her larder was all but empty. The beans wouldn't be ready until suppertime. ''Would you like a book? I have several books of poetry and two collections of essays. You might enjoy looking through *Myrven's Book of Knowledge.* I've found it exceedingly helpful.'' She had noticed him that first day, when he was barely conscious, staring at her bookshelf.

Jed could have told her what would please him most at the moment. For once, it wasn't books. Not that he was in any condition to follow through. Besides, she'd probably be shocked right out of her pretty striped stockings if he invited her to share the sofa so that he could feel her and smell her faint fragrance.

Funny woman, he thought, watching her march across to the kitchen area. She could talk the ears off a jackrabbit, but she meant well. If it weren't for her, he'd have been carrion by now. The least he could do was behave himself, listen while she rambled on and hope to hell no one found him before he could protect them both.

He tried to watch her, but most of the time she was out of his line of vision. Then he would picture her, knowing from the sounds what she'd be doing. Dragging the kindling box out from behind the range, lifting the lid to poke up the fire. The way she put one foot behind the other when she bent over reminded him of a dance step, the kind he'd seen in pictures where a fancy-dressed gentleman held out his hand and a lady wearing half a mile of shiny skirt bent a knee and held up her wrist.

He guessed it was called dancing; he'd never asked. Shuffle, slide and squeeze your partner, that was the only kind of dancing he knew about.

Did she dance? Had she ever dressed up in one of those low-necked gowns he'd seen women wearing when they went into some fancy place on the arm of a gentleman in a boiled shirt and a black tie? He'd seen that in Raleigh, right there in the hotel where he was staying. Band music and everything. Stayed awake all night, listening and wondering what was going on...and why.

He was pretty sure Eleanor didn't wear one of those stiff corselets, because he'd had his arm around her a few times when she was helping him walk. Didn't need one. Her waist was no bigger than a gnat's ass as it was.

Of course, those things also served to push up a woman's bosom, and she didn't have much to push. Had enough though, he conceded. Just about right, matter of fact. He was all for stout, shapely women, but there was something about a delicately built woman that was...

Elegant was the word that came to mind.

"Here we go," she said brightly, her skirts swishing around her ankles as she brought in his plate and cup.

"Looks good," he said, eying the ambiguous stuff in the plate. Whatever it was, he would eat it because he needed his strength.

And because she was anxiously watching him take the first bite, and he didn't want to hurt her feelings.

"Delicious," he said. "What is it?"

"Um—there's some chopped egg and some wild onions, and I cooked the cornmeal with a tiny strip of ham skin I found in the cool house. I don't think it's old enough to have gone bad."

He was sorry he'd asked.

"About my boots," he said, "I don't know much about this plan of yours, but walking out of here barefoot doesn't seem like such a great idea. I mean, sharp rocks are one thing, but you step on a pine seed or a holly leaf and it hurts like the very devil." He took another bite. It wasn't that bad, once you got used to the taste. He wondered if she knew how to make fry bread. His mother's fry bread had been the best in all Foggy Valley. It beat that dry, white-flour brick she'd served him earlier all to hell and back.

"Yes, well…I've been thinking."

He braced himself. When Eleanor Scarborough—plus all the rest of her names—got to thinking, a man would do well to be on his guard.

"I told you about all the other times I tried to get away, didn't I?" She had told him six dozen times by now.

"I believe you might have mentioned it," Jed said, suppressing a grin that would probably have hurt more than it helped. His split lip had healed, but there weren't many areas of him that weren't black-and-blue.

"Hush," she scolded, not even trying to hold back her own smile. "I know, I know, I probably told you a dozen times, but when nothing ever happens and nothing ever changes, there's not a lot to talk about."

He nodded, wondering how she ever got a comb through that mop of hers. He could still remember seeing his mother brush her long, iron-gray hair every morning before braiding it.

"Well, anyway, as I was saying, the first time I didn't even know I was a prisoner. The next few times I tried to sneak past without anyone's knowing it, but there's always someone around doing something, even if it's only throwing scraps to the hogs." She scowled, obviously recalling her failed attempts. "I hated it," she whispered, "I felt like a—a felon, being captured and brought back to my prison cell."

And he thought he'd had a run of bad luck all those years ago? Compared to what she'd been forced to endure, he'd led a charmed life. At least he had once he'd grown up and had some of the wildness beaten out of him a time or two.

"You see, I didn't think things through before. This

time I did. That's why this time I'm sure we can get away without being discovered. We'll use the chickens.''

The chickens again. Carefully, he set his empty cup aside. Eleanor squared her shoulders. She was a pretty woman. A scowl didn't take away from her prettiness, it only rearranged it. She said, ''Of course, something could still go wrong. Some of the old folks are deaf as a post—they might not hear the ruckus.'' As if she were blundering through the wilderness and suddenly came to a trail, she beamed. ''But then, they wouldn't hear us, either, would they? And as long as no one saw us—''

''You want to start at the beginning and tell me what your plan is? All I know is that it has something to do with chickens.''

Reaching for his dishes, she stacked them with her own. ''Yes, well—I explained about the animals, didn't I? I'm pretty sure I told you how Mr. Hooter tends the oxen for when there's new ground to be broken or stumps to pull, and someone else keeps the mules they use to haul heavy loads. One of the older widows tends the milk cows because hers is the best pasture and she has five children to help with the milking and churning, and she trades milk and butter for other supplies. Several families keep hogs—it's easier to feed them that way—but they all pool together when it's time to slaughter, and—''

''The chickens?''

''Oh. Well, that's the lovely part of my plan. You see, except for a laying hen or two, all the chickens are kept by this one family that happens to live on the far side of the settlement. There must be a hundred chickens there. They trade fryers for corn and milk and butter and whatever anyone has to trade, and that way, everyone gets what they need. It works out surprisingly well because there's very little cash money available, only what Alaska gets when he sells a load of whiskey to outsiders, or Varnelle, when she sells seng—that's ginseng—to the buying man who comes by once a month.''

Slowly, bracing himself against the pain, Jed leaned forward and laid a hand over her lips. ''Eleanor. Stop. Now think back to the chickens.'' Her eyes widened, but he held her gaze. ''You said the chickens were going to help us get away. Would you mind explaining how?''

The wild urge came from nowhere—at least, nowhere that made sense—to replace his hand with his mouth. To kiss her until either she started making sense or he ceased to care.

Slowly, he removed his hand. He was hurting bad, but he refused to give in to pain. She took a deep breath and it occurred to him that she wasn't quite as lacking as he'd first thought in the bosom department.

''Well,'' she said. God knows, he thought, amused, where this was going, but he had nothing better to do than listen.

So he listened. ''Dogs always bark at chickens. There are lots of dogs. There are lots of chickens.'' She looked at him as if to say, Are you following all this?

He nodded.

''So if the chickens were to get loose, all the dogs would race over to the far side of the village, yapping their heads off. Everyone able to get out of bed would rush out to see what was wrong. They all do that, like when there's a fire or something.''

God, tell me she's not planning to burn them out, he thought.

''Then, while everyone's trying to catch chickens and dogs, you and I will be racing down the hill to the old wagon road on the other side of the settlement on our way to one of the outlying farms, one that doesn't belong to a Miller.''

He was silent for so long she probably thought she hadn't made herself clear. Granted, it was a simple plan—but sometimes simple was best. She leaned forward, cheeks flushed with color. "Don't you see—?"

He nodded. "I see. Tell me this, though—how will you know when it happens?"

"We'll know when it happens because we'll hear it. Once, when a weasel got in the chicken house, the chickens set up such a fuss every dog in the valley howled for hours."

"So we wait until a weasel gets in and we hear the dogs howling?" He tapped the knot on the side of his head, diminished now, but still there. "Help me out here, I'm not up to speed."

"No, no—you see, that's the best part. All we have to do is arrange with someone in advance, and then we can be waiting halfway down the hill, ready to run. I know a good place where the deer have made a track through the bushes."

Apparently she was waiting for him to congratulate her on having come up with such a brilliant plan. "You work with the tools at hand," she said. "I read that somewhere."

Moving carefully, Jed leaned back. Leaning forward, even for so short a time, had left him breathless and hurting. With a pitying look he said, "I hate to spoil your fun, but I'm not going anywhere until I'm pretty sure I can outrun a passel of rifle-toting men high on rotgut whiskey."

Her face fell. She was so easy to read, she wasn't even fair game. "Listen, Elly," he said.

"Don't call me that. *They* call me that, and I hate it.

It's hard enough to remember who I am. Sometimes I think it would be easier just to forget, but I can't. Cousin Annie didn't sacrifice all those years to send me to college just so I could turn into a—into a—''

''Barefoot, backwoods nobody,'' he said softly. ''I know what that's like, Eleanor. I came from a valley even farther back in the hills than this one, with even fewer people.''

The difference was that there'd been a man in Foggy Valley who had showed them all that another way of life was possible. They had all hated Sam Stanfield, but he was responsible for any success Jed had achieved.

''If you can just be patient a little longer,'' he said, ''we'll both get away. I have business to attend to, and I'm sure you have plans, too.''

What plans, he couldn't have said. He knew she had no family. She'd mentioned the fact more than once. Evidently it had been several years since she'd seen her friends. He didn't know if mail was even delivered this far off the beaten track. Before he had had the misfortune to run afoul of the Millers, he'd never even heard of a place called Dexter's Cut. He was pretty sure it wasn't on any map.

She sighed. He wished he could gather her into his arms and offer her comfort, but he was in no shape to comfort anyone. The best he could do was work at getting in shape to escort her out of this forsaken place. Heiress to a gold mine or not, she didn't belong here any more than he did.

Chapter Nine

Two days later Jed was on his way back from the out house when he stepped on a holly leaf and let out a yell that echoed out across the valley. Eleanor, cooking spoon in hand, rushed outside. The moment she spotted him and realized that he wasn't seriously hurt, she glanced apprehensively toward the path.

"Sorry," he said, knowing it wasn't enough. If someone had heard him, he wasn't sure he could move fast enough to get inside and out of sight.

"You stubborn man, I warned you—" she said, moving in to support him while he picked the little sticker out of the tender sole of his foot.

"I know." She'd reminded him more than once not to go outside, as she never knew when someone might come up the hill bringing supplies.

He had replied that he wasn't going to use her damned chamber pot one more time, and if she locked him in the bedroom and barricaded the door, then she'd be to blame when his bladder burst.

She'd looked so woebegone, he'd instantly regretted his words, but dammit, enough was enough. It had been five days now. Probably. He'd asked her and they had both tried to count it up, using small milestones. How many times she'd had to spoon-feed him before he could feed himself. How many times she'd had to bathe him—at least the parts he would allow her to bathe—before he had taken over the task himself. She was a lady. Ladies didn't bathe gentlemen, much less discuss their bladders.

But then, he was no gentleman.

Sometimes it felt as if he'd been here forever.

"Lean on me," she said now, positioning herself under his arm.

"I'm perfectly capable of walking," he said, ignoring the twinges when he set his left foot on the ground.

He allowed her to help him, though, because she needed to feel useful, and because he liked having her so close. She smelled good, she felt good and thinking about what she would be like in bed took his mind off a few other problems.

And that in itself was becoming a problem.

It had been three days since she had changed his bindings. The weather had turned off warm. Hot, for late April. "I can do without all this bandaging now," he'd told her earlier when she popped her head in to ask if he wanted one egg or two for breakfast.

He'd said one, knowing that one was likely all she had.

"Boiled, fried or poached, and no, you can't take off your binding. I don't know how long it takes ribs to mend, but if you undo all the good we've accomplished, we might never get away from here."

"Fried, and I promise not to twist, bend over or turn any cartwheels. Believe it or not, I'm as anxious as you are to get off this hellish mountain."

Yesterday they had argued about whether it was a mountain, a foothill or only a bump on the side of a ridge. They had argued about a lot of things to pass the time.

Sometimes he won, sometimes she did. Forced to concede a point, she was surprisingly good-natured. He tried not to feel too smug, but he couldn't help but take satisfaction in besting a schoolteacher.

What would she say, he wondered, if he admitted that his education, such as it was, had come from a circuit preacher who'd spent a few days every month in Foggy Valley, teaching anyone who was interested, child or adult, how to read the word of God.

Thanks to the preacher's patience, he'd been able to take advantage of public libraries once he'd discovered them, but that had been years later. Then, too, experience had taught him things no classroom ever could. But he was forced to admit that there were holes the size of a buffalo-wallow in what passed for his education.

Come to think of it, he owed a lot to various preachers. One of these days he might even take up churchgoing, but not quite yet. First he had a couple of debts to settle.

She insisted on helping him up the steps, which at this stage of his recovery, was more hindrance than help. He thanked her, though, and said, "I'm fine now. Go do whatever you were doing."

"I will as soon as I've had a look at those ribs of yours."

His eyes widened in mock horror. She couldn't always tell when he was teasing, and that made it even more tempting to tease her. "You planning on skinning me out?"

"If I have to," she shot back without a moment's hesitation.

Tell the truth, he was itching like crazy. Had been for days, but scratching didn't do a speck of good through all those layers.

Bracing his feet apart, he insisted on standing while she

unwrapped him. She called him stubborn, which he easily admitted.

"I need to practice being on my feet," he said. "Besides, my bum hurts from sitting so much."

"What's a bum?" she asked, all innocence, and then she caught his meaning, rolled her eyes, and muttered something under her breath that sounded almost like an oath.

"Ladies don't swear," he said piously.

She jerked out another stick and peeled off a length of sheeting. "Gentlemen don't refer to their—their posteriors in a lady's presence."

"Ah, come on now, El, aren't we beyond all that?"

Her lips twitched as she tried to repress a smile. "Your bruises have turned yellow," she told him. When he tried to look down, she said, "Hold still, I'm not through yet."

She was fast and efficient, reaching around him to grab an end, freeing it and then reaching around him again. When her fingers brushed across his navel, he sucked in his breath.

"Sorry. Did I pinch?"

He closed his eyes. "Ticklish," he said. He didn't specify which body part was itching now.

"That feels good," he admitted when she finished unwrapping him. He flexed his shoulders. "How about scratching while you're back there."

"Scratch what?"

Lady, don't ask. "My back, what did you think? I can reach my front."

So she scratched his back, gently dragging her short fingernails over his tingling skin. "Harder," he said, wanting her to dig in, knowing she would dig only so far. He could have done better using a long-handled cooking fork, but he didn't tell her so. No point in hurting her feelings.

She stepped back and gathered up the rags and sticks. "I'll bring your shirt," she said.

"No hurry. It feels good." The air on his skin. Being able to scratch freely. Being able to breathe without being jabbed by a stick of kindling. Had any man ever had such unorthodox treatment for cracked ribs?

Or such a temptress for a nurse?

"Just don't move suddenly," she said. "Wait right here and let me bring a basin of water. We'll rinse you off and then I'll dust you down with cornstarch, that should help your itches."

A few of my itches, he thought wryly, but not all of them. "Why don't I go out to your rain barrel and dipper myself off instead? It'd be faster and save you the trouble."

"Well for one thing, you don't need to tackle those steps again. For another, my basket is due today or tomorrow and I don't want anyone seeing you out there, that's why."

He couldn't argue with that. It was a pain in the butt, though, having to sneak around. He couldn't even go to the outhouse without her standing guard at a front window, ready to signal if someone came up the path. Once he'd narrowly missed getting caught by that Goliath in bib overalls she called Hector. He'd had to duck behind the outhouse and wait until the oaf took a notion to leave.

He'd made it back inside, but Eleanor had been furious when she'd found out. He'd defended himself by saying, "I thought you said no one ever stayed long enough to visit."

"Usually, they don't, but for some reason, Hector seemed to want to talk."

That had been yesterday, maybe the day before. It was easy to lose track of time. He hadn't been able to hear their conversation, but all manner of things had run through his mind. He had questioned her about it later.

"Was he suspicious? Is he trying to court you?" She'd told him about the parade of bachelors, all wanting to marry her for her inheritance.

"He was asking me if I'd seen any strangers, or heard anything unusual. He said he'd seen a lot of buzzards circling overhead the past few days."

"Godamighty," Jed had said reverently. "McGee."

"McWho?"

"My horse. I told you I had a horse when they caught me, remember? We were taking a drink from the creek when they jumped us. Last I remember, McGee was hightailing it down the road."

"They've probably caught him by now, then. He'll be all right. The Millers would never mistreat an animal. Not a domestic animal, at least."

Jed thought McGee hardly qualified as domestic, but he'd nodded, still thinking about those buzzards. Not that buzzards weren't a common sight here in the mountains. Something was always dying.

She had lain a hand on his arm then and hastened to reassure him. "I'm sure they would never hurt him. They might catch him and try to sell him, but they would never shoot a valuable animal. Not even Alaska."

"Shoot Alaska?" he teased. But by then he'd heard all about the bootlegger with the beautiful sister.

McGee, you old devil, he thought now, wherever you are, I'm not leaving here without you. Idly, he scratched his belly, the marks left by his fingernails blending with the horizontal crease marks left by his bindings.

"Let me get the basin, I'll be right back," she said, and reluctantly, he gave up on the notion of dousing himself from head to toe with the water from her rain barrel.

* * *

Eleanor hurried away, exasperated, but encouraged that Jed was able to move about so easily now. Well...hardly easily, she amended, but at least he was no longer bedridden. He'd slipped outside to the privy half a dozen times and hadn't fallen yet. Another few days—a week, at most—and he should be ready to travel. All she had to do was keep him hidden until then.

With the feel of his firm, warm body still tingling on her hands, the scent of him, all earthy and male, in her nostrils, she hurried through the house and dropped the rags in the tub to be dealt with later. With any luck they'd be left behind with almost everything else she possessed, but she had learned the folly of premature chicken-counting.

Mercy, he was an attractive man, she mused as she went about filling a basin with warm water and gathering up what he'd need for bathing. Stubborn, but then, all the men she'd ever known were that. Devin had been stubborn, too, only, he'd managed to get away with it for the first few weeks they were married by couching his demands in sweetheart language. "Honey, we can't do this," or "Sweetheart, we're going to do that."

Jed didn't bother with the sweet talk, he simply acted. Got up when he wanted to, exercised that leg of his whenever he felt like it, slipped outside without even asking her. It was a wonder he hadn't been caught the other day, with Hector sitting right there on the porch, smoking his pipe and looking at her in a way she still found puzzling. Almost as if he were considering if it was worth the trouble to keep her there.

Perhaps...

No. Her first plan was still the safest. She might not have much experience in matters of the heart, but even she could see the way Varnelle looked whenever his name was mentioned. She was no real threat—for heaven's sake, she was years older than Hector, but if Varnelle perceived her as a threat, then it was in the girl's best interest to help them get away.

She heard the door squeak open and there he was, just as she was getting ready to take his bathwater to the bedroom. Before she could set the basin down again, he was headed out the back door. "Come back here this minute," she ordered, using her best schoolteacher tone.

"Told you what I was going to do."

"Have you lost your mind? I told you I was expecting my supplies today."

"You said today or tomorrow. I'm not waiting another week to get a decent bath."

She slammed a basin down on the table, sloshing water that dripped off onto the floor. "If Alaska takes a notion to come up here with my basket this morning, he's not going to care if you're dirty as a pig, he'll—"

He grinned at her, and then he was gone. Eleanor sighed and shook her head. Snatching one of the rags from the washtub to mop up the water she'd spilled on the floor, she caught the scent of his body—ripe, but not at all unpleasant. Earthy, masculine...

"Well, my mercy, woman," she muttered, "why not make a complete fool of yourself while you're at it?"

She decided to wait five minutes, giving him long enough to pour a few dipperfuls of water over his body, dry off and get dressed again. He'd been wearing his Levi's and he'd taken his shirt out with him. She only hoped it didn't set him back, two trips in the space of an hour, up and down those steps.

She waited another five for good measure, then, with an

anxious look toward the front path, she stepped out onto the back stoop, ready to call him back inside.

And there he stood, bold as brass, strip-stark naked and dripping wet. While she watched, he poured a dipperful of cold water over his head, tilted his face back, and bared his teeth. He did it twice more before she caught herself staring and stepped inside again.

Breathing as heavily as if she'd been running uphill, she leaned against the door, unable to erase the striking image. If Michelangelo's David had come alive, he couldn't have looked more perfect. Or more beautiful, right down to the gleaming wet hair that dripped over his forehead and the pattern of dark hair that formed a T on his chest before arrowing down his middle to...

"Oh, for heaven's sake, woman, haven't you learned anything?"

Snatching up her egg basket, she hurried out the front door and around to the henhouse, which, fortunately, was on the other side of the cabin from the rain barrel. If she heard or saw anyone headed up the path, she would start singing. Something. Anything, as long as he didn't barge out into the open like a sitting duck.

A naked sitting duck.

There were no more eggs.

"Well, of course there aren't, you've already collected them once today," she said.

What she needed was red meat. Jed needed to build up his strength quickly if they were going to get away. If he was strong enough to defy her now, he should be strong enough to walk down the hill and through the valley. But first she had to arrange for an accomplice.

She would pay a visit to Varnelle tomorrow, Eleanor decided. They would have to go for a walk, though, because she wasn't about to tip her hand where there was danger of being overheard. Once she explained what she had in mind and why it would be to Varnelle's benefit, she might even offer an additional bribe. Her only jewelry was a watch that no longer worked and a wedding band she no longer wore because it turned her finger green, but there was her wedding dress. It would be too tight and too long, but it could be altered. Of course, rose wasn't the best color for a redhead, but Varnelle might like to have it anyway. Goodness knows, they weren't going to be able to take much with them.

All right then, she thought decisively. Today to make plans, tomorrow to make arrangements, the next day to pack and rest up and by that time, Jed should be ready.

Jed watched her hurry inside, wondering if she would mention what she'd seen. He knew she'd seen him. He'd heard her come outside, but by that time he'd managed to get shed of his jeans and pour half a dozen dipperfuls of water over his sore and itching carcass. He hadn't been about to risk damaging his ribs by bending to scoop his Levi's up off the ground, much less hopping around like a one-legged chicken to put them on again.

Now he toweled off, enjoying the caress of fresh air on his naked skin. Hated like hell to get dressed again, but there was no way he could face her the way he was, even knowing she'd already seen all there was to see.

Not quite everything, he corrected, amused and impatient with his body's reaction to his prurient imagination.

Prurient. Now there was an interesting word. He'd found it when he was looking up prudent—which someone had told him he wasn't. Dictionaries were almost as interesting as encyclopedias. He had already snuck a few looks at hers. It was a lot smaller than the one in the library, but just as interesting.

Dressed, he made his way up the steep steps, well satisfied with the progress he'd made. He'd been afraid being trussed up like a sausage might have weakened him, but it hadn't. At least if he sneezed or drew a deep breath, he wouldn't jab himself in the ribs with one of her blasted sticks.

She was standing at the stove when he went inside. He knew very well she'd heard him—the top step creaked—but she didn't look around.

"Is that bacon I smell?" He could've eased on past to the bedroom, where his clothes were.

"No, it's not," she snapped, glaring at the kettle that was just now beginning to steam. "I haven't had bacon in ages. If I'm lucky, they bring me some ham or sidemeat now and then."

"Just as well, I reckon. I can really make a pig of myself when it comes to bacon." He said it with a straight face and waited.

It took a minute. He watched her profile, saw her begin to crumble. Then a giggle escaped her and he felt as if he'd won a bull-riding event at the county fair.

"Sit down, it'll be ready in a minute." She tried to sound stern, but she wasn't fooling him one bit, nosiree. Not anymore.

"Yes, ma'am, just let me get rid of this towel. I forgot to leave it out back." On his way inside he'd seen the washtub filled with the strips she'd used to bind his ribs. He felt guilty as the devil, adding more to her workload, but he didn't know what else to do. "Make a deal with you," he said. "You fill the tub, I'll scrub, wring and hang everything."

"Don't be absurd."

"I thought I was being reasonable."

''I don't mind doing laundry, I have little enough to do, as it is.''

''A whole lot more since I've been here,'' he reminded her. ''I'd like to help.''

Her nose went up in the air, but she didn't take him up on the offer. Work aside, when Eleanor Miller missed a chance to talk, something was wrong. Offhand, Jed couldn't think of anything he'd done to offend her…if you didn't count getting caught buck naked with his pecker at half-mast just from seeing her standing there gawking at him.

She must have noticed, he mused, wondering what she'd thought of him. Wondering what the hell he was doing even thinking about such a thing. She was a schoolteacher, for God's sake. She was older than he was—not that that bothered him. He was years older in experience, and when it came to the crunch, experience counted a damn sight more than book learning.

To cover the awkward silence, he started talking. ''My mama—her name was Bess, but she's dead now. She used to keep her washtub—thing was cast-iron, weighed a ton—she used to keep it out in the backyard, turned down when she wasn't using it. On wash days she used to set it on three flat rocks and build a fire under it. Once the water started to boil and the suds started to make, she'd drop in the dirty clothes, poke at it 'em with a stick to loosen the dirt, then twist everything on the same stick to wring it out.''

She went on frying whatever she was frying. Griddle cakes, from the smell of it. Smelled great.

'''Course, you being a lady and a schoolteacher and an heiress and everything, you use a galvanized washtub and a washboard. I don't know about wringing, though. Can you twist things around that washboard of yours? What d'you do, plant a foot on it to hold it in place?''

He waited for her reaction. It wasn't long in coming. She held back as long as she could, then she burst out laughing. "You're a scamp, Jed Blackstone. You and that horse of yours must be quite a pair."

"Hey, don't go maligning my horse. McGee's got character." He hoped she was impressed with his vocabulary, he'd been working on it for years now. It was getting pretty impressive, if he did say so himself. "Eleanor, in case I forgot to thank you...thank you." Women, he knew for a fact, didn't always get the thanks they deserved. Some of them, like his mother, died without ever hearing the words.

She shook her head dismissively, but he thought the flush in her cheeks deepened. It occurred to him that if a sheep had long, golden wool, it would look like Eleanor's hair. She said, "I'm sorry I don't have any bacon. I'll put a note in the basket, and maybe if we get some before we leave I can fry it up to take with us."

"I didn't mean that, I just meant thank you, that's all. For everything."

He broke off. By now he was standing so close he could see the faint freckles on the back of her neck. They matched the ones across her nose and cheeks. If anything, they were even more tempting.

Spatula in hand, she turned just as he moved closer, mesmerized by those small, pale speckles. Startled, she stepped back, bumped against the hot stove and yelped. He caught her before she could fall, but not before she reached out to catch herself and burned her left hand.

"Jesus," he muttered, shaken. Holding her tightly with one arm, he jerked her away from the heat of the stove. "Jesus, Eleanor, I'm sorry. It was my fault."

She sucked her breath through her teeth in a way that told him how much she was hurting. "Let me see," he said, trying to get a look at her hand without releasing her.

"It's nothing." But she said it between clenched teeth.

"It's something. Burns hurt like the very devil. I know about burns." Oh, yeah, he knew about burns, all right. Had the scars to prove it, too. "Water," he said. "Hold it under water, they say that puts out the fire."

Nobody had offered to plop his tail in a bucket of water. Instead, they'd tossed him across his horse, slapped the critter on the rear end and laughed as he'd tried to hang on.

"Grease," she said, glancing at the can of lard on the shelf over the big range.

"Butter," he said, thinking of how soothing her buttery fingers had felt on his lips.

But neither of them moved because he was still holding on to her, as much for his sake now as for his. *Behave yourself down there, dammit!*

This was what came of not wearing underwear. She'd whacked his union suit up so bad it was all but useless.

Shaking her injured hand in the air as if she could fling the pain from her fingertips, she said, "It'll be better in just a minute, it doesn't really hurt very much."

"Yeah, I can tell." Wasn't she even aware of what was happening down there?

He knew the instant she figured it out. She looked startled, glanced down, then closed her eyes. Her flush deepened.

"Eleanor, no disrespect, but would you mind ignoring, uh—that? Please?" He thought longingly of the barrel of cold water outside under the eaves. A dipperful now, and he'd start steaming.

"Lard's good," he said hurriedly, hiding his embarrassment, "Lard works just fine."

She slipped from his arms and turned away. "There, I've gone and let the griddle get too hot."

That wasn't all that was hot. *Think cold water. Think standing under an icy waterfall.*

He was largely recovered from his brief exposure to the Miller clan. As for his exposure to Eleanor, that might take a little longer. Say a hundred or so years.

Chapter Ten

Once safely inside the bedroom, Jed leaned against the door and closed his eyes. Ready or not, he had to get away. He was beginning to think about things he had no business, and definitely no time, to think about. George was waiting for the money. For all Jed knew, the farm could already be gone, stolen out from under the family that had lived there for three generations, like too many others in the valley had been stolen. Stanfield knew exactly where to apply pressure. If there were no weaknesses, he and his band of hired hooligans would create one.

"Not this time," Jed whispered, drawing in a deep, resolute breath. Unless the old pirate had bought out the entire county seat and every judge east of the Smoky Mountains, this time he had met his match.

He didn't sit down because getting up again was still a slow and uncomfortable process. Pretending it wasn't only made it worse. That was something he was going to have to work on. He flexed his ankle a time or two to gauge the degree of discomfort. It was better, a lot better, but probably not up to a hellbent footrace down the mountain.

His ribs were another matter. He would just have to take his chances there. He didn't know enough about bones to know how long it took them to mend, but he wasn't fool enough to test them, not unless he had to. It was hardly the first time he'd taken a beating, although it had always taken more than one man to do it. What he lacked in brawn he made up in speed and experience.

Over the years he'd been lucky—in fights, with women and with cards, winning more often than he lost. But luck could change in an instant. He was going to need both luck and speed this time. He might hold a winning hand, but first he had to get back in the game. After all the times George had bailed him out of trouble when they were kids, it was his turn now to return the favor.

Loran Dulah had been a cold man, a narrow-minded man who hadn't been able to see beyond his own prejudices. A Cherokee housekeeper had been good enough to raise his firstborn son when his wife had taken to her bed with a wasting fever. She'd been good enough to take to his own bed after his wife had died, but not good enough to marry, damn his stone-cold heart.

There was a certain degree of satisfaction—all right, a whole lot of satisfaction—in being able to keep old Loran's farm in the family. The Dulah family, if not the Blackstone portion.

"You're a small-minded bastard, you know that?" he muttered, sucking in his belly to shove in his shirttail. Not as much belly as he'd ridden in with, but a few good meals should take care of that.

"Your breakfast is ready," Eleanor called from the other side of the door. "Such as it is."

"Coming."

"Such as it is" turned out to be griddlecakes laced with blackstrap, the molasses strong enough to bite his tongue. He devoured the stack without looking up, still embarrassed by what had happened earlier. She'd seen all of him he'd cared to reveal, without having to witness his embarrassment.

"Varnelle," Eleanor said, reaching across to take his plate once he'd scraped it clean.

"What about your hand?" She'd wrapped it in the same kind of sheeting she'd used on his ribs. Done a sloppy job of it, too, but then, bandaging one hand with the other was never easy. He knew, having done it a few times, himself. "Does it still hurt?"

"It throbs some, but it's not a bad burn—not even blistered, just pink and shiny." With a shake of the head she dismissed her injury, saying, "I've decided Varnelle is the one to help us. I'm pretty sure she will, because of Hector."

Following the way her mind worked wasn't always easy. From chickens to Varnelle and Hector, Hector being the cold-eyed fellow who had sat on her porch and offered to bring her candy. As for the lady, he'd heard her name mentioned, but he had yet to see her. "Go on," he said, knowing she needed little encouragement.

It struck him all over again how lonesome she must have been, a city woman, used to being around people, living here all alone for so long. Those throwbacks could at least have taken her down to live in the community where she'd have company.

On the other hand, judging from what he'd seen, she might be better off here. "Go on, I'm listening."

"Yes, well…I'd pretty sure Varnelle loves Hector, only she's afraid he might decide to marry me for my shares. That is, he might ask me. Not that I'd have him, of course, but if Varnelle loves him, she won't believe that. She probably thinks any woman would jump at the chance to marry him."

That bug-brained, barefoot galoot and *Eleanor?* Not in

a million years. They were barely the same species. Jed had enough book learning, even if self-imposed, to know that much. "So you figure that to take you out of the race, this woman might be willing to help you get away? Why haven't you asked her before now?"

"I never thought of using the chickens as a distraction."

He turned it over in his mind a few times and nodded. It was as simple as that. She could hardly have waited for a presidential visit, or even a county fair. Dexter's Cut, tucked away as it was in a narrow wrinkle in the foothills, was so small that he doubted if anyone more than ten miles away even knew it existed.

"I'm ready to travel any time you are," he told her, knowing it fell a few yards short of the truth. All he had to do was find McGee. The old devil was fast as greased lightning in the short run, slow and steady on the long haul. He'd be carrying double this time, though. Jed didn't know how he was going to react to that.

One thing he did know. By now, he'd have taken a chunk out of anyone who tried to throw a saddle on his back. Mean McGee didn't care for saddles. He put up with Jed's saddle only because Jed always bribed him with a lump of sugar or sweet potato, preferably baked, although he tolerated raw.

Somewhere in the valley a dog bayed. Soon the strident cry was taken up by a dozen other hounds. A man's voice could be heard in the distance, singing, yodeling or maybe swearing. Sounds in the mountains could be deceptive, ricocheting from rock face to rock face before dropping into the valleys. Some days, in certain places, a whisper could be heard for miles. Other days, other places, a shout died before it traveled a hundred yards.

"What's all the hullabaloo?" he asked as Eleanor stood to put the dishes in to wash. "Here, I'll do that," he said, easing her away from the dishpan. "You don't want to get that hand wet."

Without arguing, she moved toward the door to look out over the valley. Due to the height of the trees farther down the slopes and the thickness of the nearby laurel thickets, not much could be seen from the hilltop. Smoke from a few chimneys, a few outlying fields—that was about all.

"Anybody headed this way?" he asked, pouring water from the kettle onto a sliver of soap.

"Not so far as I can tell." She sounded wary. She was hurting more than she let on, holding her bandaged hand shoulder high. Regardless of what she'd said, he knew from experience how much a burn could throb. Trouble was, when it was your ass that was smoking, there wasn't a whole lot you could do about it.

The noise was growing louder, the voices coming closer. Someone yelled, "Grab that sunovabitch, he's a-gettin' away!"

Eleanor turned, wide-eyed and suddenly so pale her freckles stood out like pepper on grits. "They're coming this way," she whispered.

From the sound, Jed figured they were still a good five hundred yards away. Depending on how fast they were traveling, that should give him at least five minutes. Selecting a butcher knife, the blade honed down to less than half an inch wide, Jed said quietly, "I'll be around back." At her look of alarm, he said, "Don't worry, I'll stay out of sight. If they want to come inside, let 'em. There's nothing of mine to find."

"Your jacket," she said, reaching for it just as he did.

Their hands met—her good one, his free one. Impulsively, he caught her to him and kissed her. One hard, damp smack, all the more disturbing because it invited more, and there was no time for more.

He pushed her away, whispering, "Go out onto the front porch and smile. You're always wanting company, remember?"

He saw her draw in a deep breath, her eyes dark with something that might be fear…or might be something entirely different. A pulse at the base of her throat was fluttering like a handheld hummingbird.

Why? Because she was frightened?

Or because he had kissed her? Had she liked it as much as he had? Was she as disappointed as he was that there was no time to follow through and see where it would lead?

Oh, yeah, he liked women, all right. He particularly liked this woman for a lot of reasons, not the least because she was totally without artifice. He liked her frankness, her kindness, the feel of her hands on his body and the way her eyes crinkled at the corners just before she laughed. It never failed to get to him, the way laughter seemed to well up inside her like a bubbling spring until it spilled over.

He liked the way she smelled, too, but that was another matter, one he had no business even thinking about. Not at a time like this, with trouble coming up the front way and no way out the back unless he dived off the edge of the mountain.

Easing out the back door, he told himself that if he were a free man, a man without obligations, he might try his luck with her. But he had places to go, people he needed to see. He would help her get away from here—he owed her that much and more. But that was all he would do. He respected her too much to start something he couldn't finish.

Hearing voices coming up the path, he knelt carefully and leaned down to peer under the house, to see how many men were headed this way. Blasted weeds—she called them flowers, but they were weeds to him. Couldn't see a damned thing. He was laboriously getting to his feet again, one hand braced against the rough log siding, when he heard a familiar whuffling sound.

He started to grin. McGee? Had to be. According to Eleanor, the only four-legged creatures around besides the hogs and hounds were a team of oxen, a team of mules and half a dozen milk cows.

"McGee, you old devil's spawn, don't give me away now," he whispered.

He heard her greet the visitors, her voice a shade too loud, like she was deliberately wanting to be overheard. *Easy does it, sweetheart, just act natural.*

"Good morning, Alaska. That's a mighty fine animal you've got there."

Mumble, mumble. The horse whickered again. One of the men swore. The voice sounded familiar.

Eleanor laughed. "My, and he looks so gentle, too," she said, and Jed nearly laughed aloud. He'd learned the hard way that once you climb down off McGee's back you'd better duck out of the way fast if you didn't want to lose a chunk of whatever body part was in reach of those big yellow teeth.

He heard her say, her voice more natural now, "Do you think we're in for some rain?"

A familiar voice drawled, "Not till after midnight. Then I figger we got us about a three-day wet spell comin' on."

Oh, yeah—he definitely remembered hearing that nasal voice while he was having the daylights kicked out of him a week ago. The other two—so far as he could tell, there were three of them—muttered so that he couldn't make out what was being said.

"See that there pale streak, like buttermilk spilled onto a washboard? That there's a dead giveaway."

Unless he missed his guess, that would be the moonshiner, Alaska. Wasn't he the brother of the woman Eleanor was counting on to help them escape?

"What we come for is to ask if ye seen any strangers around these parts." The other voice. High-pitched, younger sounding.

"Strangers?" She repeated it loud enough for him to hear. Jed knew the way her mind worked by now. While she wouldn't lie outright, she didn't mind occasionally bending the truth. "Mercy, so far as I know there's not a stranger within miles of here. Funny you should ask, though. Hector was asking the same thing the other day when he brought my basket."

Not a stranger within miles, huh? Jed shook his head admiringly. When a woman had seen a man jaybird naked—when she'd cleaned him up, doctored him and bound him up in sheets like one of those Egyptian fellers he'd read about in the encyclopedia, why then, she could hardly call him a stranger.

"Is that a new horse, Alaska? He's…um, big, isn't he?"

"Yep, got him off'n a feller t'other day. You don't want to stand too close, though, he ain't been trained right."

Understatement of the year, Jed thought, amused. Why the devil were they hanging around? According to Eleanor, nobody ever stayed much longer than it took to drop off her supplies.

"Smoke don't rise, neither." Back to the weather again. Stalling while they looked around. "Hangs real low. You gotta be smart 'bout these things, Elly Nora, else you might get caught out in a bad storm."

Listening from the other side of the small cabin, Jed wondered if that was a warning. Did they suspect her of harboring someone who might help her escape?

Damned right he would help her, and the sooner, the

better. She didn't belong here any more than he did. Foggy Valley might be a few years behind the times when it came to modern conveniences, but Dexter's Cut hadn't even made it out of the Dark Ages.

Her voice came from farther away now. Evidently she had come down off the porch and was trying to draw them away from the cabin.

"Wa-aall…we jest thought we'd ride up here, see if you'd seen any strangers hanging round. If you do, you yell down the hill, y'hear? I don't want you a-getting' mixed up with some no-count flatlander."

There was a general muttering of agreement from the other two. Yeah, they definitely sounded younger. Evidently they were on foot, if what Eleanor had said was true, and there weren't any other horses in the valley.

Eleanor assured them she would call for help if need be. Jed heard the three men talking as they moved off down the path. He waited a full three minutes before easing around the corner. She met him there, nearly plowed right into him. He had to catch her to keep from knocking her down.

"They're gone," she whispered, looking both relieved and harried. "They were drinking, I could smell it on them." She shuddered. Her hair had fallen out of its knot to tumble across her face. Impatiently, she shoved it back.

Jed wanted to assure her she had nothing to worry about, but he couldn't do it, not with a clear conscience. The truth was, they had a lot to worry about. The fact that those weasels had come calling when she said they almost never came up the hill was enough to raise his hackles. Either they suspected something or…

Or they were after something.

If a single one of the bastards laid a hand on her, they were dead meat. Buzzard bait, Jed vowed silently. "That's my horse,'' he said. ''That's McGee, I'd know that braying jackass anywhere.'' His arms tightened around her as they stared out toward the place where the visitors had disappeared.

''I think he bit Alaska,'' she confided. ''Did you hear what he called him?''

''Probably nothing I haven't called him a time or two. Did he get him good?''

''He didn't do it here, but I think it must have been his shoulder, from the way he kept rubbing it.''

''Probably what all the ruckus was a little while ago. Must've been trying to strap a saddle on his back. McGee's not real partial to saddles. I always bribe him.''

Some of the tension had left her face. Something—possibly the thought of Alaska tangling with McGee—brought forth an impish grin that made her look like a girl. For all her troubles, she hadn't lost the ability to laugh. It was just one of the things he'd come to lo—to like about her.

''McGee's going with us when we leave here.''

She started to speak, but he laid a finger over her lips and said, ''We need him, Eleanor. They know this country a lot better than either of us. We're going to have to take off like a bolt of lightning and outrun them, at least for the first few miles. McGee's not much on looks or pretty manners, but he can outrun any horse I've ever owned.'' For five, maybe ten minutes, he added silently. If they played it right, that should be enough to give them a good head start. After that, he'd have to count on guile and a moonless night.

They went in through the back door and moved directly to the front window, watching the place where the path opened onto the clearing. Jed said, ''I don't trust him not to double back. It's what I'd do in his place.''

''That's what bothers me. The twins have been here

before to deliver my basket—not that they ever stay." His arm was across her shoulder, and she edged closer. "But Alaska must suspect something, because the last time he came here was when he caught me trying to get away. I hate it when he's the one."

Hearing the soft fervor of her voice, Jed hated it, too. Hated the thought of that bastard laying a hand on her. She had no business being within a hundred miles of this place. "It won't be long now," he promised. Cracked bones or not, he was getting her away before those devils got high on popskull and decided to get better acquainted with the widow Miller.

Chapter Eleven

For supper, Eleanor sliced and fried the cornmeal mush. There was a time when she would have been horrified at serving such a meal to anyone, but that time had long since passed. The "Miz Scarb'ra" who once taught third grade at Corner Gum Academy had been replaced by someone named Elly Nora Miller, a woman whose only concern was survival.

"I think they suspect," she said, searching Jed's face for the reassurance she so desperately needed. "I know something has changed, I can tell by the way they're acting. The twins' eyes never stopped moving, not once. I'm surprised they didn't climb up on the roof and look down the chimney."

"Even the dumbest animal is smart in his own way." Jed forked up a golden-brown bite and said, "Mm-mm. This reminds me of something my mama used to make."

"But then if they'd insisted on coming inside I might have screamed for help. I don't think Hector or Miss Lucy would have approved of their breaking into my house." Leaning back in her chair, she raked her hair away from her face and sighed. "Oh, I don't know. Everything's falling apart. We need to get away."

"No argument there." He scraped his plate clean, glanced at the empty skillet and looked away. "All they know is that I disappeared. Unless I was dragged off by a bear or crawled into a hole and died, there's only one place I could be hiding. The question is, do you know I'm here, or am I hiding from you, too? Maybe they're only trying to look after your interests."

She glanced at him, lifting one eyebrow, and he chuckled. Amazing, she thought, how two people could become so attuned in such a short period of time. They were nothing at all alike, yet more than once when one of them would start a sentence, the other one would finish it. As if their minds were two sides of the same train, on separate tracks, but both headed in the same direction.

At the moment, they were both aimed at getting away. She refused to let herself think beyond that.

"We can't wait much longer," he said, fingering his empty coffee cup.

She rose and pulled out the drawer under the grinder. There was perhaps half a cup of grounds there, the last of what she'd ground earlier. She reached for the gray graniteware coffeepot, but he shook his head.

"Let me make it," he said, and took down the two-quart pot from the nail behind the stove. "I can stretch a few beans further than you can."

Boiled coffee. It seemed almost sacrilegious to drink the muddy brew from a bone china cup when she still had a tiny hoard of tea. But if thick boiled coffee could bolster courage, then she would drink it black and bitter and not complain.

They waited silently as the aroma filled the room, then she stood and was preparing to slide the pot off the fire when he leaned across the table and caught her hand. "Quiet," he signaled. "Someone's outside."

Her eyes widened. "Again?" No one ever came back the same day. Occasionally, not even the same week.

Jed lowered his voice until it was barely a whisper. "You go to the front door. I'm going to slip out the back way. If they want to come inside and look around, let them. I won't be here."

He had scouted out the terrain earlier, sensing that the time might soon come when he would need to disappear in a hurry. The shed wouldn't hide a sparrow and the privy was too obvious. Besides, both were too easy to search. There was only one possible place to hide. It wouldn't be easy, but as long as he was careful...

They were both standing by then, out of range of anyone coming up the path. Jed gave her hand an encouraging squeeze, then reached for his coat that was hanging on a peg beside the back door. "Go," he mouthed, and waited a moment until she headed for the front door, a stiff smile fixed on her face. *Sweetheart, you're going to have to do better than that,* he thought. *You couldn't fool a dead possum with that smile.*

"Hello again," he heard her say as he eased off the back stoop and ran, doubled over, toward the edge of the property. "Did you decide to bring me some meat?"

Eleanor stood in the doorway, watching as Alaska slid down off the horse and tied him off to a holly tree, taking care to avoid teeth and hooves. *Bite him, McGee! Take a big chunk out of the bully!*

He didn't bother to reply, but swaggered directly up the steps to confront her. "You sure you didn't see no strangers hanging round here?" His breath nearly sent her reeling. He'd been drinking, but he was far from drunk. She hoped.

"You asked me that earlier, and I told you I haven't

seen any strangers.'' Did lying count as a sin when it was in a good cause?

''Got to be som'eres around here, 'cause if'n he'd a gone through the Cut, we'd a' seen him. Onliest other place he could be is up here. Mind if I take a look around? Wouldn't want him to sneak in on you.''

You lying, conniving, mean-spirited horse thief! ''That's a fine horse, Alaska,'' she said. ''He seems to be a sweet-natured animal. I've never been much of a rider myself. Actually, I was never able to afford a horse, but...'' But what? she thought frantically. She needed to engage him in conversation long enough for Jed to hide.

Where on earth could he hide? There was nowhere to go unless he hid in one of the tunnels. But to reach those, he would have to pass right by where they were standing and go a third of the way down the path.

''Why don't I jest take a look inside, see that he ain't hidin' under Dev's bed?''

It's not Dev's bed, it's mine, she wanted to shout. Instead, she smiled and said, ''Let me show you around, then. I haven't had time to sweep since supper. The house is in a mess.''

The dishes. Dear Lord, two plates, two cups, two of everything!

''In fact, I haven't even washed the dishes all day. Shamefully lazy, I know, but then, it doesn't seem all that important any more.''

''Hurt yer hand?''

''My hand? Oh, my hand. I burned it. On the stove. It hardly hurts at all now.''

''Need a man to take care of you,'' he said, his expression dangerously close to a leer.

He didn't quite shove her out of the way, but it amounted to the same thing, Eleanor thought despairingly as she stood back and allowed him inside the cabin. She willed Jed to hide quickly, because there was something different about Alaska this time. Something she didn't like at all. Thank God he hadn't brought the twins to search outside while he looked in every corner of her house.

Eleanor stayed three steps behind him, her mind working rapidly on what excuse she could give if by any chance he came up with something inexplicable. The sheet she'd torn into strips? Scraps of Jed's underwear?

Dust rags. Scrub rags. She hadn't scrubbed her floors in more than a week, but Alaska wouldn't know that. Chances were he wouldn't even notice such a thing.

As the bedroom was the only room with a door, he chose to look there first. The space was scarcely large enough to hold a bed, a washstand and her small trunk. Most of her gowns still hung in a corner behind a panel of cousin Annie's burgundy brocade dining room draperies. A few things were in the living room, but she could explain that if she had to. Changing over from winter things to summer things. He would hardly know the difference, as he wore the same filthy overalls winter and summer alike.

Lifting aside the curtain, he fingered her gowns as if he expected to find someone cowering behind them. She would have to wash everything he'd touched, she thought, shuddering.

He got down on his hands and knees to look under her bed, and she took great pleasure in silently ridiculing the position. His butt was so skinny the bones showed through his patched overalls.

She couldn't help but compare him to Jed, who compared favorably with any man she had ever known, including the male lead in the only professional stage play she had ever seen.

"He ain't here." Under any other circumstances, the look on his face would have been comical.

"Of course he's not here. If anyone had been in my house, I would certainly have noticed." And had, she added silently. Oh, she most certainly had.

After a cursory look through the rest of the house—there was obviously no place a full-grown man could have hidden—he went out onto the back stoop.

The outhouse. Surely Jed would know better than to hide in there, Eleanor told herself as cold sweat beaded her skin. That was the first place anyone would search. And the shed was open on two sides. Didn't used to be, but last winter's ice storm had collapsed part of the roof, which had caved in one wall. There was nothing in there except for a broken-handled wheelbarrow. Every speck of mining equipment had long since been carted down the hill.

Alaska stood in one place in her backyard and circled slowly, a frown on his bony, bearded face. On the back stoop, her arms crossed over her breast as if to contain her wildly beating heart, Eleanor watched him like a hawk. He might be ignorant, but he had the cunning of any wild animal that survived by hunting smaller, weaker prey.

It seemed as if hours had passed by the time he turned and shambled off toward the front yard without so much as a glance in her direction. It would serve him right if McGee were no longer there. If Jed had taken the opportunity while they were inside to reclaim his property and flee. There was nothing to stop him. Nothing at all.

A sense of profound bereavement came over her as she waited for Alaska to disappear down the path. She could hear him cursing the horse at every step, and that alone helped lift her spirits.

It was growing dark, the western sky streaked with slate

gray against a dull gold background when she finally deemed it safe for Jed to come out of hiding. "Come out, come out wherever you are," she called softly.

No response. Could he have crawled under the cabin? Alaska had forgotten to look there, but there was space enough. Once a family of skunks had taken up residence under the house. Dev had had to chase them out with the dogs. It had been a horrible experience for all concerned, one she would long remember.

"Jed," she called softly after several more minutes had passed.

Nothing.

Something?

A *groan?*

Hurrying in the direction of the sound, she called softly again. "Jed, he's gone now, it's safe to come out."

Out from where? There was no place to hide, only the sheer drop where a rockslide had occurred when Dev had tried to widen a fissure in order to use a windlass to bring up the ore. He had miscalculated his load.

That time, he'd gotten away with it.

Another groan, this time from directly below where she was standing. Dropping to her knees, she leaned over the edge of the slide, looking for a rock—for anything that could hide a man. Except for a few straggling weeds near the edges, the steep slope was clean. On the northwest side, buffeted by fierce winter winds, little had grown back since the topsoil had been blasted away.

"Over here." Jed's voice! He sounded as if he were in pain. "Get a rope."

Still on her knees, she leaned over to the right and peered to the left, where branches from the surviving trees swept the ground. "Jed? Oh, my God! Hang on!"

He was hanging on. On the edge of the slide, part of a

root emerged from the rubble, shielded almost completely from view. "How did you get over there?" she called, and then said, "No, don't talk, just hang on while I go find a rope!"

What rope? She thought frantically.

Clothesline. Knife.

In no time at all she was back, testing the strength of the thin rope between her fists. It was meant to hold wet laundry, not a full-grown man. "Now what?" she called, knowing it would do little good to throw him the rope, even if her aim was accurate.

"Listen carefully," he said, his voice sounding strained. "Make a slip loop in one end, can you do that?"

"Like crocheting," she muttered as her fingers worked at knotting one end of the line. She tested the knot, then poked the free end through and pulled it until she had a sizable loop. Lord in heaven, if Alaska were to come back now—

Absolutely not, I'll shove him down the blasted mountain, horse and all, before I'll let him take you away! "Done," she yelled softly.

"Now tie the standing end around something solid."

"The standing end?" She looked at the loop in the worn gray line.

"The other end!" Was it her imagination, or was his voice trembling?

"I'll tie it off to one of the posts outside the shed." It was closer than the house, and probably strong enough. It would have to be.

She hurried to do that, taking care to tie the kind of knot that wouldn't slip. She didn't know what it was called, but she knew how to tie it. "There, that's done," she called breathlessly.

"Throw the rest of the line down, but swing it this way, you hear?"

"I hear. Get ready to catch it, here it comes!"

They were both shouting, but softly, knowing how voices carried in the mountains. Luckily, they were on the other side from Dexter's Cut.

Unluckily, the loop fell a good ten feet short of where Jed was trapped, dangling from a root that was no bigger than his wrist.

"Hang on," she called, knowing that trying again would do nothing to lengthen the line. It had been shortened on both ends, first by the loop, then by having to stretch it all the way to the shed. "I'll be back in a minute!"

Jed had no choice but to hang on. He might not survive the trip to the bottom if he turned loose. Or if the root pulled free. Or if Eleanor couldn't find another piece of rope. He tried to remember if he'd seen anything of the kind, but couldn't.

Dirt trickled from where the root emerged from the earth, striking his face. He didn't bother to curse. Better to save his strength for whatever came next.

"I'm back," she called down after only a few centuries had passed. "It'll take me a minute to tie this to the end of the clothesline, will you be all right until I get it done?"

"Be fine," he assured her, forcing a smile. It wasn't the first time he'd felt helpless, but it wasn't a feeling he would ever get used to. How the devil did a mostly law-abiding farmer's son from Foggy Valley manage to get himself into so much trouble over the course of twenty-five years?

Memories swept past in rapid succession. He hoped he wasn't seeing his whole life pass before him. When that happened, or so he'd heard, a man was on his way out.

Vera…

God, why think of her now? But she'd been sweet as honey and wild as the wind. She'd been his first, and he'd been her first. Or so she'd said. He'd been too ignorant to know whether or not she'd been telling the truth. Not that it had mattered. They'd had some wonderful times in that old lineshack before her papa caught her climbing out her bedroom window and had one of his men follow her.

Vera had been his lodestone, his North Star. Everything he had achieved since then had been for her, even after he'd heard she was married. He might not still love her, but he would damn well show her that he was as good as any Stanfield. Better.

"All right, try this," Eleanor called down to him. "It's old, but I don't think it's dry-rotted."

Attached to the far end of her clothesline was about twelve feet of something thick, lumpy and purple. God knows what it was—it looked familiar. He only hoped it was strong enough to hold his weight, but beggars couldn't be choosers.

"Got it!" he cried triumphantly after the third try. "What do I do now?"

"Nothing. I'll do the rest. If I don't make it, get in touch with George Dulah in Foggy Valley, over near where Cane Creek runs into the Broad River, and tell him—"

"Hush! Don't even think that way!"

She was hanging over the edge; he could see her head and shoulders. With the last rays of sunset backlighting on her matted yellow hair, she looked like one of those pictures done in colored glass on a church window.

It wasn't the first time he'd had the same thought. Funny how a woman he'd known for less than two weeks could become such an important part of his life.

Chapter Twelve

Time hung suspended as Jed lay there unable to move, barely able to speak. His eyes were closed but he could feel her hovering over him. Her hand was warm on his back, which was one of the few places that didn't actually hurt. On the way down, afraid that bastard would catch him—and then again on the way up, he must have slid over a thousand tons of granite, most of it jagged and knife-sharp. The rope was still looped under his arm. He was lying on the knot. And while her knot had held fast when it counted, it was no thing of beauty. It felt like another fist-size rock, in fact.

"Jed?"

"Mm?"

"Are you all right?"

He couldn't swear to all right, but at least he was here, not fresh kill at the bottom of the mountain, waiting for the local predators to stop by for supper.

It was growing dark. The shadows were reaching out for him. "Yeah, I'm fine, just give me a minute to catch my breath."

She hovered the same way his mama used to hover over

him when he was little and ailing, as if she had to assure herself that he was still breathing.

Suppressing another groan, Jed rolled over onto his back and managed to sit up without passing out. "Get this thing off me," he said. His sides hurt. His hands hurt. His shoulders hurt most of all from hanging on to the only thing within reach he could find after sliding some twenty-five feet down sheer rock face.

"What happened?" she whispered.

Glancing past her, he didn't see anyone moving in on them, so he gave her the short version, leaving out his stark terror when he'd lost his grip and grabbed on to a fistful of vines only to have them break away in his hands. "Climbed over the edge, figured I could take cover under the vines and wait him out. Foot slipped. Caught myself on a root…or something."

"You've cut your cheek," she said, as if scolding him for some boyish prank.

"Yep." That was the least of it. If he'd jarred his ribs loose again, undoing all the healing that had taken place, he might need another day or so to recover. A day or so they didn't have. "Just a scratch," he said.

"We'd better get back inside. Since he's already searched the house once, I doubt if he'll insist on coming inside again even if he does come back."

No, but someone else might, now that they had the wind up. No point in pretending it wasn't a likely possibility. The real mystery was why they had waited this long. Evidently a few of the ones who knew about him were starting to worry that he might have survived their beating. Lack of buzzards circling overhead might have tipped them off.

Eleanor helped him ease onto his knees, then stood and

pulled him up by the arms. He stopped just short of crying out, but couldn't stifle a soft moan.

Together they managed to reach the cabin. Once inside, Jed gave up all pretense. Dropping onto one of the two kitchen chairs, he wrapped his arms around his chest and closed his eyes. He couldn't seem to stop shaking.

Next thing he knew she was on her knees in front of him, lifting one of his feet. "You were limping. I don't think it's your ankle again, but you'd better let me see."

While he leaned back, gripping the edge of the chair with both hands to keep from sliding off onto the floor, she pulled a thorn the size of a nail from his right foot with her fingernails and held it up for him to admire. "Mercy, I've never seen such a big splinter. I'd better pour turpentine on it and make you a poultice."

If she'd poured kerosene on it and set it on fire, it could hardly have burned worse. Only reason he hadn't noticed was that he was hurting everywhere else almost as much. "Lesson here somewhere," he said through clenched teeth. "Tenderfeet got no business losing their boots."

She laid her head on his knee, damned if she didn't. A minute later she lifted her face and said, "We have a slight problem, then." Her lips were smiling. Her eyes weren't. "Because I only have one pair of shoes that don't have holes in the soles, and they don't even fit me any longer. I can't imagine they'll fit you."

"I'll survive." He would wrap his feet in rags if he had to. The important thing was to get the hell away from this place before Alaska came back with reinforcements. He didn't want to think of what would happen if they found him here. He was no coward, but this time he wouldn't be the only one to suffer consequences.

She sat on the floor, her knees drawn up and her ankles crossed like a little girl instead of the proper lady he knew her to be. But child or lady, when the chips were down she had come through like a champion. You'll do to ride the trail with, sweetheart, that you will, he thought admiringly.

"We can't let your foot get infected because once we leave, we're going to have to run like the wind. It'll be pitch-dark, and even in broad daylight the downhill path can be hazardous. Slick places where moss grows—rocks where the dirt's worn down around them. In some places, the pine needles are so thick you can lose your footing if you're not careful, and there's always the possibility of a fallen branch to trip on."

"It won't be a problem, believe me," he said, trying to ignore the persistent ache in his foot and his shoulders. The rest he could manage. Not without pain, but if it meant getting out of this crazy nightmare he'd blundered into, it would be worth any amount of pain.

"At least this time of year it's not all that cold," she said. "Well, actually, it is once the sun goes down, but even so, I think we'd better figure out a way to protect your feet."

He waited. There was a connection in here somewhere. She wasn't as scatterbrained as he'd first thought, it was only that she was used to talking to herself and filling in the blanks in her own mind.

"Moccasins. I think I mentioned making you a pair from one of my quilts, but leather would be much better."

"You don't have to do that, we'll be riding once we reach the bottom of the hill."

"McGee, you mean. I wouldn't count on finding him— we won't have much time, and anyway, first we have to get there. It's a twenty-minute walk even when you can see where you're going." Her brown-gray-green eyes looked so earnest he was tempted to kiss her. As if he weren't in enough trouble.

"First, though," she said, "let me get something for your foot."

She came up onto her knees and he stopped her there. Leaned over until his face was within inches of hers, and said, "Eleanor? Thank you. This makes twice you've saved my life."

She flustered so easy it was almost a crime to tease her. Not that he'd been teasing, it was no less than the truth. Without her, he'd be dead meat now, and George would lose the farm. By the time the state got through handing over his assets, Stanfield would have already foreclosed. Even if the conniving bastard couldn't convince the railroad to buy him out, George and his family would be homeless.

"Jed?" she whispered. "What is it? Are you hurting so much?"

"Hurting?"

"For a minute you looked...strange."

He felt strange. Hell, he *was* strange. For lack of a reply that she could even begin to understand, he caught her face between his hands and ground his mouth into hers.

Granite dust, sandstone and red clay were pressed between his raw hands and her tender cheeks. His teeth touched hers and then he used his tongue on her, needed to taste the very essence of her—to reaffirm the fact that he was here with this woman instead of lying in a mangled heap at the bottom of the mountain. That he was alive and able to experience all the good things life had to offer. The heat of the sun on his naked skin, the smell of wood smoke in the fall, of rain on a spring morning. A woman's lips, her soft breasts, the heat and scent of her body.

It never occurred to him that this was one of the most

basic reaffirmations of life, he only knew he had to kiss her. Wanted to do more than that, but he would take what he could get.

She made no effort to escape, even though he kissed her as hungrily as if she alone could stave off starvation. Not until he encountered the buttons at the neck of her dress did he draw back, his fingers growing still. Seeing the streaks of dirt on her pale skin and on the bosom of her dress, he closed his eyes. "Eleanor, I'm sorry. I didn't mean for that to happen."

Still on her knees, Eleanor blinked and settled back onto her heels. She was embarrassed. Mortified at the way she had greedily accepted his kisses. And now he was *sorry?*

She took a deep breath, unaware that her dress gaped open to reveal the shoulder strap of her camisole. Unaware of the streak of dirt on her throat, all the way down to the swell of her breasts. Of the grime smeared on her cheeks from his hands.

You'll never learn, will you?

"I'll get the turpentine, you wait right here." Her voice sounded remarkably calm considering she had knelt between the man's thighs and let him kiss her senseless while his—while that—that *thing* grew larger and larger, bumping against her stomach like a puppy nosing her for attention.

She felt his eyes burning through her clothes as she stepped out onto the back stoop and dampened a rag with turpentine from the jug. Let him watch. She had done nothing to be ashamed of, kissing was no crime—even if he was sorry afterward.

If she'd had sugar she'd have made a poultice from that. As it was, she used salt. It should draw off any suppuration and help the wound to heal. She tied the ends together to make a neat package.

"Whiskey."

"What?" Confused, she turned to confront him.

"Whiskey's as good as anything I know of for cleaning out a puncture wound."

"Well, I don't have any whiskey, all I have is turpentine and lamp oil." She grabbed his foot and lifted it by the ankle, her grasp none too gentle as she muttered something about blood poisoning. She could feel his eyes boring a hole right through her, but she worked doggedly, refusing to meet his gaze. If he thought he could embarrass her by kissing her senseless and then telling her he was sorry he'd done it, he was dead wrong.

She slapped the poultice over where the thorn had come out and said, "Hold it there," waiting until his hand replaced hers to step back.

"How long?" he asked meekly.

"Till hell freezes over."

He closed his eyes. Eleanor closed her own. "I'm sorry, I didn't mean—it's just that…"

"I know." He sighed. "If it's an apology you're wanting, then consider it said. For everything."

Standing tiredly in her filthy gown, half her buttons still undone, she studied the man sprawled before her, all six feet of him in his dirt-stained blue jeans that emphasized far too much of his masculinity for her peace of mind. They were as different as day and night. He was dark; she was light. He was powerfully built, she was scrawny. He was—she wanted to say as ignorant as she was educated, but it wouldn't be true. He might lack formal schooling, but he was by no means ignorant. He had a wonderfully inquiring mind and besides, he knew things that she'd never even heard of.

But then, she knew things that he didn't. And if only because it was going to take their combined efforts, their combined skills, to get them away from here, this was no time to start bickering, much less to get involved in anything of an intimate nature.

"For what it's worth," he said quietly, "I really am sorry."

She nodded. A hairpin, one of the few she still possessed, struck her shoulder and fell to the floor. "The exigencies of the moment. I understand."

Was that a twinkle in those fathomless eyes of his? "Is that what it was?" he murmured. "An exigency. Never would've figured it for that."

She, who had never flounced a single flounce in all her twenty-seven years, flounced away. Trouble was, in a three-room cabin, there was not much flouncing room. As a grand exit was out of the question, she said, "Eggs," and fled.

Jed was leafing through her dictionary when she returned. He had laid the poultice aside. The homely room smelled of coffee and turpentine.

"Two eggs," she said. "I forgot to collect them, so much has happened." Heat rushed to her face and she blamed her discomposure on him. Smug devil. Exigency, indeed.

"If you have a needle and thread, I think I might be able to piece together something from my coat sleeve that'll get me down the road a ways." He laid the dictionary aside.

Without a word, she went in search of her sewing basket. When she returned, he was fingering his torn coat. "I can wax the thread if you think it'll help. I have paraffin."

"Not worth the trouble," he said, and started cutting the dangling sleeve apart into sections.

Well, if he could put the kiss they had shared behind him so easily, so could she. "That reminds me, there was a letter in your inside coat pocket. I put it under the pepper grinder.''

She retrieved the stained and wrinkled paper, folded into thirds, and held it out. "I didn't read it," she hastened to assure him.

He glanced up. "Wouldn't have mattered if you had, it's nothing important."

If it weren't important, then why had he carried it with him all these years? she wondered. She'd been tempted to read it when she'd first discovered it. In case he died, she would have eventually had to notify his family.

"It's from a girl I used to know," he said, laying aside a section of buckskin and starting another cut.

"Vera," she said. And when he looked at her, she had to explain. "I might have glanced at it once—I needed to know who to notify in case you—that is, if…" She closed her eyes, wishing she'd never even mentioned the darned thing. "All right. I read enough to know it was deeply personal, so I set it aside and then I forgot it."

"Mmm."

Mmm, indeed. The man was purely insufferable. She was tempted to hand him the dictionary and tell him to look up the word. But she didn't, because she was knew she was being childish. And because there was no room for childishness, not with all there was still to accomplish.

"Gracious, would you look at that, it's almost dark already," she said, sounding insufferably cheerful. "I'd better light a lamp if you're planning to do close work. I'll just go—"

"Eleanor," he said calmly.

"What!" she snapped, feeling heat rise to her face again.

"Are you all right?"

"I'm fine. No, I'm not. I'm embarrassed. And I—I have

a headache.'' So now he'd think she was crazy. Maybe she was. Otherwise she'd be back in Charlotte grading yesterday's spelling test. ''I'll get the lamp and start on supper. First thing in the morning I'll speak to Varnelle. If you're able to travel, I don't think we should waste any time, do you?''

Once supper was over, Jed went back to working on his moccasins. His mother would have been horrified at the results, but he thought he'd done a pretty fair job considering what he'd had to work with.

The letter was still lying on the workbench beside the sewing basket where he'd left it. The thought of seeing Vera again after all these years left him feeling…

Curiously, feeling nothing at all. When George had written to tell him she'd married her father's foreman, he'd celebrated by getting drunk and buying himself a woman for the evening. The next day, after he'd recovered enough to remember, he'd thought about it—about Vera being married to the same man who had burned her father's initials into his ass. Funny thing—even then he couldn't recall feeling much beyond minor irritation.

''How soon can you be ready to leave?'' he asked when Eleanor dried the last plate and hung the towel on the rack.

She pursed her lips in thought, reminding him all over again of what those lips had felt like under his. How they'd tasted. He knew how she felt in his arms now—the way her soft, small bosom felt pressed against him—the way her belly snuggled into his groin. He was almost sorry he did. If they were to stay alive these next few days, he had to keep his mind focused on one thing only—getting them away from here undetected.

Trouble was, it was getting so he couldn't look at her without thinking things he had no business thinking. Even now, he thought, disgusted, he was sweating like a horse.

"Tomorrow night if Varnelle agrees. She hasn't been at all friendly since Devin died."

"Tell her your company doesn't think much of the hospitality around here. He's ready to move on." He was only half joking, but she actually appeared to consider it.

"I could do that. On the other hand, she might feel obligated to tell Alaska. I think I'd better not tell her anything other than to remind her that if I leave, she'll have Hector all to herself. Not that I was ever any real competition, but she won't believe that."

Jed could only hope she was right. The fly in the beer might be if Hector wanted what Eleanor called Dev's shares more than he did the other woman. "Better hope she doesn't give us away instead," he said dryly. "I never heard of a shotgun wedding where the bride was the one being ramrodded, but around these parts, nothing would surprise me."

She looked at him for a long time, saying nothing. Her eyes said it all. She was counting on him to see that things never came to that point.

He heard the kettle start to boil. The bottom was warped so that it always rocked as it started to steam. She slid it off the fire, poured it into a fat brown pot and reached for the cups, his big one and her dainty china one. He hoped to hell she wasn't planning on taking along her dishes.

As if reading his mind, she said, "I don't have that much left to take. Nothing important, anyway."

"Lay out what you want and I'll tell you whether or not it'll fit into the saddlebags."

"You're not going to give up on that horse, are you?" She poured him a cup of black tea, steeped instead of boiled. Not that he could tell the difference, but he'd learned a few things since he'd been her guest, one thing being that while it was all right to boil coffee, it was a crime against nature to boil tea.

"I can't rightly leave him behind. Besides, we've got a pretty fair ways to travel, even after we get past Dexter's Cut."

Silently, she sipped her tea, her eyes avoiding his. Jed suspected she was thinking about the fact that she had no place to go. No home, no family, no job and, unless he was mistaken, no money. Her in-laws had seen to that. Nice family.

"Did I tell you I'm taking you with me?" It came out of the blue, taking him by surprise.

"Well, of course you are."

"No, I mean all the way." He waited for it to sink in, knew the moment it had. Just about the same time the full impact of what he'd just said soaked into his own thick skull. Hell, when it came to having a home, he was in no better shape than she was. The house where he'd grown up now belonged to his half brother, George's wife and his family.

She didn't argue, she just sighed. "At this point, I don't have much choice, do I?"

In for a penny, he told himself. "Look, I've enjoyed your hospitality. Now it's my turn to return the favor."

Right. Now all he had to do was get there before Stanfield called George's loan, else they might all be sleeping under the stars.

Chapter Thirteen

Eleanor hardly slept at all that night. Judging from the sounds coming from the bedroom, Jed was every bit as restless. They had talked far into the night about what to take and what to leave. She knew he wasn't interested in anything but getting away—he had nothing to leave behind. But she'd needed to talk and he'd been kind enough to listen. He'd even made comments at the appropriate times.

His determination to get his horse back worried her. It was going to be a problem, because the Hootens lived near the middle of the settlement, and while the noise might wake him up, Alaska wasn't one to go dashing out into the night just because the dogs were barking.

What if he stayed behind? What if he caught Jed trying to steal his horse back? What would he do to him? To them? Because, of course, Eleanor would be right there, too. She wasn't about to allow him to go off on his own. For one thing, he didn't even know where the Hootens lived.

On the other hand, it was a long walk to the nearest market town, and by morning they needed to be out of reach of anyone who'd ever heard of the Millers of Dexter's Cut.

The sky was already growing pale when she gave up any hope of sleep. She could sleep once they got away from here. Until then she needed to gather her most persuasive arguments and pray she didn't run into a suspicious Alaska when she went down to talk to his sister.

Her luck held. Judging from the sounds coming from the cove where Alaska had his still, he and several of his friends were sampling his wares. Considering all the sampling that went on, she thought wryly, his must be the finest whiskey east of the Mississippi.

Varnelle was flapping a bedsheet on the front porch when Eleanor hurried up the path. Keeping house for two lazy scoundrels like Alaska and Digger had to be a thankless task. She was doing the girl a favor, she assured herself. Hector, for all his faults, was several cuts above the Hootens.

"Good morning." Eleanor pasted on a smile, hoping it looked convincing. She had never come calling before, not even back in their friendlier days.

Varnelle looked at her and waited. Not so much as a civil greeting. Gathering her courage, Eleanor said, "I see you've already got started on your garden. I haven't even laid off my rows yet." Nor would she. Not if her plan succeeded. "May I walk out there and look at what you've got coming up?" She needed to get away from the house before she brought up the reason she was there.

Some ten minutes later Eleanor hurried up the hill again, hardly able to contain her glee. She waved to old Miss Lucy, and shooed away a curious hound. Better not act too cheerful, she cautioned herself, else they'd be certain to wonder.

Bursting into the cabin, she hurried to the bedroom and flung open the door. "It's worked! She's going to do it!"

Her mouth fell open. She blinked twice and spun around. "I'm sorry, I—please excuse me, I didn't know…"

Jed, dressed only in the bottom half of his mutilated union suit and that hanging low on his hips, was carefully scraping away his beard, using her mirror and washbowl and her sharpest butcher knife.

"You don't ever want to startle a man when he's holding a knife to his own throat." The warning was tempered with amusement.

Without turning to face him, she said, "I should have known better than to barge in. I've forgotten how to live with another person."

"No harm done," he said, sounding as if he truly meant it. "You're among friends."

That was the trouble. If he were only a stranger she would have begged his pardon and left. As it was, she knew too well how that smooth back felt under her hands, knew just how silky his thick black hair was. Knew the taste of his mouth and the way his beard ignited nerve endings she'd never even known she possessed.

"Yes, well…it's tonight. When we're leaving, that is. We decided on midnight, when everyone will be asleep. It's bound to be more confusing then, don't you think so?"

"Bound to be," he said equably, as if he'd taken it for granted that everything would go as planned.

Eleanor had been a bundle of nerves ever since she'd set out, not knowing if Varnelle would hear her out or tell her family.

"Does she know about me?"

"I'm not sure. I think she might suspect something. She might've heard Alaska talking, but I didn't mention anything and she didn't ask. She knows how long I've wanted to get away.''

''What was the clincher?'' He scraped off the last of his beard, slung the soap off the knife and laid it aside. Then, holding her small mirror, which was all she had since Devin had sold her large oval gold-framed wall mirror, he turned his face to one side and then the other, examining his clean-shaven jaw.

She had almost forgotten what he looked like without a beard. It had grown so fast that by the second day, she had trouble seeing the shallow cleft in his chin. ''The clincher?'' she asked belatedly.

''What does she want for her services? Most women want something. Turn around, Eleanor, I don't want to talk to your back.''

Without appearing more a fool than she already did, she had no choice but to obey. Pretend he's Devin, she told herself.

Small chance. Devin had never, at least not since the first few days they were married, made her breath catch in her throat the way this man did. My word, the way that cotton knit clung to his buttocks was purely sinful!

''What does she want? Oh. My rose silk dress,'' she said. ''That and Hector, not that I even mentioned him, but it was understood between us that I'd be leaving the field clear for her.''

He reached for his shirt and shrugged into the sleeves, but not before she had seen the fresh bruises on his chest and side. Evidently, his tumble down the mountain had been rougher than he'd let on.

''Didn't you tell me that was your wedding dress?''

She shrugged. They both knew—at least she knew and he had probably surmised—that the last thing she wanted was a reminder of her brief marriage. ''It won't fit her. It probably won't be very becoming either, with her coloring, but she wanted it, so I said I'd leave it here for her.''

"Then I guess we'd better sort out and pack the rest of what you want to take, and then we'd do well to get some rest. I don't know about you, but I didn't sleep much last night." As if to prove it, he yawned, and then winked at her. "And no, I'm afraid there's no way we can take your books."

"I hadn't planned on it," she said, thinking longingly of the dozen or so volumes she had nearly worn out by now.

"Maybe the dictionary," he said. "Never can tell when you might need one of those."

She felt like weeping. Dear Lord, how does he do it? she wondered. Big, strong, dressed like a—like a scalawag, and he could melt her heart with something like that. A dictionary, of all things!

She got out three towels and set them aside. A small pot for dipping and heating water, two spoons, two forks, two cups. It would take up a lot of room, but they might need them along the way.

Jed selected two knives, her butcher knife and a smaller one she used for peeling potatoes when she was lucky enough to have them to peel. He laid out her hammer to take, and poured salt into a smaller container.

Eleanor set out her other pair of shoes, then shook her head. The ones she was wearing had holes in the soles, but lined with a strip of elm bark, they served well enough. Her good shoes were not only impractical, they pinched her toes. And so she set them aside with the rose silk dress. Varnelle was welcome to them if they fit...and even if they didn't.

Finally, she had everything, including her dictionary, crammed into two pillow slips. Good thing, she thought guiltily, that Jed didn't have anything to take, because there wouldn't be room if everything had to fit in his saddlebags.

That was something else she hadn't mentioned to Varnelle. McGee. She would leave it to Jed to explain when the time came. He was standing before her makeshift bookshelf, studying the dozen or so volumes there. Without turning around, he said, "I wish we could take every one."

"I know. It's a shame, but I've read them all so many times I've practically memorized them."

"I haven't."

She didn't know what to say to that, and so she said nothing. "I doubt if anyone will ever read them again. Or maybe Hector, if he and Varnelle move up here. He's had a few years of schooling."

It occurred to her that a man's pride was a funny thing. Hector had bragged about finishing the third grade. She knew for a fact that Jed was a proud man, yet he hadn't been ashamed to expose his lack of formal schooling. Ironically, she thought, it required a good deal of strength to be able to admit to weaknesses.

"We'd better get some sleep," he said some time later. It was late in the afternoon. Jed had just come in from checking the shed for anything that might prove helpful. They had taken time to eat a hasty supper of corn bread and molasses, and Eleanor had said feelingly that she hoped she wouldn't have to see another pan of corn bread for another year.

Jed had said she might change her mind if the trip took much longer than he planned. "You take the bed," he said flexing his back. "I'll take the sofa, I don't need much rest."

"You certainly do. May I remind you that it's been little

more than a week since you were beaten nearly to death? You haven't even recovered from that, much less from sliding halfway down the back of a mountain and hanging there by your fingernails. Your chest is all purple and blue again."

"What about my poor arms?" he teased. "Wonder they aren't five inches longer after hanging on to that root all day."

"A few minutes," she scoffed. "Trust a man to make something out of nothing."

He grinned at her, and Eleanor thought of how much she was going to miss this man when it came time to say goodbye. Not only the fact that he was so attractive she was physically aware of him every minute of the day, but the fact that he was such good company. She would have given anything to have met him under other circumstances.

But then, under any other circumstances, he wouldn't have given her the time of day.

They shared the bed. "We both need our rest," Jed insisted. "That thing you call a sofa was invented by that guy, Markwiss de Sadie. If you insist on sleeping there again, I'll be forced as a gentleman to sleep on the floor."

Eleanor swallowed her laughter and didn't correct him. He had told her enough about his background so that she understood his shortcomings. Understood, too, how far he'd come unaided. He was a man to be admired, not ridiculed.

Lying stiffly on the far edge of the feather mattress, she considered placing pillows between them, but that might imply that she was uncomfortable sharing a bed with him.

Uncomfortable? She was burning up, and it wasn't just the warm, sultry breeze that drifted in through the window. Not until the sun had set would the air even begin to cool off.

Thunder rumbled in the distance. She waited to see a flash of light, then muttered, "Backward."

He rolled over. She lay rigid on her back.

"Backward?" he echoed. "You want me to sleep on my back?"

"Not you, the lightning. I was counting from the thunder, not the flash."

Long seconds ticked by. After a minute, he said, "When we were kids, George and I used to share a bed. That was before my father added another room onto the house. When one of us wanted to turn over, we'd say, 'Flip.'"

She rolled over onto her side, facing him. As if on cue, a flash of lightning brightened the room, followed almost immediately by an explosion of thunder. Eleanor drew her knees up and ducked her head under the sheet.

"Don't tell me you're afraid of a little thunder."

"No, I'm afraid of getting struck by lightning. We happen to be the highest thing around, in case you hadn't noticed."

More lightning, followed by more thunder that rumbled off interminably, echoing from mountain to mountain.

She felt a hand grip her shoulder. "Come here," Jed said gruffly.

Without a moment's hesitation, she scrambled over the lump of feathers pushed up between them and fell into his arms, burrowing her face against his chest. If she were to die in the next few minutes, at least she wouldn't die alone. As for anything else, she would worry about that after the storm passed.

"Wake up," Jed whispered, nuzzling her ear through the thicket of wild curls. "Time to go."

Eleanor came instantly awake. It took only a moment to

realize where she was, who was holding her, and what the effect was on both of them. She'd been dreaming....

Judging from the evidence of his arousal, Jed had been dreaming, too.

Embarrassed, she edged to the far side and lowered her feet to the floor. She had slept in her clothes, as her best nightgown was packed. Jed had slept in his clothes because he had nothing else to sleep in. Probably a good thing, too.

"Rain's over. Let's head on down the mountain."

They had arranged to meet at a certain flat rock near the creek, less than a quarter of a mile—a hoot and a holler, as Hector would say—from Alaska's cove.

Eleanor had taken time to clear away any fallen branches on her way back up that morning, but the squall had tossed a few more across the path. The air smelled of resin and wet earth. It felt cool, but not unpleasant.

They didn't talk on the way down, but she could tell Jed was having trouble keeping his homemade moccasins on his feet. She heard him cursing under his breath. Finally, he bent and snatched them off, shoving them into the pillow slip he carried.

Varnelle was waiting for them by the rock. In the light shed by a cloud-veiled moon, she gave Jed a long, unsmiling look. "This the one they beat up?"

Eleanor nodded. Jed said nothing.

After a moment, Varnelle said, "I knowed they was a stranger messin' around here. 'Laska, he told Pap some man traded him a horse for a gallon of shine, but I knowed better. I heard what went on up there, all the ruckus. You was supposed to 've left."

"Are you going to help us?" Jed asked. He didn't have time for a lengthy discussion, especially not with the sister of the man responsible for his being here. He still wasn't certain she could be trusted.

"Wait here. Gimme ten minutes to get over to Jessie's place."

"Jessie keeps most of the chickens," Eleanor explained.

"When you hear the dogs start up, then take off a-running. I ain't promisin' nothing, but I'll do what I said this mornin'."

Eleanor nodded. "I left the rose silk hanging in the bedroom, and some shoes, too. Anything else you want, you're welcome to take."

"My horse," Jed said.

"I didn't figger on no horse," said the sturdy redhead dressed in men's boots and a faded print dress. In the light of the quarter moon, everything was painted in shades of gray, Varnelle's red hair included.

"I'm not leaving without him," Jed stated flatly. Behind him, Eleanor huddled on the rock, two large, lumpy bundles beside her. At the last minute she'd crammed in what little food had been left, not knowing how long they'd be traveling, nor even where they were headed.

Foggy Valley? She'd never even heard of the place before Jed had erupted into her life. Had no real idea where it was located, but decisions about where they were going could wait until they were clear of the valley.

"I'm not leaving without McGee," Jed repeated, his voice quiet, but rock hard. "I wouldn't mind having my hat and boots back, but those are replaceable. McGee's not."

"'Laska, he might sell him to you if you was to ask. Might beat the tar out of you ag'in, too."

"I'm not buying my own horse."

"How do I know he's your'n? 'Laska caught him fair'n square. He was a wanderin' loose."

"We can't waste any more time, we need to get started," Eleanor said, breaking up the duel.

"If this here fool don't mess ever'thing up over some dumb old horse, you'll be free an' clear 'fore anybody knows you're gone."

Turning to Jed, she said, "You're plumb crazy if you think my brother's gonna give up that ol' horse, mister. He don't cotton to strangers."

"I noticed," Jed said dryly.

"No telling what he might do if he was to catch you still hanging round here."

"There's laws against horse stealing," Jed said, his voice still smooth as butter. "Laws against ganging up on a man and beating him half to death, too, come to that, but I won't press charges. All I want is my horse."

Varnelle stood on first one foot, then the other, as if she needed to relieve herself. From her place on the rock, Eleanor watched the two of them, wishing they would stop bickering and get on with setting things into motion. The last thing they needed now was for Varnelle to change her mind.

Sliding down from the rock, she joined the other two. "Please, can't we just forget McGee? I'd rather walk a hundred miles than have to spend one more night here."

"All right, I won't go after my horse." Jed nodded to the redhead. "Get started then. We'll wait until we hear the dogs and then light out for the road."

Varnelle's eyes narrowed. Even in the near dark, Eleanor could tell that she was suspicious of Jed's easy capitulation. Thinking quickly, she said, "I'm sorry not to be able to tell Hector goodbye. Will you tell him for me? And thank him for all the lovely things he's done for me? The candy? He knows the kind I like best and always tries to bring me some little thing."

That was rubbing it in, perhaps, but she had to do something.

As if she'd needed the reminder, the other woman turned and disappeared in the direction of the village. "Wait for the dogs to start up," she called back softly.

They waited. For several minutes neither of them spoke. The settlement below was silent. There were fourteen houses in all, with the usual assortment of outbuildings. Eleanor happened to know that the chicken farm was some quarter of a mile away.

"Maybe you could come back for McGee," she suggested, knowing she didn't really want him to take the risk. If Alaska or any of his friends caught him a second time they might kill him to keep him from bringing the law down on their heads.

Jed claimed to be part Cherokee. When it came to sheer wiliness, she would match his Indian blood against any other man she had ever met, but he, better than anyone, should know that the Millers didn't fight fair.

Jed was so silent, she wondered if he could have fallen asleep. Had ten minutes passed? Five? It seemed hours since they had left the cabin, leaving a lamp lit in case anyone was watching.

"You know where McGee's being kept?" he asked suddenly.

She started at the sound of his voice. Except for a chorus of tree frogs, it was dead silent. "The Hootens live over in that direction, about the second house over." She pointed in the general direction of the house she had visited only that morning.

Jed turned in the direction she had indicated. He lifted his face as if he were listening. And then he placed two fingers between his lips and let out a soft, penetrating whistle.

Chapter Fourteen

Without a bribe it took several minutes, but Jed managed to gentle the skittish horse. Eleanor thought McGee must be glad to see him after spending a week with Alaska, who wasn't known for his kindness toward any creature, two- or four-legged.

"I'll need a minute to tie your bundles on," Jed said softly. "Stand clear, he doesn't like strangers, remember?"

Didn't like anyone, so far as she could tell. He bumped his head against Jed's a time or two, hard enough to cause Jed to stagger, but perhaps that was considered affection.

"Stand still, you damned churnhead, or I'll send you back where you came from," Jed growled.

The horse bared his teeth, but stopped trying to knock him over. Eleanor said, "Good horsey," and felt like an utter fool.

Thunder rumbled sullenly. Wind sent a flurry of leaves showering around them as Jed fashioned a bridle from the clothesline he had coiled over his shoulder. Cutting off the excess, he used it to tie together the two pillow slips. "You heard the lady, dammit, be a good horsey and stand still while I—" He positioned the makeshift saddlebags and stepped back, "There, that does it."

Eleanor wondered how he could see in the darkness. She could barely make out what he was doing. The white shirt helped. Lifting his hands to the horse's head, he whispered words that were part profanity, part encouragement. "Easy, boy, there's a lady present. I can't talk to you the way I usually do, so be a good fellow now, y'hear?"

McGee stomped impatiently and tossed his head. Eleanor had visions of racing headlong through the pitch-black night on the back of a runaway horse.

A clap of thunder seemed to ricochet forever before grumbling off into the distance while a single star hung in the sky. Even as she watched, it was swallowed up by the same clouds that had swept over the moon only moments earlier. Rain was on the way, and would likely overtake them before they found a place to stay for the night. She had no idea how far it was to the nearest boarding house, much less the nearest town.

From a distance came the constant din of the hounds, their barking, howling and baying punctuated with shouts and sporadic gunshots.

"They shoot chickens around here?" Jed asked. She knew he was trying to ease the tension, but Eleanor wasn't fooled. Neither was McGee, judging from the way he was dancing around. Danger surrounded them like a cold wind, sweeping up from the valley below.

"Come here, let me lift you aboard."

"I think I'll walk." Danger or not, she wasn't ready to climb up on a fidgety horse named Mean McGee, not if she had to run every step of the way to freedom.

Ignoring her protest, Jed lifted her by the waist. Holding her in midair, he said, "You gonna ride sidesaddle or sensible? Make up your mind fast, we've got to move out."

"Put me down, I've changed my mind." She grabbed

his shoulders and struggled to free herself as another gun-shot rang out.

"Lift your skirts," he said, any hint of teasing now gone from his voice. "It's now or never, Eleanor."

Oh, God. They were coming closer.

She hoisted her skirts above her knees and he settled her astride the skittish animal and swung up behind her. The tiny part of her brain that wasn't paralyzed pondered how he managed to pull himself up when there were no stirrups, no saddle horn—nothing at all to grab on to.

By then they were moving, though, and all she could do was dig her fingers into the sinewy thighs that cradled her hips and pray that they wouldn't be shot in the back or garroted by a clothesline as they made a mad dash though the very heart of the settlement.

"I th-thought—we were g-g-going to t-take the road," she chattered, bouncing like a rubber ball on McGee's bony back.

"Shortcut. No time."

The next shot was closer. Something zinged through Miss Lucy's apple tree. "Hurry, hurry," she urged, her fingers digging deeper into his thighs.

They had just cleared the last barn in the settlement when the rain began. In reaction to an unspoken command, McGee settled into a bone-shaking lope that quickly ate up distance. Even so, by the time they were halfway across a newly plowed field they were both soaked to the skin.

Blinded by rain and pitch darkness, Eleanor swept an arm across her face. One of Jed's arms came around her waist to steady her and she cried, "Hold on to the horse!"

"McGee knows what he's doing. Can't have you slipping off, I'd never find you in this rain."

A little farther on, the field began to slope steeply up the hillside. Searching desperately for something to lighten the moment, Eleanor tried to think of all the jokes she'd ever heard about mountain cows being born with one set of short legs so as to graze on the steepest pastures, but nothing could take away from the gravity of their situation. Jed would have heard them all, anyway, and besides— McGee's legs were all the same length.

"Oh, God," she whimpered when she felt the gelding's hooves slip on the rain-slick mud. She bit her lip to keep from crying out in panic.

"Easy, we're almost clear," Jed said as they skirted past one of the outlying farms.

A non-Miller farm, she was almost sure of it, belonging to one of the few families that had been "allowed" to go on living there. How on earth could such a people exist in this enlightened age, she wondered, not for the first time. To think she had almost become one of them. Trapped forever in the Dark Ages....

They kept on going, and Eleanor breathed a sigh of relief. Just because these people weren't Millers didn't mean they would protect a pair of strangers from an armed mob.

It seemed like hours later when, numbed by cold and the relentless pounding of her tender behind, she felt McGee slow to a walk. Jed whispered to him, talking him down as if he were a blooded racehorse, and the miserable creature finally came to a halt.

"Attaboy, easy does it, take a breather now—you did good, real good." And to Eleanor he said, "Sorry. I was afraid to try to hold him back until we were in the clear."

The rain drummed down steadily, chilling her to the bone. Her damp drawers had slipped up, her sodden hose down so that her knees were completely bare. Everything else was soaked through so that it stuck to her like a cold second skin. Her whole body ached, her hair was plastered to her face, and she had no idea where they were, much less how far they still had to go. What's more, she didn't care, she simply didn't care.

"D'you think they could still be following us?" she whispered through chattering teeth.

"No." He mouthed the word against her ear. From his very stillness she knew he was listening.

"Why did we cut through the settlement instead of going around?"

A long moment passed before he answered. "They expected us to take the road. Your friend might even have told them that's what we were planning."

The meaning of his words sunk in slowly. Would Varnelle have done that? Eleanor didn't want to think so, but the woman was half-Miller. Her allegiance must surely lie with her family. Besides, even Miss Lucy, matriarch of the secretive, obsessive clan, recognized the dangers of too much inbreeding.

"What do we do now?" she asked, pressing her back against his reassuring warmth. Except for a few scattered drops, the rain cut off as suddenly as it had begun. A faint iridescent glow marked the position of the moon as the clouds moved off to the northeast.

"We cut across that low ridge up ahead until we're clean out of sight of the valley, then we find a dry place and rest until morning."

A dry place to rest until morning. It sounded like heaven. No matter how tempted she was to simply slither to the ground, fall in a heap and let the mud keep her warm while she slept, she knew they had to get as far away as possible. If the dogs tired of chasing chickens, they might pick up the trail.

"I hope none of the chickens got hurt," she said, knowing that some might even have given up their lives for her freedom.

"I expect they're all safe for now. What are they, fryers?"

Well, she thought—that put things into perspective. "I'm ready whenever McGee is."

"How about it, fellow? The lady's ready to move on."

An hour later, well clear of the last of the outlying farms, they crossed a low, thickly wooded ridge. The rain had stopped some time ago, but the air was still damp. And cold. From nearby came the sound of running water.

"Cave would be nice," Jed said. Hands on her hips, he steadied her for a moment, then slid down and led the horse under the shelter of a stand of black gum trees. Eleanor sat like a lump on the creature's back, bereft without Jed's arms to support her, his warm thighs no longer cradling her hips, but too tired even to attempt to slide off.

Moving unerringly in the darkness, he lifted her down. "Don't try to walk yet. Give yourself a few minutes."

"I think it must be the color of your eyes." Her voice was flat with weariness. Leaning her head against his chest, she said, "Dark absorbs light. I think I read that somewhere."

"Mm." He held on to her for a moment until she no longer swayed on her feet. "You all right now?"

She nodded, then, in case his light-absorbing eyes hadn't seen her, said, "I'm fine, just fine. Thank you."

Unexpectedly, he laughed aloud. It was the last straw. When she burst into noisy tears, the laughter ended abruptly and he caught her to him again, rocking her in his arms and murmuring soothing sounds against her wet hair. "Easy now, it's all right, you're going to be just fine."

"I know, I know," she sobbed. "I don't know why I'm acting like a baby, I'm just so…"

"So relieved to be free," he finished for her, and she nodded, her matted hair tangling in the buttons of his shirt.

It took both of them to untangle her, too many fingers for true efficiency. Lacking light, she was ready to ask him to cut her free when the last snarl was freed.

"There now, no harm done," he said, sounding so endlessly patient she felt like bawling again.

"To think I could have done this months ago," she said bitterly.

"What, tied yourself to my shirt?"

"Asked Varnelle to help create a distraction. Instead, I kept sneaking away and getting caught. Over and over. Did I tell you that?"

"Over and over," he said solemnly.

Her watery chuckle was weak, but it was better than weeping. "Lord, I'm hungry," she whispered. "And cold. And wet. And tired."

"Whoa, one thing at a time." He used the same soothing tone of voice on her that he did his horse. She might have resented it if she'd had the energy.

He led her several feet away to an overhang that felt almost dry. "I'm going to collect enough wood to build a small fire, then we'll see about something for supper."

"Breakfast."

"Mm."

It probably was closer to morning, she realized. The night wasn't particularly cold for a late-spring night in the mountains, but they were both soaked to the skin. At least she had a dry change of clothes. Jed had nothing.

She made out two pale shapes suspended from a dead branch. The pillow slips. Her monogrammed linen pillow slips edged in Cousin Annie's tatting, that had spent countless years in Annie's hope chest before being transferred to her own.

The wet pillow slips.

"Well, damn blast it all to hell," she muttered just as a load of kindling was dropped at her feet.

"Not enough? I can find more, but I thought we could get started with this."

"Not that—that's wonderful. Where did you find dry wood on a night like this?"

"Deadfalls. What were you cursing?"

"My dry clothes. They're all wet."

Without comment he knelt and built a small pyramid of sticks over a bundle of dried grass. She could barely make out the shape of his white shirt as she inhaled the subtle masculine scent of his body, taking comfort from his nearness. It occurred to her that in any wilderness, on the darkest night, she would have felt safe as long as this man was near.

Which told her something, only she wasn't quite sure what it was. Probably be better off not knowing, she admitted silently. It was hard to be rational under the circumstances.

Arms wrapped around her knees, she shivered as she watched him arrange a circle of rocks around the kindling. When a tiny flame flared larger, sent up a shower of sparks and began to blaze, she asked wonderingly, "How did you do that? I didn't hear the sound of flint striking flint. Was it a—a fire stick?" She had once seen a demonstration utilizing string, a stick and a wad of dry grass to spark a fire.

He chuckled. "You might say that. I dipped a few of your sulfur matches in melted paraffin before we left."

His laughter warmed her even more than the thought of a roaring fire. "Jed, are you sure we're far enough away to be safe?"

"Any luck, they're still searching along the old wagon

road. Probably stopped off at Alaska's cove to refuel before they set out after us.''

The tiny fire popped and snapped as the kindling caught up. Eleanor untied her wet shoes and slipped them off, then peeled off her soggy hose. Cupping her bare toes, she tried to warm them with cold hands.

As light from the fire spread in a larger circle, she noticed that Jed was barefoot, too. ''What happened to your moccasins?''

''Fell apart while I was tracking down lightwood.'' He tugged a few scraps of shaped buckskin from his pocket and tossed them on the ground. ''Don't reckon I'll ever be a cobbler.''

They spoke of inconsequential things while Eleanor wondered how a bitty little fire could keep them warm until the sun rose again. She hated to complain, but she was freezing and starving, and what's more, she had no idea where they were or where they were going, much less how long it would take them to get there.

He'd said he was taking her home with him. She didn't even want to think about his family's reaction if he showed up with a dirty, bedraggled stranger. From what little he'd said, she gathered they weren't at all close.

What if he changed his mind and left her somewhere along the way? ''This Foggy Valley place you mentioned. Is it very far from here?''

Without answering, Jed moved over to where McGee stood, snorting occasionally, but otherwise apparently content. He returned a moment later with a bundle rolled up in the remnants of his buckskin coat. ''Bread, cheese and the last two eggs.''

''Oh, my mercy, my hens! They'll starve!''

''I doubt that. Once the sun's up, I expect there'll be a

steady parade up the hill, claiming everything you left behind. That includes your chickens.''

Jed produced her small boiler, filled it from the nearby creek, dropped in the two eggs and set it near the edge of the fire. ''About where we're going,'' he said, settling down on the other side of the fire. ''I think I told you this before—it's a few miles from where Cane Creek flows into the Broad River. Fifty, sixty miles or so from where we are now. Maybe more.''

In other words, she thought, discouraged, we might be lost in this wet, cold wilderness forever. She didn't know what to say. At least he'd brought her this far. She was no longer a prisoner.

''I reckon the dictionary's ruined,'' he said, sounding so wistful she was ashamed of her own lack of gratitude.

''We could dry it, but it would take forever and even then, some of the pages would probably stick together.''

They were talking about a book when they were lost in the mountains, miles from civilization? When she was wet, cold, hungry and destitute, totally dependent on the dubious hospitality of strangers?

''Eat a biscuit and some cheese,'' he said. ''You'll have to wait until we're done with the boiler to drink.''

Before they'd left she used up the last of her flour, knowing they would need food on the road. The cheese was moldy, a rind she'd been saving in case mice invaded the cabin again. Using the paring knife, he peeled the blue fur from the outside and divided the sliver that was left into two small squares.

''Oh, for a handful of dried apples to go with it,'' she said.

He was sitting cross-legged on the other side of the fire. ''Or apple dumplings.''

''Or roast beef and potatoes.''

"How about fried squirrel with baked sweet potatoes?"

They went on naming their favorite foods while they munched cold biscuits and nibbled the hard cheese. Then Jed emptied the pan, refilled it from the creek and they took turns sipping cold water while they waited for the eggs to cool. Eleanor said, "Should we save them for tomorrow?"

"We'll do better than that tomorrow. You need food tonight to keep you warm."

She needed more than food, but she didn't see any point in saying so. Her quilts were back at the cabin. She'd thought about bringing them along, but they'd both had enough to carry. Besides, they'd have been soaking wet by now, and would probably weigh a ton.

But if Jed thought he was going to sleep on one side of the fire while she slept on the other, he was sadly mistaken. Body heat, she had recently discovered, was the best kind of all. Soothing and exciting, all at the same time.

"Oxymoron," she said.

"Damn, I'm sorry that dictionary got ruined."

It was a game they had played before, once she'd discovered how inadequate his education was and realized that instead of being sensitive about it, he was determined to fill the gaps.

She told him what the word meant. He thanked her gravely and handed her a warm egg, freshly shelled.

"How far do you think we've come?" she asked after she'd finished half her egg.

"About four miles, way I figure it. If I pace him just right, McGee can do five on flat ground before he starts wheezing."

"Then why did we stop?"

He looked at her across the fire, his eyes impenetrable. "Because you needed to stop."

She didn't know what to say to that. How any man could be so kind, so gentle, after being treated the way he'd been treated, passed all understanding. She remembered the first time she'd been on the receiving end of Devin's temper. He'd tripped over a keg of nails, sprawling on the ground in front of the shed, scattering cut nails all over the ground. Hearing his curses, she'd come racing out of the house to see what had happened. When she'd tried to help him to his feet, he had struck her a glancing blow and blamed her for leaving the keg in the middle of the shed, as if he hadn't unloaded it from the wagon and left it there himself.

Never even apologized for it, either.

She had since learned that among the Millers, women were always the scapegoat for anything that went wrong. She had rejected the role and made no bones about it. After that, it had never happened again, at least, not to that extent.

"We'd better try to get some sleep," Jed said, offering her a last drink of water. "I'd like to make an early start tomorrow."

"How long do you think it will take?"

"Less than four days if we make good time."

Four days. Walking most of the way, probably, because McGee couldn't be expected to do all the work. He had done the important part last night. He'd gotten them clear of Dexter's Cut.

"There's some good roads farther north, but we'd lose too much time cutting across to reach them."

"Railroads? Isn't the Carolina Northwestern supposed to be laying more track through the mountains?"

"I'd like to avoid using the railroad. Personal reasons."

"Just as well," she said sleepily. "Neither of us could afford a ticket."

"Oh, I reckon I could get us aboard all right, but McGee

might be a problem. Can't leave him behind. See, I already told him about George's south pasture, and he's been looking forward to it. New strain of grass they're trying out."

"Yes, well…" She yawned once and then again, barely managing to cover her mouth in time. "Can't disappoint McGee, can we?"

Jed waited several moments before replying. "I just hope you're not disappointed. It's not a fancy place, El— not like you must be used to in Charlotte."

She'd told him about the house where she'd grown up— the house she had inherited from her cousin. The house Devin had sold to buy mining equipment. Whenever he heard of any new invention in mining technology he'd been eager to try it, convinced that only the antiquated equipment was keeping him from discovering the mother lode.

She yawned again, and Jed said, "Bless you."

"That's for sneezes."

"Bless you anyway. Time to go to sleep."

She would simply have to trust him, Eleanor told herself, remembering the last time she had trusted a man enough to follow him into the wilderness.

Chapter Fifteen

They slept cupped together, with Eleanor facing the fire and Jed curved around her back. The ground was hard even though he had padded it with leaves, moss and fir boughs. The clean, resinous smell helped, but no scent could make up for the ridges and rocks underneath, or the cold that crept up from the ground. Toward morning Eleanor woke and wondered if it could have snowed in the night. She was half-afraid to open her eyes until the increasing urge to relieve her bladder became too pressing to ignore.

Jed was already up. She had missed his comforting warmth against her back, which explained why she'd grown so cold. On the far edge of the small clearing near the creek, he was doing something with McGee's make-shift bridle, talking softly to the horse. Other than nipping occasionally at his backside, McGee ignored him.

A bright sun glinted off a sea of wet leaves. The fire had been rekindled and several strips of what looked like bark simmered in a pot of water, sending up fragrant clouds of steam.

Eleanor sat up and yawned, filling her lungs with fresh mountain air, her spirit with sheer optimism. Someone—

Jed, of course—had spread her clothes out on the bushes to dry. Ordinarily she would have been mortified to see the stockings she'd worn yesterday and the ones she had packed, along with her two petticoats, all her bloomers and her best flannel nightgown, all spread out for anyone to see.

Today there was no room for embarrassment. "What *is* that wonderful smell?" she called out, rubbing the sleep from her eyes.

"Sassafras. Best I could do. Can you drink it without sugar?"

"I'm sure I can, but first..."

"Right over there." He gestured to a thick clump of laurel farther upstream.

Gratefully, she hurried away, picking her way carefully over the slippery ground. Dexter's Cut was miles away on the other side of the ridge. From here, there wasn't a sign of smoke other than their own. Filled with sheer, unreasonable relief, she felt like singing back at the birds. "I hear you, mockingbird," she whispered. "Repeat after me." And she whistled softly the first few bars of her favorite Sousa march, not at all surprised when the bird flew away.

A few minutes later she knelt beside the creek and prepared to splash her face with the icy water. Catching a glimpse of her reflection, she tried to remember whether or not she had packed her comb and brush. She recalled setting them aside to pack, but had she ever actually done it?

If not, Jed would simply have to shear her like a sheep. She wasn't a prideful woman, but she did have standards. The thought of turning up uninvited on the doorstep of Jed's family in filthy, ragged clothes with her matted hair filled with all manner of leaves and twigs simply would not do.

"The salt's melted, but I can drizzle a few drops on your fish if you'd like. Watch out, it's hot."

"My *fish?*" Forgetting all about her matted hair and her rumpled dress, Eleanor could only gape at the magician who had managed to produce a feast from nothing at all. "Remind me if I'm ever lost in the woods again to be sure to take you along."

"I'll remind you," Jed said, his eyes lending added significance to the words.

They ate quickly because they were hungry, and because there wasn't much, and because they needed to be on the way. Eleanor pulled on her dried hose and reached for her shoes. Jed had cut the tongue from each one and carefully positioned it over the holes in the sole.

She could have cried. Dear, thoughtful man, how did I ever survive without you? she wondered. How am I going to survive once this journey is over?

It didn't bear thinking about, and so she turned her attention to getting ready to ride. Or walk, as the case may be.

She put on her shoes—they were still damp, but the kidskin lining helped enormously. Why hadn't she thought of it herself?

"Thank you," she called, wriggling her foot in his direction.

"Won't last long," Jed replied. "I saved some buckskin, we'll use that next."

Carefully looking away from where she sat lacing her shoes, her face still creased from sleep, Jed rolled up her nightgown and crammed it into a pillow slip, then began scouring the soot from the boiler before packing it in the other one. The dictionary was ruined but he couldn't bring himself to leave it behind. That went in on top of the boiler, which also held their cups and cutlery.

She purred like a kitten when she slept. He'd never heard a woman purr before…but then, he'd never before spent an entire night with any woman. Certainly not Vera, and not the women who charged by the hour.

Two nights they had shared now. A few more they would share before they reached the farm. It would have to be enough, he told himself, knowing it wouldn't. Knowing that forever wouldn't be enough.

"Looks like McGee fared pretty well," he said without glancing up from the bridle he was reworking. "Found him a patch of new grass."

"How far do you think we'll get today? I just hope it doesn't rain again."

This time of year, showers could pop up out of nowhere, but Jed didn't see any reason to tell her that, if she didn't already know it. For a schoolteacher, there was a surprising lot she didn't know.

"Probably won't. I know of a cave about eight hours' walk from here," he said. "We'll try for that, but if we don't make it, there's other places we can stop."

"How do you know all these things? There's nothing here—no roads, no towns…"

"Be surprised how much traffic there is in these hills," he said calmly. "Hunters, trappers, sang-getters." She would know about ginseng, a valuable commodity for those who knew where to find it. She'd mentioned one of the Millers—he'd forgotten which one—who collected the herb.

Chances were small, but he'd just as soon avoid meeting anyone on the trail. George needed every advantage he could hang on to, and the element of surprise was a big one.

They didn't talk much for the first few hours. As the trail was clear and easy to navigate, they started out walking. Surrounded by millions of trees, some the deep color of evergreens, others a tender shade of green that would turn the hills into a blaze of red and gold in another few months, they trudged on, crossing the next ridge at an angle. Occasionally Jed would lead them off onto a shortcut, a track left by animals on their way to water. Eleanor kept a wary eye out for possible predators, but he assured her she was safe.

"They kept my gun, dammit. I should've gone after that, too, before we left."

"Would your gun have come to a whistle?" She knew he didn't really mean it. Guns could be replaced. Lives couldn't. No telling what would have happened if he'd gone after whatever else Alaska had stolen from him.

"You'd think we were the only two people in the world," she said later on when they paused at a convenient flat rock for a breather. She examined the sole of her shoe with her fingers.

"How's it holding up?" he asked, meaning the improvised patch.

"It's still there," she said, not bothering to add that it was thin as silk and probably wouldn't last out the day.

"You can ride for a spell."

"I'd rather walk, but thank you. You don't have enough leather to line my…" She broke off, closing her eyes.

"Behind," he said, chuckling. "We'll save McGee for when the going gets rougher then. You ready to go?"

If there was a village or even so much as a single cabin anywhere nearby, Eleanor never saw it. Once she thought she smelled smoke. Another time she was almost certain she heard the sound of a distant train whistle, the melancholy "whoo-woo" so familiar she nearly cried.

They passed two waterfalls, one with a small pool that she eyed longingly. As cold as it was, she would have loved nothing better than to submerge her entire body and stay there until hunger drove her to surface.

They met up with the creek again a few miles farther on. It was well past noon, judging by the angle of the sun. Eleanor's stomach growled. She was so weary she was beginning to stumble, and so they made camp in the middle of the day. Jed built a fire and heated water, boiling the last shreds of sassafras bark. She was growing almost used to the taste by now. With sugar and perhaps milk, it would have been an acceptable substitute for coffee.

"How are your feet?" Jed asked.

In a movement that would have shocked her senseless only days earlier, she lifted her left foot and propped it on her right knee. "Well, I can't quite see my stocking through the hole yet, but it won't be long."

While they waited for the tea to brew, Jed cut two strips of buckskin and handed them to her. "Might as well do it while we're stopped, else you'll have blisters, sure's the world."

He knew her too well. She might be somewhat lacking when it came to common sense, but she had copious quantities of pride. "How are *your* feet?" she countered.

Grinning, he shook his head. "Give me another few hours and I'll be an inch taller than when I started out this morning."

"My blisters are bigger than yours," she taunted.

"Wanna bet?"

"Did I ever tell you about my little boys? How they always had to be the biggest or the best? If one of them claimed to have been bitten by a black widow spider, the other one would swear he'd been bitten by a boa constrictor, even after I read them about the way boas dealt with their prey.''

''Both of 'em lived to tell the tale, though, huh?''

''That tale and many more.''

They talked about silly things, avoiding uncomfortable reality. Travel was going to be increasingly difficult before they reached Jed's valley, but they had no choice but to go on. Jed had important business—he'd told her about the trouble his family was in, and the means he had to deal with it. She had an idea there was more to the story than the simple repayment of a debt, but he hadn't gone into detail, and she hadn't asked.

Weariness was a constant companion as they trudged on, taking turns riding, but mostly walking as the terrain was increasingly difficult. It was too early in the season for nuts or wild fruit. Greens were easy enough to find near the streams, but without seasoning, they were tasteless and did little to stave off hunger. Twice Jed trapped squirrels, which he roasted on a spit over the fire. Even without salt they were delicious. Eleanor knew she would never again look at a squirrel in the same way.

''I could probably catch us another trout, but it would take too long. We need to move on unless you need to rest your feet some more?'' They had just finished the midday meal on the second day—or was it the third? Time had lost all meaning.

She really did need to rest. Not only her feet, her entire body. Jed insisted she ride for a part of every hour, but watching him leading McGee and knowing that his feet were as sore as her own, she pleaded the need for exercise.

Walking behind him gave her ample opportunity to study the way he moved. Sore feet or not, he moved as if he owned the forest. As if he were intimately acquainted with every rock, every tree—every faint game trail along the way.

Watching the easy way his limbs moved, the way the muscles of his narrow hips bunched with each step, she thought about that odd mark on his buttocks. He had mentioned a man named Sam Stanfield. Did the double S have anything to do with the man who held the mortgage on his family's farm?

There was so much she wanted to know, but lacked the courage to ask. So much she knew without having to ask. Honor and integrity were qualities she had once assumed that most men possessed—train robbers, bank robbers and a few politicians excepted, of course. That was before she had learned that men could smile and say nice things and all the while be thinking of ways to rob a woman of her possessions.

"I'm a bloody idiot," she muttered, stepping over a sharp ridge of granite.

"You say something?" Jed called over his shoulder.

Twitch, twitch, twitch. If there was a reward for following the leader, she thought, half amused, half shocked at her own boldness, it was watching the leader's muscular behind and picturing him in the altogether.

"I said, I hope it's not going to rain again," she replied.

"We'll stop in another hour or so. I think there should be another cave somewhere ahead. If it does rain, we'll have a dry place."

"Us and how many bears and snakes and wildcats?"

"Pick one. They're not likely to hole up together."

She shuddered. "Rain's not so bad. I really do need a bath, anyway."

They walked another few feet and then Jed stopped to pry a rock from McGee's hoof. He used one of her knives

for a pick and it occurred to her that, left to her own devices, she would never even have thought to bring a knife.

But then, left to her own devices, she would still be up
on Devin's blasted hill, waiting for someone to bring her
a sack of flour and a jar of buttermilk, and perhaps stay to
exchange a few words. "Jed, have I thanked you yet for
helping me get away?" she asked, taking the opportunity
to sit while Jed dealt with McGee.

"Believe you did. Couple of times, in fact. You
could've done it without me."

"And how far do you think I'd have got? Anyway,
thank you again. I can't imagine where I thought I was
going, all those times I tried to get away on my own. I
certainly couldn't have walked to Charlotte, even if I knew
how to get there."

"You'd have stopped at one of the outlying farms and
they'd have helped you."

"How can you be so sure? They might have kept me
on as an indentured servant." She was only half joking.
Without help, without friends or family to search for her,
to make inquiries, she could have spent the rest of her life
lost in the hills, less than thirty miles from civilization, yet
unable to find her way out.

"You good for another hour or so?" he asked, holding
out a hand to help her to her feet.

Just then they heard another distant train whistle.
Eleanor lifted her face, blinking away the sudden tears.
"How is it possible," she whispered, "to be so close and
yet so far away?"

It was the most natural thing in the world for Jed to pull
her into his arms, to hold her, swaying gently, murmuring
soothing, meaningless words. "Wanna call it a day?"

She shook her head, her face burrowed against his neck.
He smelled of sweat, horse and earth. So did she. "I'd

give a hundred dollars for a bath,'' she said, laughter struggling against tears of sheer exhaustion.

"I'll send for the maid and have her draw you a tub. You want some of that sweet-smelling stuff ladies dump in their bath water?''

"To be sure. Gardenia, if you please, and lotion to rub on afterward. Oh, and have her lay out my best blue muslin with the matching shawl. I do believe it's turning off cooler, don't you?''

They had played the same game before, when the going was hard and seemingly unending. She knew he was worried about the time it was taking them to get there. Knew also that without her, he would have made far better time, riding partway, walking fast the rest, taking steeper, faster trails instead of the easier switchbacks.

Holding her away, he plucked a twig from her hair and brushed it off her forehead. It was now matted beyond recovery. Laughter caught in her throat and she said, "You might as well do my hair while we wait for the maid, Blackstone. Shorter, I believe…much shorter, in fact. Start whacking and don't stop until you see the pink of my scalp.''

"Hmm, words have a familiar ring to 'em. Didn't some famous general say something like that?''

"You've been reading the encyclopedia again, haven't you?''

"Not lately, love, not just lately.'' Cupping her face in his hands, he searched her eyes for a moment, then leaned closer and touched her mouth with his. He tasted of sassafras and the wild mint they both chewed while they walked.

His kiss was so sweet, so giving, not at all demanding. She could have wept all over again. She knew he'd been aroused the past two nights when they'd slept curled together under layers of her clothing, yet not once had he touched her improperly. With her bottom cupped securely against his hard groin, she had lain there, afraid to move a muscle, wondering what would happen if he were to touch her breast.

Now, shocked by her own thoughts, she drew away. Jed didn't try to hold her. He smiled, his dark eyes tired, but still twinkling. "Thank you, ma'am. I needed that," he said.

"I'm the one who needed it. But I think if we're going to find accommodations for the night, we'd better hurry. We don't have reservations, and I don't like the way those clouds are moving in."

Not even to himself would Jed admit he was lost. Going east all those years ago had been easy. Relatively easy. The first time he'd cut cross-country, wanting only to get as far away as possible from the pain and humiliation of what had happened, he had simply followed the first trail he'd come to. Two days later, by following wagon roads and ducking off to the side whenever he heard a traveler coming, he'd reached the Catawba River. Too miserable to go on, he had bedded down a few hundred feet off the road, uncertain where to go from there, not sure he could make it, even if he knew where he was headed. He'd still been there when a circuit-riding preacher had come along, needing help with a loose wagon wheel.

By that time he'd been feverish, his wound badly inflamed. Walking had been miserable, riding out of the question. The Reverend Pepperdine had nursed him back to health and talked him out of going back to the valley for revenge. He'd ended up staying with the preacher—a learned man, if a bit narrow-minded—for nearly two months, finally parting ways on the outskirts of Hickory.

By that time the inflammation on his buttocks had healed to the point where he could sit without suffering the agony of the damned.

By then he had also worked out a plan for the future— a plan that included riding triumphantly back to Foggy Valley on a fine, blooded stallion, wearing fancy boots and expensive clothes, just in time to save Stanfield from some horrible unnamed fate. And of course, a weeping Vera would throw herself at his feet, thanking him for saving her father and pleading with him to marry her.

Eight years was a long time, he thought now, carefully picking his way along the abandoned trapper's trail. He was returning, all right, barefoot and wearing rags—penniless until he could claim the money he had wired to the bank in Asheville. By no stretch of the imagination could McGee be mistaken for a fine, blooded stallion, not that it mattered. Somewhere over the past few years the revenge that had driven him for so long had lost its power.

He thought of all the days he'd spent reading after Pepper had introduced him to the public library. He had stumbled over half the words until he'd discovered dictionaries. Once he and the preacher parted ways, he'd spent his nights refining a modest skill at cards, building on each small win, never betting his last cent but keeping back enough to stay in the game.

Luck had been with him over the years, but luck hadn't been entirely responsible. He had learned a lot about judging his opponents. For instance, he could tell by a fleeting smile when a man thought he held a winning hand. Eye movements, posture—something as subtle as swallowing, could signal either an opportunity to grab or a risk not to be taken.

Now, looking at the woman up on McGee's back, her slight body drooping with exhaustion, he had a feeling this game might well be the most important of his life. And as high as the stakes were, he had a feeling he just might be holding a winning hand.

Time would tell.

Chapter Sixteen

It was the direction of the rain that gave him a rough idea of where they were. It blew in from the west, gusts of wind-driven leaves and creaking branches preceding the first wave of showers. "Over here," Jed yelled, pointing to a jutting rock formation. It wasn't one of the caves he remembered from years past, but it should keep them dry as long as the wind didn't switch. Once a long time ago he had spent a few days in this same area, hiding out, healing and plotting revenge. That was before he'd met Pepper. Thanks to the reverend, he had eventually gotten past his initial rage.

They were both soaked to the skin by the time they huddled in the shallow shelter made by an uprooted tree and a small rockslide. Jed gave Eleanor a gentle push, tossed the two grimy pillow slips in after her and then led McGee to a place farther downhill where there was a stand of knee-high grass beside a sliver of a stream.

"Another few miles and we'd have made it," he said, ducking into the scant shelter and flinging water off his face with one hand.

"Foggy Valley?"

"The cave I promised you," he said ruefully. "The one with the pond."

"Oh. Then I suppose my warm bath will have to wait."

"And the beefsteak and fried potatoes."

"And the gardenia bath salts."

"And the coconut pie and brandy."

She sighed. It had been hours since they had stopped to eat, and even then, it had only been wild greens seasoned with wild onions. As hungry as she was now, she'd have given a fortune to be clean, even if she had to wade out into an icy creek and soak until all the dirt and any insects that had set up housekeeping in her matted hair floated off downstream.

Only, not when it was raining too hard to see. Not when thunder rumbled just over the mountain. Now when even her cabin on Devin's Hill was beginning to look good to her in retrospect.

"Wait here," he said abruptly, after studying her forlorn face long enough to make her even more uncomfortable.

"Where else would I go?" she whispered as he disappeared into the gray nothingness.

With the rain had come fog. Absently, she wondered how that could be. And then she wondered if they were lost.

And then she wondered what Jed would say—that is, if he came back—if she were to ask him to make love to her.

She would pretend that she was clean and fragrant, dressed in something becoming instead of the dirty remnants of her oldest dress—that she was beautiful, her features flawless, her body perfect, with plump, pink-tipped breasts and shapely hips, like a Botticelli Venus. And as long as she was wishing, she might as well wish that he loved her.

It took him more than an hour, during which the rain slacked off but the fog had grown even thicker, but Jed managed to find his way back. Recognizing the trail as another trapper's run, he had followed it until he'd come across a rabbit gum. Cleaning one small rabbit had been the easy part. Finding dry tinder and kindling had taken much longer. Keeping it dry on the way back had been damned near impossible. He'd ended up stuffing everything inside the boxlike rabbit gum and carrying the whole thing back with him. He would leave the trap in the shelter, where eventually it would be found. He didn't know what else to do.

Eleanor was asleep when he made it back just before dark. The fog, if anything, had grown thicker. It would take several hours of strong sunlight to burn it off come morning. Hours they didn't have to spare. He was too far behind schedule as it was, after wasting nearly two weeks, thanks to the Millers.

But gazing down at the sleeping woman, he thought, not a total waste. Far from it.

While Eleanor slept, he built the fire, rigged a spit and set the rabbit to roasting. Later he would venture out to collect enough water for drinking, but for now he needed a few minutes to think. And to warm his hands and feet. Where there was wind, any rain at all was miserable, even a cool spring shower. He wished he had something to wrap her in. A blanket, or even his old buckskin coat. Sleeping raw didn't particularly bother him, he'd done it too many times in the past, but Eleanor was a lady.

"Damn those heathens, every blasted one of them, for doing this to her," he whispered fiercely as he shifted his bare feet closer to the flames.

God, he missed his boots. They weren't just any old boots, they were his lucky boots, the first pair of custom-made boots he'd ever owned, paid for by his first big win. He'd worn them the night he had won nearly three hundred dollars and shoved half of it back to the center of the table against a deed for a few hundred acres of land that might or might not be worth a plugged nickel. He'd taken the pot that hand. According to the loser, it wasn't that big a deal, as the property was practically worthless, more than half of it so steep even goats had trouble negotiating the slopes.

Turned out the fellow was dead wrong.

Jed had been wearing his lucky boots again—hell, they were the only pair he owned, his old ones having finally worn out—when the railroad agent had tracked him down to his hotel and offered him two hundred dollars for the same worthless land.

They were still dickering five days later when George had wired him that Stanfield was going to take over everything unless George could come up with two thousand dollars by the end of the month.

That settled the matter. The next morning, wearing his lucky boots and a store-bought suit, he had tracked the agent down to a hole-in-the-wall office and stated his price. Twenty-five hundred dollars.

While Jed might have resented the fact that his father had seen fit to leave everything to George, he'd been born in that ugly old house. He had grown up planting Loran Dulah's tobacco, suckering the plants, picking the leaves, bundling them into hands and racking them up in the barn to dry. He had nursed his father's dumb cows through colic, scours and difficult calving, driven the small herd from one pasture to another and bottle-fed the orphans.

Whether he wanted to admit it or not, that land still meant something to him, even though he hadn't been back in eight years.

It had taken a few days. The land agent was wily as a fox. But Jed was good at reading his opponent. He had carefully read, without seeming to, the man's face, his hands and his posture while he'd driven the price up to nine hundred dollars. And then he'd collected his hat, thanked him for his time and left.

Next day, the agent had sought him out. Jed had held out for twenty-five hundred and made his point. The fact that the agent had been willing to pay that amount told him more than words or plats on an office wall ever could. He knew—he *knew*—where the next section of Carolina Northwest tracks were going though, and it wasn't Foggy Valley!

Two thousand and two hundred dollars had been wired directly to the bank in Asheville the next day. The other three hundred, less the amount he'd owed the hotel and the livery stable, had been in his saddlebags when he'd been jumped, beaten and robbed beside Miller Creek. He hoped whoever was wearing his lucky boots now was enjoying them.

Like hell he did. The drunken dumb-asses had damn near broken his leg twisting them off. He hoped the bastards ate bad meat and caught the world's worst case of back-door trots. He hoped their hair fell out. He hoped their dogs turned on them and their wives took off with a traveling salesman. He hoped—

"What are you so angry about?" Eleanor asked, her voice thick with sleep.

From across the fire, he saw her eyes widen as she yawned. Watched the way she winced as she sat up. "Not angry," he corrected. "Just hungry. You about ready for some roasted rabbit?"

Dinner was quickly devoured. They tried to make it last, as the next meal might be a long time coming, but there wasn't that much meat on a spring rabbit. Hands and face gleaming with grease, they faced each other across the fire. For once Jed could find no telltale signs to read. No smiles, no frowns, no shifting of the eyes. No lust lurking just under the surface.

Another time, he thought.

Or maybe not.

"You might as well know, I'm slightly lost," he said after checking to see if the water had started to boil.

"How slightly?" She didn't sound quite as upset as he'd have expected. Too exhausted to react, probably.

"When the sun comes up tomorrow I can probably give you a better idea. Let's just say that as the crow flies, we're still about a day and a half from where we're headed. Trouble is, we can't fly. All we can do is switch back and forth over the top of the next ridge and work our way down the other side. Near as I can figure, we're somewhere near Cat Cove."

She hesitated, then asked, "House cats?"

It took him a moment, then he said, "Could be, I never heard what it was called for." He'd lay odds it wasn't for any tabby cat, though.

Carefully, Jed poured hot water from the boiler into the two cups he had brought along, knowing in advance what kind of trip lay ahead of them. Wrapping her grimy fingers around the delicate flowered china cup, she said wistfully, "I'd almost rather use it for bathing, but there's not much use in getting clean and having to put on filthy clothes."

"Build up a good enough layer of dirt, it'll keep the bugs from biting."

She laughed, and he felt something inside him turn over. After all she'd been through—not just today and yesterday, but being held prisoner for so long by a bunch of wild, gold-crazy heathens—she could still laugh. A woman born into a world of china plates and lace-trimmed gowns. A woman who called a sofa, a chair and a makeshift bookshelf crammed into one corner a parlor.

A woman who not only knew things, but knew enough to teach school.

"Did I happen to mention how much I admire you?" he asked.

He thought at first she was going to cry. Instead, she bit her lip, tilted her head and said, "Thank you. If this is—"

From several yards downhill where McGee was hobbled, came a sound that brought Jed instantly to his feet. "Wait here," he said tersely. Then he drew the butcher knife from his belt and handed it to her. "Use this if you have to. I won't be far away."

Jed moved silently, using instincts born of experience and bred into him by generations of Cherokee ancestors. The fog was thick enough to cut with a knife and he'd left the knife behind. If the horse had been spooked by a bear or a big cat, chances were he'd have heard it moving through the underbrush. This time of year, with the warm days and cold nights, copperheads and rattlers came out after dark to soak up heat from sun-warmed rocks. Not that there'd been much sun in the past few hours, but if he had to bet on it, he'd bet on a snake. McGee hated snakes.

The gelding sounded off again. From fear, not from pain. After traveling together all these years, Jed knew the difference.

Easy, boy, hold your water—I'll take care of it.

His bare foot came down on a fallen branch. Quickly, he withdrew his weight before it could snap. When he judged the distance to the place where he'd hobbled the horse to be about five yards, he paused to listen, all his senses alert, open and receptive.

Definitely not a bear, then. This early in the year they still stunk of the cave.

But cats had their own wild smell, the same subtle, distinctive gaminess he detected on the damp air now. Not that a bobcat was any real threat to a full-grown horse unless the horse was already foundered. With plentiful small game, a horse was hardly worth the effort, but some cats were just plain mean.

Then again, so were some horses.

McGee knew he was close by. So did the cat. Now let's see which one of you fellows is going to spook first, Jed thought, bracing himself to make his move.

First making sure of his footing, he suddenly leaped into the air, clapped his hands loudly and shouted at the top of his voice. "Yip, yip, yip, oolay! Oolay! Scat, scat, scat!"

The trick was to scare the cat away. Sounding like a demented fool was irrelevant. McGee wouldn't spook. Recognizing the sound of his voice, the horse whuffled a greeting. As for what Eleanor must be thinking, he couldn't worry about that now. He stomped and shouted a few more times for good measure.

The threat, whatever it was, took off through the underbrush and moments later he was leading McGee back to the shelter, back to the fire that would keep any would-be predators at bay. Once there, he tied him off to a dead pine, giving him as much slack as possible. What with one thing and another, the clothesline was getting damned short.

Out of gratitude, the horse only tried to bite him once.

"See if you can stay out of trouble until morning, will you?" He slapped the gelding on the hindquarter and turned away.

"Is that you?" Eleanor called softly. All he could see through the thick fog was the rosy glow of the small fire.

She was huddled near the back of the shallow overhang, watching with wary eyes as he approached. Not until he dropped down on the other side of the fire did the tension appear to leave her. "What was it?" she asked.

"Cat. Probably a half-grown bobcat, feeling his oats."

"I didn't know cats ate oats."

"Figure of speech." He grinned, grateful once again for her resilience. He'd heard it said that city-bred ladies were made of sugar and spice. This one was made of grit and gumption. "Whatever it was, I put on the whole show, chapter and verse."

"The show?"

Holding his hands over the fire, he rubbed them together. "Stomping's for snakes, shouting's for cats."

"What if it had been a bear?"

He peered into the boiler to see if there was any hot water left. There wasn't. "Reckon I'd have tried to slip in and cut McGee's line, then we'd have both run like hell."

"And ended up at the bottom of the mountain with a broken neck," she said dryly.

"Yeah, I tried that recently. Didn't much care for it." He deliberately made light of what had happened, just as he made light of how he'd been feeling just before McGee had sounded off. If he remembered correctly, he had just told her they were lost.

Sliding around to the other side of the small fire, he took one of her hands in his, caressing the calluses that marred the satiny skin. "Eleanor, listen to me. Wherever we are now, we're safer than we were a few days ago. Will you take my word for that?"

She nodded. A thatch of matted hair flopped on top of her head like the broken blade of a windmill.

"I'd rather come up against bears, bobcats and a whole passel of snakes than face another run-in with those in-laws of yours,'' he made an effort to inject a little humor into the situation.

He heard her stomach growl and wished he had something more than water and another day and a half of rough traveling to offer her. Maybe more than that if they were too far off track.

"Better get some sleep,'' he said. It was the best he could do for now. "Tomorrow the fog's bound to burn off. Once we see which way the wind's blowing and hear that train whistle again, I can pretty well tell where we are.'' To within twenty-five miles or so, he added silently.

"Mm,'' she said, picking up on his usual way of answering the unanswerable.

They slept spoon fashion again. Jed thought he just might qualify for sainthood, holding her in his arms throughout the long, chilly night, feeling her soft bottom press against his aching groin. Smelling the ripe woman scent of her body.

She had to know how she affected him. There was no way she could mistake his erection for anything other than what it was. Rampant, unabated, unsatisfied lust.

If she was offended, she didn't show it, knowing that it was either put up with his embarrassing condition or sleep cold. Spring or not, the hours just before daylight were cold as a banker's heart.

Once her breathing evened out, he moved his face closer to the back of her neck. The shallow valley there was one of the most beautiful places on a woman's body, to his way of thinking. Gently, he laid his lips against her skin, tasting the salt there, feeling the grit—inhaling the essence of something so uniquely Eleanor he knew he was doomed.

She's under your protection, you randy bastard!

Evidently he was more of a gentleman than he'd thought. After a while, he sighed, moved away slightly and eventually slept.

Chapter Seventeen

Eleanor woke and lay still for several minutes, flexing various parts of her body that were stiff and aching. She was too grateful to be alive for another day to complain. Not that complaining would do any good.

Hunger gnawed painfully at her belly. Water would help—lots and lots of water, but that would mean stopping to duck behind the bushes every few miles. Just as well she was long past embarrassment. How much more humiliation could she possibly face, as Jed had already seen her at her worst?

Carefully, she lifted his arm from her waist and rolled a few inches away. He snorted in his sleep, but didn't open his eyes.

Good. She could do her business behind the bushes, splash her hands and face as clean as possible, perhaps even wet her hair and pat it into some semblance of order, never mind that it was matted beyond repair, and then greet him with a cheerful smile.

Men couldn't abide a miserable woman. Devin had told her so too many times to forget. She hadn't bothered to remind him that if he hadn't brought her to his back-of-beyond cabin, sold everything of worth she possessed and then blown himself up, leaving her to the tender mercies of his crazy cousins, she might not have been quite so miserable.

Lifting her skirts, she squatted behind the thicket of rhododendrons, making mental lists of all she needed to do before they set out again. There really wasn't much she could do.

Suddenly, pain streaked through her. She screamed, jumped up and slapped a hand to her bottom, feeling something there besides her own flesh.

Eyes wide with fear, she danced around in a tight circle, screaming for Jed. "Hurry, it's a snake!"

He thrashed through the bushes, knife in hand. "Where? Did he bite you?"

Wailing as much in embarrassment as in pain, she thrust her bottom at him. "Right here," she sobbed. "On my— under my—my skirt."

Casting a swift glance around, he bent over. "Let me see."

She glared at him and dropped her skirt, horrified that he would even suggest such a thing. "I can't do that."

"Eleanor, if it was a blacksnake, the bite wouldn't have hurt. If it was any kind of a viper, I'll have to cut through the bite and suck out the venom. It's the only way. Now be sensible."

"Where is he? Go find him and cut off his head before he bites you, too."

"That won't cure whatever happened to your, uh—your behind."

She swayed on her feet, her hand never leaving the burning lump. "Am I going to die?" she whispered.

Without bothering to answer, he caught her to him, looked over her shoulder and lifted her skirt. He had to pry her hand forcefully away from the site of her injury.

She waited, her heart pounding so loud she could actually hear it. She knew all about snakebites. At least, she'd read about how painful they were, and how the victim could swell up, turn black and die within minutes.

"How—how long?" she whispered, meaning how long do I have to live.

Gravely, he said, "Be still, I'm going to have to use the knife."

A poisonous snake, then....

She braced herself. "Lord, I wish I'd been a better wife," she muttered. "I wish I'd been a nicer person, but I guess it's too late now. Tell cousin Annie I'm sorry about her pump organ and all the other things, and I—"

She broke off when Jed stood up again. Her skirt tumbled down unevenly and she waited to hear the sentence of death pronounced.

Wasn't he supposed to—to suck the venom from the wound? As mortifying as the thought of such an intimacy was, if it meant she might live, she would bear it gladly.

He was grinning. "Bee sting," he said. "Hurts like the dickens, but it probably won't kill you unless..."

"Unless?" Her ears were already ringing, but that could be from holding her breath.

"Take a deep breath and let it out."

She did, her eyes never leaving his face. "Unless—?" she prompted.

"Now swallow."

"Swallow what?" She gulped twice.

"How's your throat feel?"

"I didn't scream all that loud," she said, indignation beginning to replace the paralyzing fear of a moment ago. "It feels fine. What hurts is my—my—"

"Tail. I can take care of that for you."

A bee sting. Oh, for heaven's sake. She could have taken

care of it herself if she'd thought to bring along her baking soda. "It'll stop hurting after a while," she said, summoning all the dignity she could gather, which under the circumstances, wasn't much.

Mystified, she watched as he glanced around, plucking a leaf here and another there. Three leaves in all. He put them into his mouth and began to chew, never taking his gaze from her face.

Eleanor could only wonder if this were some mysterious Cherokee ritual meant to drive out evil spirits. "If that's supposed to make me feel better, I can tell you right now, it's not working."

"Bend over," he said, and spat the green wad into his hand.

"I beg your—"

"Bend over, Eleanor. For once, forget you're a proper lady and do as you're told."

Hands on her knees, she bent over, closed her eyes and wondered, not for the first time, just when her entire life had turned into a farce.

Something cool touched her bottom. Within seconds, the pain began to fade. She stayed in that position, skirt laid over her back, bloomers around her knees, and waited for him to laugh.

"Laugh and I'll kill you," she said grimly.

"Wouldn't dream of it," he said, but she could hear the laughter simmering just under the surface. "How's it feel now?" he asked after another few minutes had passed.

"Fine. Good. That is, it doesn't feel at all."

"Then I'll go on back to camp. I'm going to try and snare us something for breakfast, but we need to get on the road as soon as the fog burns off."

On *what* road, she wondered as she adjusted her clothing and struggled to find a single shred of dignity. If they'd waited to find a proper road instead of streaking off across country like two felons fleeing in the night, none of this would have happened. They would have reached a village by now, or even a town. New towns were springing up almost as fast as new train tracks could be laid. Surely they could have found some place to stay—to rest—to work, if they had to, to earn enough to travel the rest of the way with some degree of comfort and safety.

"We'll have our tea first," Jed said by way of greeting when she returned to camp. "Sweet birch. Ever tasted it?"

She shook her head, unable to look directly at the man who had witnessed perhaps the most embarrassing moment of her life.

"You'll like it. I wish I had time to hunt down a bee tree, but it's almost sweet enough as it is. If there's time before the fog burns off, I'll boil us some greens. Won't be as tasty as your fried cornmeal mush, but it'll fill up the empty places. McGee seems none the worse for his near miss last night."

It occurred to her that he was talking more than usual in order to allow her time to find her composure. She didn't know whether to cry or to thank him for his sensitivity. "That's nice. I'll gather up everything and get ready to travel."

Gather up her three dresses, her petticoats and bloomers and the flannel gown they used for cover during the night. Everything was damp, most of it soiled, all of it beginning to mildew. She thought about her rose silk and was glad Varnelle had it, whether or not she was ever able to wear it.

"I think I'll leave my shoes here and go barefoot the rest of the way," she said, as if the idea had just occurred to her. The buckskin patches were nearly worn through and without the tongue, the laces cut into her swollen feet.

Jed lifted one shoe and studied it inside and out. "I've got another few scraps of leather. It'll protect your feet from thorns, at least."

"Until it wears out. I think I'll just watch where I step. I'm getting used to going barefoot. What about you?"

He ignored that. He had stopped complaining years ago, knowing how little good it did. "You can start out riding today. Once we hit a steep stretch, it won't be safe without a saddle, but long as we're on fairly level ground, McGee might as well earn his keep."

It was an indication of just how weary she was that she didn't argue. Knowing how miserable that bony back was—knowing she would have to be on constant guard to keep those yellow teeth from taking a bite of her foot, she only nodded.

"We'll move out once we've eaten. Just before daylight I heard the sound of a train coming from over there." He pointed to a ridge that appeared to float on a sea of fog. "Once it got light enough I climbed a tree and took a look around. Fog's still too thick to be sure, but I think I've figured out where we are, give or take a few dozen miles."

He looked directly at her then, his bearded face every bit as grimy as her own. And then he smiled, and it was as if the sun had come out and burned off not only the fog, but the memories of the past three days—even the past three years.

It was late that afternoon, after topping another ridge and zigzagging down a narrow trail, when they came upon the pond. Hollowed out by eons of rushing water that had since been diverted by a rockslide, it glittered in the golden sunlight, as inviting as the finest porcelain bathtub. A trickle of water leaked through the slide, just enough to keep it filled.

"Did you know this was here?" she asked, seeing Jed's expectant gaze on her weary, grimy face.

"I was pretty sure I remembered where it was, but it's been years since I've been along this way. You game to try it?"

"Just try and stop me." She lifted her head and inhaled, smelling honeysuckle and something even sweeter…black locust?

She had started out the morning riding, feeling guilty because several times she saw Jed wince as he stepped on something sharp. And while riding might spare her feet, it was anything but restful. She'd been almost relieved when he'd told her she would need to walk the next few miles. Walking under a midday sun was hot work.

"Going to be cold, you know. Take your breath away. Best way is to jump in and get it over with. Your body'll take over and warm you up."

Beyond any pretension of modesty, she was already unbuttoning her bodice when she saw him pull his shirt off over his head. She could hardly begrudge him a bath. The pool was certainly large enough for two.

"Is it very deep?" she asked, hesitating on the last button on her dress.

"It's not even up to your neck," he assured her. "I'll be nearby just in case, though."

"Well…all right, then." She tugged her dress down over her hips, unbuttoned her limp petticoat, leaving on only her bloomers and sleeveless camisole.

Moving to the edge of the bank, she drew in a deep breath, shouted, "Last one in is a rotten egg!" and sailed off, bottom first, arms and legs out before her. She wasn't actually afraid of water, she'd simply never learned how to swim.

Jed shed the last of his clothes and dived in after her.

Taking a deep breath, he submerged and swam the length of the small egg-shaped pool. Even with the sun overhead, the water was shockingly cold. He came up, tossed his hair from his face and looked around for Eleanor.

"Sweet Jesus," he whispered, oblivious to his own nakedness. She had waded to the far side of the pool, putting as much space between them as possible.

It wasn't enough. Five hundred miles wouldn't have been enough. He remembered seeing another woman wearing wet cotton underwear that stuck to her skin like paint, showing off every secret it was designed to conceal. It was while standing under the edge of the roof of Sam Stanfield's lineshack on a hot summer night, taking advantage of a cooling rain and the tantalizing view, that he'd first learned that veiled secrets were more tempting than secrets clearly revealed.

Vera hadn't needed a bath that night. She'd always smelled of the store-bought perfumes her daddy gave her. After working fence from sunup till sundown, Jed had been the one who'd needed the bath. Rank as a polecat.

Vera had stripped down and joined him, giggling the entire time. He could still remember the way she had wriggled her plump bottom, eyeing his naked privates like a hungry bobcat sighting a big, fat rabbit.

With her long brown hair and her pale blue eyes, Vera had been the prettiest woman in the whole wide world as far as Jed was concerned. Of course, back then his entire world had consisted of Foggy Valley and the territory immediately surrounding it. Other than the circuit-riding preachers and peddlers who came through at irregular intervals, sometimes traveling with their families, there were precisely four women under the age of forty living in the area. Two of them were rarely seen without a lip full of snuff, and another one had a disturbingly vacant stare.

And then there was Vera. Her daddy's little darling, the secret dream of every man in the valley under the age of fifty. Hell, even crazy old Elbert, said to be close to a hundred years old, would have gotten a rise out of seeing her the way Jed had seen her almost every night that summer he'd turned seventeen.

Realizing belatedly that he was standing in water scarcely up to his hips, he lowered his body, still thinking about a time so long ago that it might as well have been another lifetime. He'd kept her letter to remind him of just how far he'd come in the eight years since he'd been driven out of the valley.

And now, there in the shallow end of the pool, a near-naked Eleanor was standing with her back to him, dipping her head under and swishing her hands through her hair.

Turning, she startled him out of his trance. ''Jed, get over here.'' She sounded more riled than demanding.

Lowering himself under the surface again, he moved smoothly through the crystalline depths until he was only a few feet away.

''I'd forgotten how good swimming feels,'' he said in a valiant effort to keep his mind off what was within reach of his hands. ''I've been swimming since I was knee-high to a grasshopper.'' As if she'd be interested, he thought ruefully. Focusing on her nearness—not to mention her near-nakedness—he rambled on determinedly. ''There was a spring-fed pond on the farm where the cattle drank. George—he's four years older than I am—anyhow, he taught me to swim one summer by throwing me overboard. Said one of these days I'd thank him for it. Turned out he was right. Couldn't always find a bridge when I happened to want to cross a river.''

She yanked irritably at a section of matted hair. Jed tried not to stare. Did she have any idea how naked she looked, covered from neck to knees in transparent cotton under-wear? Despite the cold water, his body had reacted enthu-siastically to the first glimpse of her stiff, rosy nipples and the faint shadow between her thighs.

"I want you to cut it off," she said while he shook the water from his hair.

"Cut what off?" He asked, alarmed. He cast a quick glance beneath the surface to see how much was visible.

Everything, unfortunately.

She grabbed a handful of long tangled curls and tugged. "This. I can't get even a comb through it now and my brush just slides over the surface."

Oh. She was talking about her hair. Relieved, he said, "What you need is a curry comb."

"What I need is a sheep shearer. Can you do it with a knife? I didn't bring my scissors." She stood there, not three feet away, facing him with her feet planted apart, both hands clutching chunks of dripping hair.

He blinked, swallowed twice and remembered to breathe. Oh, man, she was something. Mad as a wet hen—*wet* as a wet hen—every glorious inch of her glowing pink through her thin white underwear. She might as well not be wearing anything. "I reckon I could," he said judi-ciously, "but it'd be a real shame."

"Just do it. It'll grow back enough before I get back to Charlotte so I can do something with it. Buy a switch or something. Two bugs floated out the first time I dunked my head under water. *Bugs!*"

"I'll have a go at it. Might just cut out the worst tan-gles—you can probably comb the rest across the bare spots." He knew as much about cutting hair as he did about toe dancing, but if it meant this much to her, he'd try his best. Bald as an egg, she'd still be beautiful. He would have liked to tell her that, to reassure her, but he'd never been good at fancy words.

"Why on earth didn't I think to bring soap?" she wailed. "Not that even soap would help at this point."

"Because leaving came up in a hurry? Because we had to pack just what we'd need for the trip—no room for anything else? You can't be expected to think of everything."

"Well, I should certainly have thought of soap," she said as if he'd lost his mind. "That's a basic necessity."

In her world, it probably was. "Come on over here to the bank." Averting his eyes, he took her by the hand and led her to the steep side of the pool, where the bank had been worn away. "Reach down, dig your fingers under the top layer of pebbles and you'll find sand and gravel. Works as good as soap when it comes to scrubbing dirt off a body."

Shooting him a skeptical look, she pinched her mouth shut, closed her eyes and submerged. A moment later she came up sputtering, holding a handful of coarse gravel that leaked through her fingers before she thought to cup her hand.

"Here, let me help you," he said, and before she could protest he had scooped up two handfuls and was scouring her arms and shoulders.

Gently, though, because he didn't want to hurt her.

"Ohh, that feels good," she purred.

"Turn around partway," he said gruffly, and dutifully, she revolved until she was side to him. He lifted her arm and lightly scoured underneath. The light dusting of golden hair there aroused him almost as much as had the sight of her pale thatch.

Jesus, don't let her look down, he thought, embarrassed at his body's reaction. "Look over there," he said, pointing to a dead pine that rose above the lower canopy of trees. "Pretty sure I saw a bobwhite."

"I didn't know quail perched in trees."

He didn't, either, he'd simply said the first thing that had popped into his head. Trust an educated woman to call him on it.

Taking her by the shoulders, he turned her so that she was facing away from him. Scooping up another handful of fine gravel, he applied it to her back. "It would help if you lifted your thingamabob," he said.

It would help if you stripped off everything, climbed out onto the bank and put me out of my misery. He thought it, but didn't say it. She was in his care. A gentleman didn't take advantage of a lady who was dependent on him for survival.

On the other hand, he'd never pretended to be a gentleman. Might have claimed it a time or two when it had been to his advantage, but he'd been lying.

"That feels so-oo wonderful," she crooned, holding her camisole up under her arms so that he could scrub her lower back.

And lower, and lower. He couldn't help himself, his palms slipped under the waist of her bloomers to cup her buttocks.

She stood stock-still. Hearing her catch her breath, he closed his eyes and wondered if he could just sink under the surface until he drowned.

But then, she'd probably snatch him up by his bearded chin and save his worthless life. Again.

"Eleanor, I'm sorry. I didn't mean…"

She turned to face him, causing his hands to tangle in the clinging wet muslin. "I'm not sorry. I wanted you to touch me," she said so softly at first he wasn't sure he'd heard her correctly. "Jed, would it be so wrong to—to—"

"Make love?" His eyes bored into the depths of hers, seeking...

Seeking something. He'd used the word deliberately, knowing that if it happened, this time it would be different from anything he had ever before experienced with a woman. This time it wouldn't be a case of calf love—or whatever it was that drove young men to make fools of themselves. It wasn't pleasure for pay, either, which is what he'd mostly known after leaving home. Only now that it was almost within reach did he realize just how far he had come down an unknown road.

God alive, I think I'm in love!

At least he knew when to shut up. Blindfolded and bootless, he was treading uncharted territory here.

Chapter Eighteen

It was Eleanor who led him out of the pool, her skin glowing pink through the thin wet garments. It was Eleanor who stood before him, the expression in her eyes shy but determined. "Please?" she whispered as her fingers touched the top button of her dripping camisole.

Jed needed no other invitation. Whatever waited at the end of the trail, they would work it out together. They were miles apart in ways that counted most in her world. His own world was more basic. All he knew was that he wanted this woman, body, spirit and soul.

"I don't want to hurt you," he said, the words encompassing far more than the moment.

Stepping out of her drawers, she knelt and held up her arms in invitation. "I won't let you," she replied calmly. Her eyes, eyes that usually reflected all the colors of a sunlit forest, looked dark as night as she gazed up at him beseechingly.

He came down beside her carefully, fully aroused and knowing that even though she was experienced, his unchecked eagerness might frighten her.

It frightened him. Jed had known more women than he could even recall, but never—not even with Vera—had he known anything to compare with the feelings that coursed through him now. Could it be this simple? Could a man fall in love with a woman without ever having learned how to love?

He was still kneeling when she lay down, gazing up at him. After a while she said, "You could start by kissing me." A wistful little smile tugged at the corners of her mouth.

It was all the invitation he needed. Lowering himself carefully, he took her in his arms and touched her mouth with his. Easy, easy, he warned himself, don't frighten her.

But casy was impossible. The moment his lips touched hers, all rational thought fled. Hungrily, his mouth caressed, lifted, pressed and dragged gently against the moisture, parting her lips—making it impossible for her to shut him out, even if she'd wanted to.

But Eleanor was every bit as eager as he was. In the most intimate parts of her body, hundreds of soft, sweet explosions were happening, like bubbles rising from a freshly poured glass of fine wine. She only hoped the taste wouldn't prove as disappointing as her first and only taste of champagne.

She was no stranger to passion. She'd been married for nearly two years to a healthy young man who had insisted on performing the marriage act once a week after his bath.

But never, not even in those early days, had she felt anything like the urgent demands that had driven her to shamelessly beg a man to make love to her. She didn't even know why. It weren't as if she'd ever found any real pleasure in the act, yet she couldn't deny this mindless, throbbing ache that seemed to encompass her entire body.

She felt her breasts swelling against the palms of his hands as he caressed her there. "Open for me, love," she heard him whisper, and she opened. Her eyes, her mouth and her thighs, anticipating what was to follow. Hungry for the taste of him, for the devouring kisses she would never have known existed had not this man staggered up her hill, more dead than alive. And far more...

Her limbs moved restlessly. She wanted him there— wanted him where she ached the most. I never knew, she thought wildly, never dreamed it could be this way.

He tugged her arms from her camisole and tossed it aside. When he eased her damp bloomers down around her knees, his hand brushed her bottom and he whispered, "Does it still hurt?"

"Does what still hurt?" The only thing that hurt was this vast emptiness inside her that desperately needed to be filled.

"Bee sting," he said, amusement leavening the tension in his voice.

"Oh, that old thing." She kicked her bloomers free of her ankles and twisted until she was facing him, his—his part moving against her belly. She wanted it inside her where the throbbing was almost painful, but didn't know of a polite way to tell him so.

"Does your place hurt?" Maybe one day she could get up nerve enough to ask how he came by such a strange scar in such a private place.

"Oh, yeah," he said on a sigh. "But I know a remedy." Moving between her thighs, he lowered himself carefully, using one hand to guide himself to her opening.

Hurry, hurry, hurry—oh, yes, yes, yesss! Right...there!

But he didn't move. Didn't he know what came next? Was he waiting for her to do something? Waiting to see if it fit?

It fit. He slid into her slowly, stretching her like a newly dried glove. My mercy, it fit wonderfully, filling places in her that had never been filled before—places she'd never dreamed existed.

She began to twitch, restless to relieve the ravening hunger.

"Am I hurting you?" he asked.

"No! Yes—just do something!" she all but shrieked.

He did something. He touched her in a place no man, not even Devin, had ever deliberately touched her before. Stroked her there.

She couldn't breathe. Something was happening to her. Moving slowly, he started to withdraw from her body, and she grabbed him and pulled him back, but the moment she moved her hand from his backside, he withdrew again, hovered, and then thrust into her once more. Withdrew, hovered and thrust again and again, faster and faster. Her fingers bit into his shoulders, then moved over his sleek back to dig into his buttocks.

"Oh, my, oh, my—faster," she urged, angling her hips so that she could press against him.

It was like riding that damned horse of his, their gaits were so wildly mismatched. Yet the result of this particular ride was so blazingly, gloriously splendid that she could only shout out her release as pleasure swept over her like a tidal wave.

Jed groaned, and then he collapsed. Still joined, he rolled to one side, carrying her with him. His eyes were closed, his face almost the face of a stranger, she thought, staring at him in wonder. All but his tender, sensitive, beautiful mouth.

It took forever for her to recover enough to breathe, much less to speak. Eventually, she was able to blurt out the first words that came to mind. "What happened?"

"What happened?" Jed opened one eye. "I'm surprised

you have to ask. Mountains moved, that's all. The seas parted and we walked through together…that's all.''

She shook her head. "But what did you do to me? I didn't notice anything—different. I mean…''

The sound of her voice, softened by a woman's passion, yet touched by a child's innocence, was enough to start him to hardening again. Carefully, he eased himself from her body and rolled onto his back to stare up at the darkening sky.

"Was that husband of yours a eunuch?''

"Devin? Of course not, but…'' She toyed idly with one of the dark curls surrounding his flat brown nipples.

"But you've never felt, uh—that way before?''

Refusing to meet his eyes, she shook her head.

"Then he was a selfish fool. Eleanor, what just happened was only what's supposed to happen.'' But had never happened to him before, never to that degree. "Release comes easy for a man, but with a woman…''

With a woman…what? Women were as different as clouds in the sky. As pebbles in a creek. Sure, there were basic similarities, but no two women were alike, even among the professional ladies who were the only kind he'd known well enough to compare.

Except for Vera, but that had been different. They'd both been inexperienced. Come to think of it, she'd been the one to take the initiative. She'd showed him things—taught him things she claimed she'd read about in a book. He'd never even wondered where she'd found such a book.

"Sweetheart, women are as entitled as men are to their pleasure, didn't he tell you that? Didn't he show you?''

"Devin didn't talk much, not once we were married.''

Didn't *talk* much? Married to this precious woman, he hadn't even bothered to talk to her, much less to give her

her pleasure? God, the man deserved to be flayed alive, if he hadn't already blown himself up.

Her hand moved tentatively down his middle, following the trail of dark hair. If she followed it to its source, he wouldn't count on their getting any sleep tonight.

"Yes, but how does it work? I mean, I've studied the physical sciences, but nothing was ever mentioned about...well, about you know what."

"Can't say much for that school of yours." Amused, he placed a hand over her breast, feeling the nipple swell and harden to nestle against his palm. "You mean this?"

She caught her breath. "Something like that," she gasped.

He sat up and propped himself on one elbow, leaning over to move his hand down to her mound. "Or this?" he said, and touched her in a way that brought a moan to her lips.

And then he knelt over her, his beard brushing her inner thighs. "Or this?" he whispered just before his mouth covered her woman's place.

She bucked like a wild thing. With one arm over her thighs, he held her still. Bringing her to pleasure was almost enough to drive him over the edge, but this time was for her. He had little enough to offer her, but this he could do.

"Jed, you've got to—ah...to stop! I can't stand it!" Her voice was as thin as if it had been strained through three layers of silk.

She shuddered and cried out, her voice cascading over him like music, like motes of sunlight filtering through the darkest forest. And then she fell apart in his arms.

Not until she lay boneless and panting did it occur to him that the act had pleasured him as much as it had her, if in a different way. He felt hope simmering inside him like a bubbling spring.

Waiting for her to speak, he marveled at what he'd discovered, both in himself and in her. For a widow, his sweet Eleanor was as innocent as a day-old chick. She might be an educated lady from the big city, but there were some things worth knowing that even an uneducated bastard with a brand on his ass could teach her.

Some things this bastard would delight in teaching her, but first he had to convince her to throw in her lot with his, for better or worse, and pray that the worst didn't happen.

Starting over, he mused...was it possible?

"We'll have to get an early start tomorrow," he said guiltily, knowing that George was waiting for him no more than a hard day's ride away. Alone, he'd have been there by now, gone on to Asheville, reclaimed his money from the bank and shoved it in Stanfield's ugly face.

In the presence of witnesses, in case the sunovabitch tried to deny it.

"Then we'd better get some sleep," she said, staring at his erection.

He should have been embarrassed. Or proud. Hell, he didn't know how he ought to feel with a woman like Eleanor, he only knew he wanted to go on feeling it, whatever it was, for the rest of his life.

Only he couldn't afford to think about that now.

"With that bee sting on your behind," he said the next morning, "you might be uncomfortable riding."

"It's your turn to ride. I rode yesterday."

Yesterday the trail had been relatively easy. "Tell you what, why don't you start out and see how it goes? I can make it easier for you if you don't mind using your clothes for a saddle.''

He ended up padding one of the pillow slips with flat folded clothing and tying it on with the last of the clothesline. McGee tried to take a chunk out of his rear end while he was tightening the rope cinch, but other than that, the horse had been on his best behavior. Probably knew that the sooner they got to the end of the trail, the sooner he'd find himself knee-deep in pasture grass with his muzzle buried in a bucketful of oats. McGee wasn't dumb, he was just ornery.

"Up you go," he said, hoisting Eleanor onto the makeshift saddle. "Sorry, no stirrups." He'd made loops but they hung too low to do any good and he wasn't about to redo the entire mess. McGee's patience extended only so far. As did his own.

The first several miles were easy enough. Carrying the other sack—the lumpy one filled with the ruined dictionary, her shoes, the boiler and cups, the fish trap and enough kindling to get a fire started in case it rained again, he led the horse along a fairly well-traveled track that wound its way up and over Dark Ridge, the last ridge before they reached Stanfield country.

According to George's last message, Stanfield now owned everything in the valley except for the Dulah farm. As the only man in the area with money to spare in these lean times, the old pirate offered loans to anyone in need, demanding an exorbitant amount of interest. When they couldn't pay up, he took over their property.

Just thinking about the decent families that had been ruined by Stanfield's cutthroat tactics over the years was enough to make his blood boil. So he concentrated on paying off George's debt, instead. Not until that was done could he afford to think about his own needs.

* * *

They had been traveling less than five hours since they'd set out. It felt more like five days. The sun was already settling behind the distant mountains. They hadn't talked much, not even when they'd broken briefly so that she could stretch, drink from the creek and duck behind the bushes. Hanging on had taken most of her energy, as they'd traveled faster than usual. Eleanor had sensed a renewed urgency the closer they'd come to Jed's valley. Instead of walking, he'd jogged along at a slow run, leading McGee, whose gait was indescribable. She made a silent vow that once this journey ended, if it ever did, she would nail her boots to the ground before she climbed up on top of another horse.

Somewhere over to the right lay Henderson. Jed had pointed it out, explaining that his valley lay approximately halfway between there and Asheville. Perhaps she could find work in either of those cities once she'd had time to rest up and get her clothes back in order. Jed might even visit her there after she got settled and he did whatever he had to do for his brother.

She was increasingly nervous about meeting his family. What on earth would they think of her, looking like a scarecrow, having spent several nights alone with a man not her husband. A man she had come to love with all her heart, who had never said a word to indicate that he loved her back.

There was nothing she could do to make him love her. As for the way she looked after days on the trail, she would try to think of herself as a pioneer woman and hope that once she explained, they would allow her to stay for a few days.

"I smell smoke," she announced, lifting her face and sniffing.

"Farms on the other side of the ridge. Might be burning off some land."

"Could we stop?"

"Depends," he said without looking back.

"On what? Tell me they're not like the Millers."

"The ones I remember were decent folks, but they're mostly gone now. Besides, things change." Jed paused, scratched his jaw through the thick black beard and waited for her to come alongside. "Eleanor, I haven't been back in these parts for eight years. I can't swear to what we're going to find once we get there, but I can pretty much guarantee it'll be better than what you left behind. If it's not…"

He left it hanging. If George had turned bitter like their father—if he'd filled up the house with young'uns so there wasn't a corner to spare—if the woman he'd married, whom Jed hadn't seen since they were all children, turned out to be hardhearted enough to judge by appearances, then he would take Eleanor with him to Asheville and settle her there, get his money from the bank, and once he finished his business with Stanfield he would join her there.

It would mean the rest of his plans would have to wait, but if he'd learned one thing over the past eight years it was patience.

Actually, he had learned a lot, but in the long run it was patience that had stood him in the best stead, whether it be gambling, dealing with wily businessmen who took him for a witless rube, or taking revenge.

The smell of smoke grew stronger as they neared the top of the Dark Ridge. Foggy Valley was bordered by Dark Ridge on the southeast side, Notch Ridge on the northwest. By the time they stopped for a break, Jed was seriously starting to worry. The Dulah land was mostly cleared now, nothing left to burn off. Nothing except the tool shed, the feed barn, the cattle barn and the house. Surely not even Stanfield would stoop to burning a man out, not when everyone would know who to blame.

But according to George, there was no one left to know now that the Scotts and the Gillikins had left, much less to cast blame. No one left but George and his family.

Don't borrow trouble, Jed warned himself. Could be a brushfire anywhere between here and Tennessee. Wind could carry smoke hundreds of miles. Someone on the far side of Notch Ridge could be clearing new fields, not realizing what the location of the new rail line would mean.

On the other hand, it might be that George's wife would welcome Eleanor with open arms. They would just have to wait and see. "How'd you like a nice fat trout for dinner?" he asked, warily eyeing the thickening sky. It was probably low-hanging clouds that was making the smoke look so thick, he told himself, trying to disregard the pungent smell of burning wood.

"There's fish in the stream?" Leaning forward, Eleanor rubbed her bottom. Not a word of complaint had passed her lips, but the past few hours couldn't have been easy on her, especially after this morning. They'd pushed hard all day. He'd been hoping to get home before dark.

"Used to be. I came this way with an old trapper once when I was just a kid. He took four nice ones and had 'em dressed in less time than it took me to get a fire going."

She didn't have to ask how he was going to catch fish without the proper equipment. He had showed her how his mother's people wove traps they called weirs using only vines, staking them down and then driving the fish into the open end.

Instead, she slid off McGee and led him to a place in reach of both grass and water, and tied him off, warning him what would happen if he tried to kick or bite her.

"See how he minds me?" she said, rubbing the circulation back into her sore nether regions.

"Likes the sound of your voice. I don't know if you know it, but he's been on his best behavior ever since we left, afraid if he acts up we'll send him back to that nest of vipers." Grinning, Jed set the weir aside and hunted for a switch to use to swarp the fish into his trap while Eleanor found a good place and arranged the kindling in a pyramid over a handful of dry grass.

They shared three small trout and settled for cold water to drink. Seated on the ground, they spoke little, content to fill the emptiness brought on by lean rations and physical exertion. Bread would have helped. Fish slipped down too easy.

Neither of them referred to what had happened the night before. Jed knew that sooner or later they would have to talk about it. He had a case to make that wasn't going to be easy, him being who he was and Eleanor being who she was.

Trouble was, that wasn't all he had to do, and the closer he came to home, the more urgent the feeling that he needed to be there.

"Does your brother have any children? You never said." Daintily, Eleanor spat a fish bone onto the ground. Even wearing dirty clothes and eating with her fingers, she had the air of a duchess.

"Three, last I heard, with another one on the way. I've been away a long time, though, and we haven't exactly kept in close touch."

"With your own brother? For shame."

Keeping in touch was hard to do when one brother could barely read. When one of them stayed on the farm he'd inherited, working eighteen hours a day while the other one moved around, spending his nights gambling and his days in various libraries trying to make up for his educational inadequacies. Especially when the process was slowed by having to resort to the dictionary every few lines. He'd gotten better over the years, but it wasn't enough. Not nearly enough. He had nearly wept when Eleanor had decided to leave all her books behind. Not that they could have carried them, but some day, some way, he would make it up to her, he vowed silently.

"Whenever I planned to be in a place for a while, I'd wire George and he'd write in care of general delivery." He didn't say whether or not he'd written back. Didn't consider it necessary. The folks at the telegraph offices were good at wording messages and eventually, someone would ride over to the valley and deliver his replies.

"I think I'll walk for a while," she said, rising and scrubbing her hands with water and gravel, the way he'd showed her. "McGee's been a good boy, he deserves a rest."

"How're your feet?"

"Tough as shoe leather. How about yours?"

He let her get away with the lie because there wasn't a whole lot either of them could do about it. "Then why don't we see if we can make that cave I was telling you about before it gets too dark? The rest of the trail's not too bad if I remember correctly. That way we can reach the farm in time for breakfast instead of showing up in the middle of the night."

Chapter Nineteen

That quick, quirky grin of hers would be the death of him yet. Jed wondered if she was thinking what he was thinking. That once they reached the farm they wouldn't be able to share a room, much less a bed. Jed had not seen his half sister-in-law since she was a skinny, solemn teenager, daughter of one of two circuit preachers who used to cover the area. He wondered if she was as straitlaced as her parents had been. George used to suffer through the Reverend Redd's longwinded sermons, but Jed, wild as a buck, up to everything and good for nothing, had usually managed to be elsewhere.

Pepper's sermons, on the other hand, had been fairly interesting and had seldom lasted more than an hour and a half. The fact that one man was a Baptist, the other a Methodist, had nothing to do with their different styles of preaching so far as he could tell.

They trudged on for another mile or so, but the closer they came to the place where he'd planned to make camp, the more certain Jed was that they wouldn't be sleeping at all—not that night, at least.

"I've got a bad feeling about that fire, El," he said. She hated it when he called her Elly, but didn't seem to mind when he shortened her name even more. "Henderson's over that way." He pointed east. "Asheville's up there." He pointed north. "There's nothing in that direction that would put out that kind of smoke."

The smoke seemed to be concentrated to one small area. With the wind, a grass fire would have covered more ground. A forest fire would have been visible from here, racing up the side of the ridge and bursting from treetop to treetop.

By the time they started down the northwest side of Dark Ridge, the smoke had mostly died down, only the odor lingering in the air. By then, though, Jed knew. He *knew*.

"Stanfield's spread takes up the middle two-thirds of the valley, with our place lying toward the southwest." George's place, not "ours," but he didn't need to get into that now. "There used to be two more farms before Stanfield foreclosed and drove them out of the valley, though, so unless the wind's playing tricks—"

"Playing tricks?" Her eyes were as round as chestnuts.

"The way the wind currents eddy around these mountains, anything's possible, but I'm pretty sure the smoke came from our end of the valley."

She nodded as if she understood what he was saying. Maybe she did, he thought tiredly. God knows they had talked about everything in the few weeks since he'd first staggered up the hill and fallen into her arms, George and the farm included.

Eleanor barely managed to hold on to McGee's lead. She didn't know which hurt worse, her feet, her behind, or the thighs that had been rubbed raw. Her back was breaking and she was so tired she could barely stay awake, but Jed had to be in even worse shape. He'd been walking for days. He wouldn't hear of riding while she walked.

He'd insisted on giving McGee a break, but she knew what the real reason was. He was simply too much a gentleman to ride while a lady walked.

There was no question now of stopping over for the night, even if they'd found a cave with steam heat and indoor plumbing. They'd been traveling at an increasingly rapid pace ever since they'd set out this morning. "If you're right and the smoke really is coming from your brother's farm, you need to run on ahead," she said. "I can follow the trail down the ridge, or if I can't, McGee will eventually get me there."

But he was no longer listening. Instead, he'd climbed a mossy boulder and was peering through the darkness. "God, it is," she heard him whisper.

A full moon had risen a few hours earlier, but it was still hard to make out the valley below. "Is what?" she asked, almost afraid to find out. There was tension in every line of his tall, lean body.

"The fire. Hang on, we're going to take another short-cut."

Before she could protest he boosted her up again. Leaning forward, she clutched McGee's shaggy mane with both hands and tried to hook her toes under his belly. Jed claimed the horse had fallen in love with her voice. For whatever reason, he'd stopped trying to bite her, to kick her or dislodge her, but that didn't make his bony back any more comfortable.

The journey down was breathtaking, with Jed leading the way and McGee more than once overtaking him. Even before they reached the place where the valley widened out before them, she could see what was happening.

The smoke was coming from Jed's farm. She thought of it as Jed's even though she knew his older half brother lived there. Lived on whatever was left of it, at any rate.

Jed was cursing as he hurried forward. Sliding to the ground, she called after him, "Go on ahead, you don't have to wait for us, McGee and I will follow."

Without a word he turned and looked at her. Moonlight shone down on his bearded face and she thought she saw the glint of tears just before he took off at a run.

"I'm not sure what's happened, McGee," she said quietly, "but I think it's bad. He's going to need us, so don't give me any trouble, you hear?"

Several minutes later she joined the small group huddled together near the site of the fire. She hung back, close enough to hear, but not close enough to intrude. She heard Jed say, "At least he didn't torch the house."

"That don't mean he won't. He tried, but I woke up and scared him off." Jed stared at the taller man, then both men turned to watch a small shed collapse in a flurry of sparks and ashes.

"Last week it was the feed barn."

"Why the hell didn't you tell me what was going on?"

"Tried. You'd left the hotel. Figured you were on your way."

A tall, thin man, George looked nothing at all like his younger brother, one being dark, muscular and bearded, the other fair, gaunt and clean-shaven. Shirtless, George wore bib overalls with one shoulder strap unfastened, as if he'd barely taken time to get dressed. The woman standing some distance away was swollen with child. She wore an enormous nightgown and a shawl. Two young children clung to her skirts while a boy of about six stood beside the two men, his small bare feet spread, arms crossed over a scrawny little chest as he mirrored the posture of his elders.

"Why burn you out if he thinks he's got you over a barrel?" Jed wondered aloud after several minutes of silence broken only by the crackling and popping of the coals. "Doesn't make sense if he thinks he'll get it all in a week or so anyway."

Another rafter collapsed in a spray of sparks. One of the younger children let out a wail, and Eleanor stepped forward without thinking and knelt beside it—it being a little girl whose thumb seemed permanently attached to her mouth.

"There, honey, you're safe now," she murmured.

The older woman glanced at her, looked at Jed, then edged away, drawing both children with her.

George said, "Must've heard about the money. Figures to scare us out before you can pay him off. Good thing I heard the commotion and come downstairs, else we might not be standing here talking about it. I heard a jug hit the porch and run outside. It was coal oil, all right. Bastard doused the porch good, but he run off before I could catch him. It was one of Stanfield's men. Don't know his name, but I recognized his face. Shed was already burning."

"God alive," Jed said reverently. "He'd have burned the house, knowing you all were inside?"

"Old fool's lost his mind. Weren't never real smart."

"Oh, yeah," Jed said bitterly. "He was smart, all right. Just because he doesn't think like a normal man, that doesn't mean he's dumb." Just vicious, cruel and greedy, he added silently. If he had that damned dictionary, he could probably come up with a few more words to describe the man who had watched as two of his hired hands held a boy while a third man beat him half to death—a man who had held him down with a foot on the back of his neck while his foreman burned a brand on his ass.

"Might's well go on up to the house," George said tiredly. "Stay out here long enough, the sumbitch might come back and finish the job. Wouldn't put it past him."

The two men set out across the clearing, George's wife and children following behind. Eleanor brought up the rear, still leading McGee. Jed paused beside the old catalpa tree where he used to collect fishing worms and stared at the place he used to call home. In the moonlight the gaunt, two-story house looked smaller and older than he remembered, but otherwise unchanged except for a row of flowerpots on the front porch.

He waited for Eleanor, beckoning her forward. "Eleanor, this is my brother. George, this is Mrs. Miller. She's been traveling with me." He heard his sister-in-law catch her breath and recognized his mistake a moment too late. Lorly hadn't changed much. Still prim, prissy and disapproving. He wondered how George had managed to get three children on her, with another in the oven.

He cleared his throat. "That is, I was staying at Miz Miller's house when…"

Laura Lee Dulah, her voice laced with disapproval, said, "Go on upstairs, children. Hurry now, get back to bed."

Nobody moved. Five pairs of eyes turned toward Eleanor—Eleanor with her matted hair, her bare feet and her torn and filthy dress.

Jed met her eyes over the heads of the three clinging, whining children who were obviously being shielded from any possible contamination. He started to speak, but she waved him to silence.

"If you'll tell me where the stable is, I'll see to McGee," she said quietly.

If she'd been wearing a crown and one of those velvet cloaks with the white speckled fur trimming, he couldn't have been any more proud of her. "We'll both see to McGee, dammit. You got any blankets to spare," he said to the other woman, "I'd like to borrow a couple."

He had already turned away when George caught his arm. "Don't take offence, boy, Lorly don't mean no harm."

Jed looked at the big horny hand on his elbow, then looked at the lined face of his only relative. "If you can spare a stall, we'll bed down out there for the rest of the night. Come morning, I'll borrow some clothes and see about getting my money out of the bank."

"We still got three days." George's voice held an unspoken apology, his posture a picture of defeat.

"Three days is enough time to burn what's left. If you can spare those blankets and some food, Mrs. Miller and I will—"

"God's sake, Jed, come in the house! Bring your woman, Lorly don't mean nothing. She's been feeling poorly with the new babe and all."

Eleanor felt an irreverent urge to giggle. Poorly Lorly? Would that be Laura Lee, perhaps? Or Lorelei?

The mind boggled.

Jed spoke for them, as Eleanor couldn't have opened her mouth without laughing. Hysterically, but who would have known? She'd be looked on as not only immoral but insensitive, and at the moment, she couldn't have refuted either charge.

Jed said, "If you've got any coffee, I could use about a gallon. I expect Mrs. Miller would like to, uh—wash up, wouldn't you El?"

El would. But first she would like to drink her gallon of coffee, with cream and sugar please, eat everything edible she could find and then sleep for a solid week. In a barn, on the ground—at this point she wasn't particular.

After that, she would consider the situation and decide where to go from here. Because she obviously couldn't stay where she wasn't wanted, not even for a single day. Not even if it meant walking away from the most wonderful man in the world.

Eleanor couldn't get comfortable. Other than the one lumpy pillow she'd been grudgingly offered, there were no cushions on the wooden settee, as if indulging in any form of physical comfort might doom a mortal to eternal damnation. The quilt covering her had an odor she didn't care to identify. It could have served as bedding for a dog, or maybe been used by a child who hadn't been properly trained to use a chamber pot.

She would rather have slept in the barn. At least the straw would be clean. It had been George who'd insisted on their sleeping in the house, Jed in a room off the kitchen, herself as far away as possible in the front parlor.

God, she was tired. Daylight was only a few hours away, and she needed sleep to be able to think clearly about the future. Instead, all she could do was lie here on this blasted contraption and try to find a position that wouldn't leave bruises on her body. At least her old Biedermeier had been padded, even though the padding was about as comfortable as a sack full of turnips.

Thinking about the dawning look of suspicion on Lorly's face as she'd taken in Eleanor's filthy bare feet, her matted hair, and everything in between, she had to wonder what the woman would have made of her in-laws, the Millers.

And what they would have made of her. It was almost amusing, only she couldn't afford to be amused. If she started laughing, she'd never be able to stop—either that or she'd end up crying. There was no room in her life now for either tears or laughter.

She could hear them talking in the kitchen. Jed said, ''I

can make it to Asheville and back by evening, but I'll need
to borrow a horse. McGee's pretty well shot his wad. Besides, we had to leave his saddle behind and I don't know
that he'd take to wearing a borrowed rig. He's right particular.''

"You can take one of my horses. Bay's faster, but the
gray's steadier." George's voice was slower, his accent
more pronounced. Almost Elizabethan, as if he'd been iso-
lated here in the valley since the early colonial days.

"I'll take the bay. Any problems you know of between
here and there? It's been a while since I've been this far
west.''

"Rockslide last spring up near Greyson's Falls. Take a
left at the burned tree—you'll see the turnoff. You'll come
out just above Lee Fox's place. Road's clear from there
on so far's I know.''

Eleanor sat up again, sore to the very marrow of her
bones. She wasn't going to get any sleep this night, and it
was clear the others weren't even going to try. Not the
men, at least.

With a reluctant sigh, she stood and gathered up the
corners of the smelly blanket, wondering whether to leave
it on the settee or take it out and hang it over the porch
rail to air. Her hostess would probably fumigate it once
she left.

She heard a murmur coming from the back of the house,
and then Lorly said, "There's more coffee in the pot. I've
got to go out back.''

Eleanor waited, not knowing whether to join them and
get it over with, or stay here and put off the confrontation.
It wasn't going to get any easier, no matter what. Lorly
obviously considered her a fallen woman and wanted nothing to do with her.

The truth was, Eleanor was in no position to deny the

charge. She had spent the last two weeks and more alone with a man not her husband. She had slept with him and made love with him, and given a choice, she would do it all over again.

After a moment's silence, she heard George say, "I'm right sorry about that, Jed. Lorly's just broody, she don't mean no harm. She just weren't expecting your woman."

"Eleanor's not my woman," Jed said quickly, and Eleanor's hand grew still in her task of folding the thin quilt. She waited to hear just how he intended to explain her. She wasn't his woman. She wasn't anyone's woman. The trouble was, at this point she didn't know what she was—or where she belonged.

"She's right pretty, I'll say that for her. Hair's a mess, though. Looks like her head's full of nits. If she was one of my young'uns, I'd cut it off, soak a rag in coal oil and tie her head up for a few days."

Before she could take offense she heard Jed saying, "Funny you should mention it. That's just what Eleanor said—not the coal oil, but she asked me to cut her hair for her. Trouble was, all I had was a butcher knife. Maybe Lorly could lend me some scissors."

"I reckon. Jed, Stanfield's bound to know you're coming."

In the other room, Eleanor blinked at the sudden change of topic. She did *not* have lice, either. Tangles and dirt, certainly, but she would have known if she'd had lice. At times she'd seen whole classrooms affected by the pesky things. They itched.

"I was pretty sure he'd hear about it one way or another. I could've taken a train from Raleigh partway and been here a lot sooner, but I was afraid he might arrange a little accident if one of his spies sent word I was headed this way."

"Pass the molasses." There was the sound of clinking cutlery.

They were *eating* in there? Well...damnation!

"I've been looking for you ever since I got your last wire. Lee rode over with it week before last. She the reason you're so late?"

Halfway to the kitchen, Eleanor froze. Knowing that she was the "she" in question, she could picture Jed nodding. She needed to see his expression even more than she needed a plateful of whatever they were eating.

To think that only yesterday she had felt closer to him than she had ever felt to anyone, even to cousin Annie, and certainly to Devin. Hesitating outside the kitchen door, she reminded herself that regardless of all that had happened between them, Jed was with his family now. Once again she was alone among strangers.

"If it weren't for Mrs. Miller—Eleanor—I wouldn't be here at all," Jed said quietly, and she strained to hear.

That was the way Lorly found her. Coming in through the front door, the older woman paused, one hand on her swollen belly, the other still holding the china doorknob.

"Oh, I—I don't know where this belongs," Eleanor said quickly, indicating the folded quilt she was holding. "I could hang it on the line for you if you'd like. Or wash it." So now, along with all her other sins, she was caught eavesdropping.

George's wife regarded her as if she were one of the children who'd been caught wallowing with the pigs. "I expect you're needing to use the necessary," she said stiffly. When Eleanor nodded, she went on to say, "George was fixing to put in one of those fancy toilets with the pull chain and a drain pipe, but what with one thing right after another, he never got around to it."

Eleanor released the breath she'd been unaware of holding. Evidently she had passed some sort of test, but remembering Varnelle's early show of friendship, she wasn't about to put too much trust in it. She and Varnelle had shared gender, but their goals had been vastly different. She didn't know this woman. "Jed told me about the streak of bad luck you've had lately." She ventured the tentative overture.

"Bad luck? I reckon that's one way to describe calling in a man's loan and then trying to burn him out so as to get his land and his money both."

Seeing Eleanor shift her weight, pressing her thighs together, the older woman said, "Go on outside, it's right through the back door. You'll see it. There's not much privacy for a chamber pot, what with babies running all over the place. 'Sides, I get down that low anymore, I have to call George to help me up again."

The two women eyed one another warily. Lorly's lean, dark face softened into what could almost be called a smile. It was as if an invisible dam had broken.

It's going to be all right, Eleanor told herself. One way or another, everything was going to work out. Buoyed by a rash of unreasonable optimism, she hurried out the back door into the first faint light of morning.

Chapter Twenty

Judging by Jed's looks when Eleanor joined the others at the kitchen table, he'd had no more sleep than she had. His eyes were shadowed and his face looked almost haggard. Everyone else had eaten breakfast, but no one seemed eager to leave. On the back of the big iron range sat a gray graniteware coffeepot, a pot of oatmeal and one of stewed apples, lending their fragrance to the warm, untidy room.

"Help yourself," Lorly said, and Eleanor did.

The men spoke quietly at one end of the table while at the other end, three children played noisily around their mother's chair. Eleanor took a place in the middle. Eyes downcast, she strained to hear what was being said as she spooned apples on her oatmeal and added sugar and cream to her coffee.

"Stanfield knows we're up to something," Jed said. "He might even have heard about the money—probably has by now. I've got one last ace in the hole, though."

"Unless you've got some mighty powerful friends, that ace had better be a spade. Word's out all over about the money. Lee wanted to know about it when he rode over to deliver your wire. Wanted to know if you'd robbed a bank or something.''

''What'd you tell him?''

George shrugged. ''Said I didn't know. Stanfield knows, though. That daughter of his came sashaying over here the next day after I got your wire, wanting to know when you were coming home.''

''Vera?''

Eleanor quietly laid down her spoon, trying to hear more against the children's noisy games.

''Only daughter he's got. Told you she married Pete Marshall right after you left, didn't I? They had 'em a son not long after that. I reckon that pretty well fixes Pete's future if the old man ever decides to hand over the reins. Be a big improvement, I can tell you that much. Pete weren't the one who's been setting all these fires. I heard tell him and Stanfield had words after the Gillikins got burned out.''

Jed's hands gripped his thick coffee mug so tightly his knuckles whitened. ''I wouldn't count on any improvement.''

''Maybe—maybe not, but I'd sooner deal with a nest of rattlesnakes than deal with the old man. He knows every banker between Asheville and Raleigh. Sure as the world, he knows you're coming with enough money to pay him off, and he's trying to scare me out before I can settle up.''

''Yeah, well, knowing's one thing. Doing something about it, that's something else. Like I said, we're going to need us a good witness when we pay him off, else he'll take the money and turn around and claim he never got it.'' Jed scowled at his empty cup and Eleanor rose and poured him a second cupful, then looked at George.

George nodded. She refilled his cup. He thanked her and turned back to Jed. ''We can make him sign off.''

"We can make him write his name on a piece of paper, but who's going to know if he writes it a different way so he can claim later that we forged it? Simplest thing in the world to do, change a man's handwriting," Jed reasoned. "Without a witness, the law's not likely to pick up on it. It'd be his word against ours, and he's got more powerful friends than we have."

"Then we get a witness to stand by while we hand over the money and get the note back. Was that the ace in the hole you were talking about?"

Jed's dark eyes were twinkling, and Eleanor tried to picture him as a boy in this same shabby, comfortable kitchen. He couldn't have looked anything at all like George, or any of George's children. They were all fair. Jed's hair wasn't the kind that started out fair and darkened with age. He'd probably been born with hair as black as hard coal.

"Know where it's located, this tract of land I sold to the railroad?"

"Somewhere around Winston? Didn't you say that's where you were when you won it? I reckon land's pretty valuable around those parts."

"Happens, it's just over on the far side of Notch Ridge." He chuckled softly. "Know what that means?"

George's eyes widened slowly behind his gold-rimmed spectacles. "Lord ha' mercy," he said reverently. And then he began to chuckle.

Grinning broadly, Jed raked back his chair and stood. "Thank you kindly for the breakfast, Lorly, that was mighty good."

Lorly had been holding three-year-old Reba on her lap, entertaining her with a game of catch-finger while she listened to the men's conversation. Having finished her breakfast, Eleanor began collecting dishes to wash, half expecting Lorly to stop her at any moment.

George's wife obviously hadn't quite made up her mind about her. Eleanor couldn't really blame her. In Lorly's place, Eleanor might have had a few doubts, too.

The men excused themselves, Jed to get ready for his trip to town and George to get a mount saddled. The children swarmed around a basket filled with week-old kittens.

"Don't mess with those babies," Lorly warned half-heartedly.

"We won't," they chorused, and promptly reached into the basket, cooing and cuddling the tiny creatures.

Lorly sighed and patted her swollen belly, apparently content to allow Eleanor to clean up after breakfast. "George bought me that oatmeal special when I complained about having to eat grits and cornmeal mush every morning. Even with money so scarce, he treats me like I was a princess."

Eleanor couldn't help but contrast that with the way her own husband had treated her. "Your son looks just like him," she said, cautiously reaching out to accept the proffered olive branch. There was something restful about a kitchen that smelled of cinnamon, coffee and new kittens.

Three-year-old Reba climbed back up on her mother's lap, reached for her hand and placed it flat on the table. Absently, Lorly snatched it away before her daughter could slap a tiny palm down on her fingers. Reba lunged, grabbed four of Eleanor's fingers and shouted gleefully, "I winned, I winned!"

From the corner of the room by the cat basket, Zach cried, "You did not, neither. You never win, you're too little."

"I did so winned, didn't I, Mama? Didn't I?"

"Shh," Lorly patted her daughter's hand, her attention

obviously straying. "'Course you did, sugar babe. Zach, don't tease your sister."

Some twenty minutes later Jed emerged from the back of the house and headed out the back door just as Eleanor was spreading the dish towel on the rack. He was wearing borrowed boots, a clean pair of Levi's that fit like a glove—a tight glove—and one of his brother's shirts that hugged his chest and shoulders with the cuffs rolled back over his muscular forearms. He had shaved off his beard, revealing a square, oddly pale jaw.

Eleanor could only stare, remembering the man who had staggered up her hill less than a month ago. That Jed had been her secret—hers to hide and to heal.

This Jed no longer needed her. He had his family.

Zach tired of playing with the kittens and came to lean against his mother's side. "Read me a story, Mama."

"After supper tonight," Lorly promised. "Right now I've got beans to pick over and a load of your dirty overalls to wash." She said it with a tired smile.

Eleanor said, "Let me do the beans while you collect your wash. I'd do that, too, only I wouldn't know where to look."

"There's no call for you to—"

"Please?"

With a nod, Lorly indicated the bin where the dried beans were kept. "I get so tired…sometimes I wish we'd waited another year before we started this baby."

Through the back door both women could see George leading out a bay mare. Jed crossed to meet him and the two men stood talking. Eleanor longed to hear what they were saying. Instead, she sat at the table and began picking over the beans. Lorly left to collect the dirty laundry, and the children trooped outdoors, Zach helping two-year-old Sara down the steps.

Eleanor wondered what it would feel like, having brothers and sisters—having children of her own. Her hands grew still. No matter what happened in the future, she told herself, at least she no longer felt as if she were walking a fragile tightrope over a mile-deep drop.

Lorly returned, her arms layered with clothes to be laundered. "Let the beans wait. Come on out to the washhouse, you might as well make use of the hot water before I dump these filthy things in to soak. I declare, the girls are just as bad as Zach is when it comes to playing in the dirt."

Bemused, Eleanor rose and followed her to the washhouse, attached to the house by a boardwalk. Evidently she had passed some vital test.

Inside the unpainted room there was a fireplace, a small potbellied stove and two tubs, one a galvanized washtub, the other a copper hipbath that had been polished to a soft gleam. "George ordered it for me from the mail-order catalog right after we were married," said the older woman, pride lending her plain features a becoming glow.

"Oh, my...are you sure you don't mind?" Eleanor could hardly take her eyes off the tantalizing sight of the tub. Nearby, an enormous kettle sent up clouds of steam.

Lorly reached for the kettle, but Eleanor shook her head. "Let me. Please. I've never wanted anything so much in all my life as I do this bath." With soap instead of a handful of sand and gravel, she sincerely hoped. Plain lye soap would be just fine. She would take whatever was offered and be grateful.

Lorly chuckled softly. "I told you George spoils me rotten. He's got his eye on one of those big porcelain bathtubs with water piped up from the well, if we ever get through this mess."

As much as Eleanor wanted to see Jed again before he left—if he hadn't already gone—she wanted a bath even more. Once the tub was filled, cold water added to that from the kettle, Lorly produced a bar of genuine French milled soap from her apron pocket. "It's lavender," she said. "George gave me a dozen bars when I told him we were having us another baby."

"Oh, I can't use your good soap," Eleanor protested, avidly eyeing the sweet-smelling oval. "Laundry soap is just fine."

"'Course you can. I'll tell you the truth, it's so good to have another woman to talk to, I'd give most anything and call it fair trade. The only woman left in the valley now that the Scotts and the Gillikins have gone is Vera Marshall, and I'm not about to take up with the likes of her, that I'm not!"

Lorly left, promising to lay out something for Eleanor to wear until her own things could be washed and dried. "It won't be what you're used to, but I reckon it'll be some better than what you're wearing now." There was no insult intended and none taken.

Left alone, Eleanor quickly undressed and lowered herself into the warm water. Oh, bliss...sheer heaven! She ducked her head and then worked lather into her hair, knowing that it would take more than French milled soap to undo the damage done by nature and long neglect.

She was trying to rinse the soap from her hair when Lorly brought in a towel and an armful of clothes. The water had already grown cool. Longingly, she eyed the kettle, just beginning to steam again.

"I'll just put the overalls to soak in the bath water once you're done with it. George and Zack's things always take a good soaking before they're even fit to wash." She held up a green calico. "This dress used to fit me perfectly before Zach was born. After Reba came I couldn't squeeze into it. You're welcome to it if you can wear it."

She gazed wistfully at the white-collared dress and shook her head. "Lord, the dreams a woman dreams when she's young."

Eleanor knew about dreams. "About love, you mean. Did you know? I mean, what did you think the first time you met George?" Standing, she wrapped the towel around her, using the ends to blot her hair.

"Think? I don't reckon I thought at all, at least not with my head." She laughed, looking far younger for a moment. "First time I ever met him, he was twelve and I was ten. He stuck a cocklebur in my hair. Next time we came through the valley, he picked a persimmon and dared me to eat it. It wasn't ripe yet."

Eleanor laughed and reached for the coarse cotton drawers. The ring of flowers embroidered around the lower flounce gave her a glimmer of what Lorly Dulah was really like before pregnancy, overwork and worry had dulled her spirit.

"I'll do your things later in clean water." Lorly dropped the laundry into the hipbath and poked it down with a broom handle. "There, that'll wait a spell. One thing I learned after the babies started coming—it doesn't matter if a chore doesn't get done on time, it'll still be waiting for you when you get around to it."

Both women laughed, and Eleanor felt a fresh rise of optimism. For the first time since the day she had first set out with her brand-new husband for his romantic-sounding mountaintop home, she felt like the future was wide-open before her.

"Want me to trim your hair for you?"

"I doubt if a trim would be enough." Eleanor touched the wet, tangled hair that had always been difficult to manage. Devin had called the mop of tight curls her crowning glory, but then, Devin hadn't had to rinse the soap out with vinegar, then rinse the vinegar out, and then brush it until her scalp ached.

She glanced toward the window, wondering if by some miracle Jed was still there. Interpreting her look, Lorly said, "He's left. Won't get there before the bank closes, but if everything works out, he'll be back tomorrow."

Setting aside her own selfish interests, Eleanor said, "I hope it does. I'm sure it will."

"My knees are worn out from praying." With a rueful smile, the older woman added, "Can't get up from praying any easier than I can from peeing. Once this baby's born, I'm going to nurse him until he's ten years old. They say as long as you're nursing, you can't get caught." A stricken look came over her. "You did say you'd been married, didn't you? I run on at the mouth like I'd never had company before."

Smiling, Eleanor said, "I know how that is. My husband died about six months ago and I've lived alone ever since. My neighbors were… Well, let's just say they weren't very friendly. I used to talk to my two laying hens."

"I've got the children and George, when he's not out working. He's not much for talking anymore, though. Too worried, I guess."

Lorly collected her scissors and said, "Come on out on the side porch, let's cut it now before I have to go out back again. These past few months I've worn a regular trough out to the privy."

Lorly draped the towel around Eleanor's shoulders and sat her down on a backless chair. The scissors went whack, whack as clumps of matted hair fell to the floor. "Did I tell you my father used to ride through here once every month or two when I was a little girl? Turn your head this way—that's right."

Eleanor felt the cool blade slide along the back of her

neck. Her hair hadn't been trimmed in nearly five years. "I'm going to look like a plucked chicken," she whispered.

"Hush, that you're not. Papa taught George to read, did Jed tell you that? Him and Pete Marshall. Jed, he was too stubborn, couldn't sit still long enough. My, but that boy was a handful. Pretty, though, I still remember that. With those dark eyes and that wicked grin, I reckon he's got away with more mischief than the law allows. Turn this way now, let me trim around your ears."

Around her ears? "My mercy, how short are you cutting it?"

"No shorter than I cut Reba's hair starting when the weather gets warm. Hers is almost as thick as yours, but straight as a stick. Makes it easier to manage."

They were still there when the neat little trap with a woman at the reins pulled up before the house.

Lorly said, "Oh, my sakes, it's Vera."

Eleanor swallowed hard. The last thing she needed was to meet Jed's beloved Vera when she was dressed in a faded gown that didn't fit, with her so-called crowning glory lying in untidy heaps around her feet.

"Where's Jed?" the visitor demanded as she hurried up the front walk. She was short, plump, and overdressed for a morning visit in Eleanor's estimation. "Papa said he was back."

"And Papa would know," muttered Lorly. When the woman reached the steps, she said, "Morning, Vera. I'd like you to meet a friend of mine. This is Mrs. Miller. Eleanor, say hello to Mrs. Marshall, our neighbor."

"My Gawd, Laura Lee, you're fat as a pig." Ignoring Eleanor, the newcomer stopped at the bottom step. "Where's Jed?"

"He rode into town." Lorly crossed her arms over her

bulge. "Would you like to come inside for a glass of cool cider. It's going to be a scorcher today."

The visitor stood her ground, evidently untempted by the offer of a cool drink. She had three chins, one thrust forward, the other two quivering. "When's he coming back?"

"Who?"

"Jed! Who did you think we were talking about?"

"Well, it could've been George or it could've been your husband. I declare, if I have to carry all this weight around much longer, my mind's going to be full of holes as a tea strainer. Did it serve you that way before little Petey was born?"

Eleanor saw a new side of the woman she had known less than a day. Lorly was a lot smarter than she let on, definitely nobody's pushover. They sparred for another few minutes and then Vera—Jed's beloved Vera of the flowery language and the highly embellished handwriting—swung herself back up onto the seat of her gleaming black trap, slapped the small mare with the reins and left, kicking up a cloud of dust behind her.

"Notice she didn't once look over to where the shed used to be," Lorly said dryly.

"You think she knows who burned it?"

"She knows."

"You don't like her," Eleanor ventured.

"Like her? I despise the woman. The Lord says, 'Judge not lest ye be judged,' but she made a play for George right after Jed left. George says he sent her packing. He said she'd chase after anything in pants, but you couldn't tell Jed that. 'Course, that was after Jed left home and went to work for her daddy. I don't reckon George saw him much that last summer before he ran away."

As curious as she was, Eleanor knew she shouldn't pry

into something that was none of her business. Instead of asking what had happened that long-ago summer while she swept up the hair off the porch, she said, "Jed still carried a letter from her when I met him."

There, that was all right, wasn't it? If he hadn't minded her knowing about it, he shouldn't mind his own family knowing. "He said it was to remind him of all he needed to achieve before he went home again."

"I don't know about any letter, but I reckon he achieved it, whatever it was he set out to do. Lord knows, if he hadn't been able to come up with the money, I don't know where we'd be now. My folks are both dead. George doesn't know anything but farming, and after that bad drought I don't know of any farms that can afford to hire help."

Eleanor started to throw the trimmings into the trash, but Lorly shook her head. "I'll sprinkle them around the garden to keep the deer away. They say it works for snakes, too, but it's not snakes feeding on my early greens. Go on inside and look at yourself. There's a mirror in our bedroom, first one on the right at the head of the stairs."

"I'm almost afraid to." Eleanor touched her hair, tried to measure the length with her finger, and sighed. It would grow back. It might take a year, but eventually she would look normal again.

Laughing, Lorly gave her a gentle push. "Go look!"

Chapter Twenty-One

Eleanor looked. Turning this way and that, she stared wonderingly at the big-eyed urchin in the mirror. Surely this wasn't the prim Miss Scarborough, third-grade teacher at Corner Gum Academy on the outskirts of Charlotte. Surely not Mrs. Devin Miller, widow of the late miner who blew himself to smithereens trying to burrow under a hill in search of an elusive dream.

"If I thought my hair would look like that," said Lorly, coming up silently behind her, "I'd take the shears to it this minute. It's those curls of yours. Growing up, I used to pray every night for the Lord to curl my hair, then I'd have to pray forgiveness for the sin of vanity." Chuckling, she stepped back and looked at the faded green dress Eleanor was wearing. "I could take it in before Jed gets back. I'm right handy with a needle."

Reba came in and stared up at Eleanor. "What happened to her hair?"

Lorly whispered, "Hush, sugar."

"Mama, I hafta go to the pribby."

Lorly sighed. Taking her daughter by the hand, she explained, "She thinks she's too old to use the chamber pot, but she's afraid to climb up on the seat in the privy, afraid she'll fall in.''

After the two of them left, Eleanor took one last look in the mirror, marveling at the transformation wrought by a simple haircut. Simple? It was no more than two inches long, all over her head.

She tried on a smile. Even her cheeks looked plumper. If she'd known what a difference it would make, she'd have cut her hair off years ago, fashionable or not.

At least a dozen times before dark she went out onto the porch, hoping to see a lone rider on a big bay mare riding down the switch, which was what the Dulahs called the road at the far end of the property that crossed directly over the low ridge. It was possible, just barely possible, she told herself, that Jed had reached town before the bank closed, concluded his business sooner than he'd expected and headed home instead of staying over.

Either way, he wouldn't be hurrying back on her account, she told herself, but hope refused to die.

It was while they were cleaning up after breakfast the next morning that Lorly brought out a wrinkled gown of silk pongee with a small bustle and gigot sleeves. The lace overskirt had yellowed until it looked as if it had been dipped in tea. "It was my wedding dress," she confided, holding it up to her distorted figure. "Can you believe I ever wore something this size? My waist was nineteen inches then, and my bosom was...well," she said, laughing. "A lot smaller, at least. Babies will do that to you."

Eleanor thought about the rose silk she had worn as a bride. She would have preferred something else—something like this gown, in fact. Instead, she had made over one of her cousin's Sunday gowns, and Devin had claimed he liked it even better than white satin. More practical, he'd said. Rose silk taffeta—*practical?*

"I'm sure it will still be in style when Reba and Sara grow up," Eleanor said diplomatically. "Lemon juice and sunshine should lighten the lace several shades."

"I wasn't thinking about the girls," Lorly said with a sly glance at Eleanor, who was drying the cutlery and dropping it into the drawer.

"Then it's time you did. If this one's a girl, you'll have three daughters lined up waiting to wear their mama's wedding dress. Do you think George can bear giving away three daughters?"

Draping the gown over a chair, Lorly sat—sprawled was more like it—in another chair and slipped a hand behind to rub her lower back. "What kind of gown did you wear for your first wedding?"

Eleanor slammed the drawer harder than necessary. Without turning around, she spread the towel on the rack. "My only wedding," she stressed. "It was rose silk taffeta. Nice enough, but yours is truly lovely."

"What happened to it?"

And so Eleanor told her the story of their escape, which sent both women into gales of laughter. In retrospect, Eleanor could see the humorous aspects, although at the time there'd been nothing at all funny about it.

"Lord, it's nice to have another woman to talk to," the older woman said, and Eleanor nodded agreement. Then she went on to describe her wedding dress in detail, along with the shoes she'd worn with it. "Poor Varnelle probably won't be able to wear any of it, but thank goodness I kept everything, even though the shoes pinched and I would never have worn the dress again. If I'd died, they might have laid me out in it, but you know what? I'll bet anything they'd have stripped it off before they buried me.

The Millers didn't believe in wasting anything. I'd like to think Varnelle will enjoy it, but I honestly don't care if she sells it to buy sugar for her brother's still.''

"If she wanted it enough to defy her family and help you get away, I bet she won't sell it for any amount of money.''

"Actually, just the thought of getting rid of me would probably have been enough. It was Hector she really wanted, not a silk dress and a pair of spool-heeled shoes that would twist her ankle if she ever tried to walk in them. Hector didn't love me—he didn't even approve of me. The Millers like manageable women, and I'm afraid I was never that.''

She got up and looked out the window again, then sat back down. "It was Devin's shares he was interested in, like all the others. He spent a lot of time down in those tunnels under the hill, and nobody was supposed to set foot in Devin's tunnels. They were supposed to be off-limits until one of the men married me, and then everything that had belonged to Devin would be his. Me, included.'' She stared down at her feet. She was wearing a pair of Lorly's crocheted slippers. "I saw him there several times. Hector, I mean. I never called him on it, because I really didn't care where he went as long as I didn't have to marry him.''

Lorly flexed her swollen ankles. "Yes, well…all that's behind you now. Unless you're wanting to go back and claim your gold mine?''

"Ha. That'll be the day.''

The sound of children playing outside drifted in through the window. The fire had been banked after breakfast, but the room was still warm. On the far wall, a wagtail clock loudly counted off the minutes. It was almost time to start preparing the noon meal, but neither woman moved.

Lorly, a secretive smile lighting her plain features, said, "Don't be surprised if Jed brings you a bolt of dress goods and some trimmings. I don't know about the shoes, though. Does he know what size you wear?"

Eleanor's jaw dropped. Eventually, she remembered to close her mouth. "Dress goods? Why on earth would he do that?"

"Well, because he wants to marry you, silly. He won't care if you're wearing a feed sack, but I reckon he knows you well enough to know you'd be happier wearing a pretty gown. Might even feel guilty because you traded your wedding dress to help him get away."

"To help *me* get away, you mean. Lorly, I think you might have jumped to the wrong conclusion. Jed and I—that is, Jed…"

"Wants to marry you."

"Oh, my mercy," Eleanor whispered. She could feel her cheeks burning. "Honestly, there's nothing like that between us. I mean, we—that is…"

"I wasn't born yesterday," Lorly smiled, then winced and shifted her position. "This baby's kicking me in the back. I'd have sworn that wasn't possible."

"Another little boy, then."

"Sara was a kicker, too. Don't change the subject, just answer me this. Do you love him?"

Eleanor propped her elbows on the table and covered her face with her hands. "Yes," she whispered. "I'm afraid I do, but honestly, Jed's never said a word that would lead me to believe he wants to—to marry me. It's not for want of opportunity, either. We've been together almost constantly for weeks."

"Deny it all you want to, but just remember I told you so." With something that looked almost like a smirk, the older woman said, "If you don't mind, I'm going to sit here and watch you work. Just set the beans and corn bread out when they come in for dinner. There's apple butter in the pantry and buttermilk in the cool house.''

Eleanor had offered to take over any tasks that involved standing. Lorly hadn't objected. Now as she got out bowls and sorted out enough cutlery she was remembering snatches of conversation among her married friends about pregnancy and the various afflictions that went along with it. They had usually fallen silent when she approached out of consideration for her unmarried state, but she'd heard enough to know the changes could be horrendous.

Was a tendency to hallucinate among them?

She honestly couldn't remember. Now she wished she'd paid more attention. What was going on? Could Jed have said anything to lead Lorly to believe what she obviously believed? If he'd had any intention of offering for her, wouldn't he have come to her first? And if he did, would it be because he loved her, or because he thought he'd compromised her?

One thing she was fairly sure of—it wouldn't be for her supposed gold shares.

She glanced out the window toward the switch, then looked over toward the barn where George was sharpening a plow. Lorly had explained that they'd had to let the hired man go as they could no longer afford to pay him. Everything, she'd said, hung in the balance until they found out whether or not they were going to lose the farm.

Just as Eleanor brought in the things from the cool house, a lattice affair built up off the back porch where it could catch the slightest breeze, they heard the clip-clop of a horse riding in on the hard-packed soil. ''He's back,'' she whispered, her heart clutching almost painfully.

Lorly grabbed the table and used it to hoist herself out of the chair while Eleanor set the food down, then both women hurried outside in time to see an old-fashioned trap pull into the yard, the bay mare tied off behind.

Two men sat on the high seat, one of them easily recognizable. Eleanor felt her breath constrict in her lungs. The children darted past her, all but Sara, who grabbed hold of her skirt and clung. Evidently, to the two-year-old, one skirt was as good as another.

Eleanor scooped the child up in her arms, instinctively seeking a barrier as Jed climbed down and turned to assist an elderly man wearing a frock coat, a bowler hat and thick, gold-rimmed spectacles.

"Told you so," Lorly whispered.

"Told me what?"

"Brought the preacher with him."

"As a witness," Eleanor hissed. "You heard what they said. They're going to need a witness when they pay off Mr. Stanfield. George could hardly call on you, wives don't count."

"How about you? You're not a wife...yet."

Jed cautioned, "Watch your step, Pepper, there's toys scattered around everywhere."

Pepper? Eleanor was still standing there clutching his two-year-old niece when Jed helped the elderly man up the front steps. "Pepper, I want you to meet my family." He proceeded to introduce the Reverend Pepperdine, recently retired from the ministry. "Pepper took me in when I needed a friend, didn't ask any embarrassing questions, fed me real good and didn't make me listen to more than three hours of Bible lessons a day, right, Pepper?"

"Didn't do a speck of good, either. Pleased to meet you, folks. Understand I'm s'posed to witness a signature and marry Jed and his lady. Which one of you...?" After glancing first at Lorly, his gaze shifted quickly to where Eleanor stood, her arms filled with a squirming Sara.

"Potty, Mama, I need to potty," wailed the youngster, lunging toward her mother.

Eleanor grabbed the child to keep her from falling just as Reba reached up and tugged at her sister's foot. "Can I take her to the pribby, Mama?"

"No, you cannot. You all come on inside and I'll pour us some cold tea. Reverend Pepperdine, have you eaten dinner? It's ready to go on the table."

Zach raced up to the porch on his broomstick horse and stared at the newcomer. "Who's he, Papa?" the boy whispered loudly just as George walked up, wiping his hands on a filthy rag.

More introductions were made, and then Lorly reissued her invitation.

"I'd be much obliged for a bite to eat and a glass of tea, ma'am."

In all the bustle that followed, a cold meal was set out, Sara was pottied and settled for a nap and the older children were assigned to take the kitten basket out into the sunshine and then come back inside and eat their dinner.

"Did you get it?" George asked, once the children were dispersed.

"Got it. Two thousand with interest, with enough left over to pay for a lawyer if we need one. But with Pepper to serve as witness, it probably won't come to that."

Eleanor filled the men's glasses with cold sweet tea from a stoneware pitcher. Questions log-jammed in her mind, but first George and Lorly needed answers.

They talked some more about when and how to arrange the meeting with Stanfield, then Jed rose and held out a hand to Eleanor. "Come outside with me while I see to the horses. George, all right if I turn Pepper's gray into the south pasture with the bay? I reckon McGee's still in the paddock?"

George nodded. It occurred to Eleanor that he looked several years younger than he had just this morning. The lines in his face were less obvious and there was an almost jaunty lift to his shoulders.

Jed took her arm and ushered her outside. She started to go down the steps, but he held her back. "Wait up, we need to talk."

She waited, her mouth too dry to swallow. What if Lorly had been right and he asked her to marry him? Did she love him?

Oh, my, yes! With all her heart and soul.

What if he asked her what her future plans were and offered to arrange for her to ride to Asheville with Pepper, whose ministry obviously included helping those in need?

"Talk about what?" She asked the minute they were outside. She wasn't sure she wanted to hear the answer.

Instead of replying, he turned and pulled her into his arms, burying his face in her hair. She had forgotten all about being shorn. "Smells good," he said. "Looks good, too. So do you. And in case you're wondering what I'm doing, I'm courting you."

She stopped breathing. He was *courting* her?

"See, I've been thinking. It's one thing to make love to a woman—that comes natural. It's different, though, when a man wants to tell a woman how he feels about her and ask her if she could possibly see spending the rest of her life with him, even when she's fine and educated and beautiful and he's not any of those things."

She was going to cry, either that or she was going to melt all over him like a burned-down tallow candle. "You are *so* beautiful," she countered fiercely. "Besides, without you I'd still be up on Devin's Hill with no hope of ever being free. You're fine and you know far more than you think you do. So ask me."

"Come out to the barn with me. I don't need an audience."

Blindly, Eleanor followed and stood by while he unhitched the gray. He handed her the reins and untied the bay from behind the trap, then they led the two animals across to the pasture.

Neither of them spoke. Could she possibly be dreaming? Was she going to wake up any minute now back on Devin's Hill, or lying on a bed of crushed branches on the hard, rocky ground, in a filthy dress with her hair matted around her face?

How could any man love a woman after seeing her the way Jed had seen her these past few days? He'd have to be crazy, and she preferred to believe Jed was sane.

Chapter Twenty-Two

No sooner did they step inside the barn than Jed pulled her into his arms. His hands moved over her back, pressing her against him while he murmured words she was almost afraid to believe. He was completely, breathtakingly aroused. It was all Eleanor could do not to...wiggle herself against him.

"I missed you—God, how I missed you!" He kissed the top of her left ear. "I was afraid I'd dreamed you up."

"I was afraid I was dreaming, too," she confided, her voice muffled by the hard heat of his shoulder. The feel of his body, the sound of his voice, even the scent of him—sunshine, laundry soap and clean male sweat—coalesced to scatter her last rational thought.

He ran his fingers through her hair—soft now, not a tangle in sight—and held her face away. His eyes moved over her features, lingering on her mouth until she felt like screaming for him to *do* something. Anything!

"I had some words all planned out in my head, but I've forgotten what they are. All I know is, if I don't kiss you right now I'm going to explode. It's been building ever since that day by the pool when you—when we—"

"Then why don't you hush up and kiss me?"

One kiss led to another and still another. Hungry kisses. Urgent kisses—kisses like nothing she could ever have imagined, until recently. By the time they managed to climb the ladder to the hayloft, Jed's shirt was unbuttoned and Eleanor's borrowed clothes were wildly askew. She would have some explaining to do, especially if she couldn't find all the buttons to sew them back on before Lorly noticed they were missing.

They could hear the children laughing outside. Somewhere nearby, a horse whickered. They heard Lorly call the children in for dinner, and then, with feverish haste, they scrambled out of the rest of their clothes.

Jed said, "We can wait if you want to."

Frantically, she shook her head. He was kneeling over her, his face flushed, his lips thinned almost as if he were in pain. Slowly, almost languorously, she held up her arms. "I've waited three days. Three days and twenty-seven years."

He needed no second invitation. The urgency was too great. The moment he positioned himself between her thighs and touched her with his fingers, she imploded with a series of small, stunned gasps. Embarrassed, as if such indescribable pleasure were somehow sinful, she whispered an apology.

He shook his head and managed a brief strained smile. "That was just the beginning. There's more."

And there was more. A fast, breathless coupling in the slithery bed of hay from last year's harvest, followed once they'd both recovered by a slow, leisurely exploration that culminated in the kind of experience most women only dreamed of all their lives.

Before Jed, Eleanor hadn't even known enough to dream. Now a good portion of her life was gone and she was just learning how to live. "I don't suppose we have time…?" she ventured.

He laughed. Rolled over onto his back on the hard, dusty floor of the loft and drew her with him so that she was lying half on him, half on her petticoat and half on…

Too many halves, she thought dreamily. And you, a schoolteacher. For shame!

"Pepper said he could stay long enough to do it. How long does it take to make a wedding dress?"

"Not very long if I wrap the cloth around me like the ladies in India and drape one end over my head like a veil so that it covers—" She touched what remained of her hair.

"Don't dare cover your head." Jed twisted a curl around his finger. "If I'd known it would look like this, I'd have taken a butcher knife to you first time you asked me to."

She laughed. After a moment, he did, too. And although the feeling was still there—that warm, delicious tingling that could build into a raging wildfire that could be extinguished in only one way, Eleanor knew they would need to get back soon. Lorly would keep George and the children away as long as possible, but now there was another guest to accommodate. Pepper would have to share Zach's room, which meant that Jed would probably sleep here in the barn. Perhaps…

And perhaps not. If they were going to be married within a few days, she could wait. It might kill her, but she could wait.

They'd barely had time to get dressed again before Zach and Reba burst into the barn and yelled for them. Zach looked in each of several stalls while Reba started climbing the ladder. "They're up here, Zachy, I hear somebody moving!"

"Hey, can I ride your horse, Uncle Jed? Papa said I had to wait till you came back and ask you. I think he likes me. I already talked to him about it."

"Talked to McGee?" Jed called down as he hurriedly buttoned his shirt.

"Talked to Papa."

"Miss El'ner, can you make Mama cut my hair so it looks like yours? Then it wouldn't never get tangled and Mama wouldn't pull when she tries to comb it." Reba's hair was dark, thin and straight as a ruler.

Eleanor found her other slipper under the hay, pulled it on and hurried to the top of the ladder. "Move down, honey, so we can climb down. Let's see if your mama will let me do you a French braid."

And then she had to answer a dozen questions about that.

"What were you doing up there?" Zach looked curiously from one to the other. "Old cat's not there no more, she stays in the house with her babies. I know how she made her babies, want me to tell you?"

By suppertime that evening, Eleanor was beginning to get used to her shorn head. Catching a glimpse of herself in the mirror when she went to get clean sheets to make up a bed for the preacher, she touched a curl and thought that a younger sister, had she been lucky enough to have one, might have looked like this.

She still had trouble believing that Jed actually wanted to marry her. She wasn't naive enough to believe that men married every woman they made love to, else the world would be filled with bigamists. Nor did it have anything to do with gold shares, real or imagined. Neither of them would ever go back to Devin's Hill. She didn't know where they would end up—here in Foggy Valley or somewhere else. Wherever it was, as long as they were together, to have and to hold—to share a bed, to make love every night, perhaps more than once—she would be content. She could build from there. Visits to George and Lorly and their children, bringing her own babies so that the cousins could grow up together...

Oh, my mercy. Her hands fell idle in the act of flapping a sheet over the bed and she sighed.

As soon as the children were bedded down, Jed lit the lamps in the front room. George went out for a last look at the small herd of mixed-breed beef cattle and to see that the horses were settled for the night. Eleanor set out cups and a plate of ginger cakes while the coffee percolated, and Lorly and the preacher talked about what was going on in President Cleveland's Washington, about the state of the economy, which had little to do with the economy in Foggy Valley, North Carolina—and of all things, plumbing.

Then George came in and Eleanor poured the coffee and the talk turned to Sam Stanfield and the necessity of arranging a meeting as quickly as possible.

"I'll ride over first thing and set it up," offered Jed. "You want to meet here or at his place?"

George looked at his wife and shrugged. "Halfway between? Hell, I don't care as long as we get it done. Where's the money?"

"In your old saddlebags, hanging on the back porch."

"The back porch! The devil with that, man—your pardon, preacher—but couldn't you find a safer place to hide it than right out there in the open?"

"Reckon I could've buried it under the manure pile. I doubt if any of Stanfield's men would've dug it up. On second thought..."

"What about bringing it in the house?"

"What's to keep him from trying to burn you out again? You want to bet he doesn't know where I went and why?"

"I won't be sleeping tonight, I'll be standing guard. What about the barn? Couldn't you hide it there?"

"Stanfield doesn't want a measly two thousand, he's counting on—"

"Measly!" Lorly exclaimed. She had devoured four of the dozen cookies Eleanor had set out, one right after another.

"What he means, honey," George explained, "is that Sam's got his eye on a bigger prize. Railroad's going to pay big money for land to extend their line farther to the southwest."

Jed looked at George. George looked at Jed. Both men started grinning, and Pepper leaned forward and said, "What? What?" Having removed his necktie, his celluloid collar and his black coat, and with his wispy white hair awry, he looked far less like a preacher.

"You want to tell him?" George asked.

So Jed explained how he'd accidentally come by a tract of land on the other side of Notch Ridge that would serve the railroad's plans even better than the valley, as they wouldn't have to blast through thousands of tons of solid granite on either end, but instead could follow a more or less level route all the way to Asheville and beyond.

"He's bound to know," the Reverend Pepperdine said, although he was chuckling, too. "Man's as smart as you say…"

"Agent swore me to silence so property owners in the area wouldn't triple the price of their land. I made him promise not to record the deed until I wire him an all-clear, else I'd tell every property owner between Hickory and the Tennessee border. Stanfield's got spies somewhere along the line, but we've got an edge for the time being. Once we pay off the loan, there's not much the old bastard can do, beg pardon, Pepper.''

It was decided that Jed would ride over to the Stanfield Ranch early in the morning to arrange the meeting. ''Halfway between his place and yours, that suit you, George? Personally, I'd as soon not set foot on Stanfield land again, but this time I'll know better than to let him get the drop on me.''

''What if he refuses to take the money?''

''He'll take it and sign off if I have to hold a gun on him.''

Pepper tsk-tsked, but behind his smudged spectacles his eyes were twinkling. ''My, my, I feel like a character in one of those Wild West stories.''

''That what you're reading nowadays?'' Jed teased.

Pepper had been the one to find Jed the night after he'd been driven out of the valley.

Two people, Jed thought now, had seen him at his worst—a loser. A beaten man. Both had earned his everlasting gratitude. Both were in this room together.

It was almost scary, come to think about it. Not that he necessarily believed all those Bible stories he'd heard—although the one about the Good Samaritan definitely had the ring of truth.

''My back hurts, I'm going to bed,'' said Lorly. ''I've got a lot of sewing to do starting early tomorrow,'' she added with a sly look at Eleanor.

George stood. ''Preacher? Did Lorly show you where you're sleeping? You and Jed can share Zach's room, Eleanor's in with Lorly, and Zach can bunk in with the girls.''

Well, that answered that. ''What about you, George?'' Eleanor asked.

"I won't be able to sleep much tonight. I'll just sit up and keep an ear out for anything…unusual."

"I'll spell you after a couple of hours," Jed said quietly. He looked at Eleanor. Soon, his eyes promised. They still had a few things to do first, a few details to work out, but as long as she was where he could see her whenever he glanced up—where he could hold her when no one was looking—then he might be able to survive the wait.

The night passed quietly, with the two men talking in a way they never had before. Before, they'd been too young. George had always been serious; Jed, wild as a buck. They talked about old Loran and his first wife, George's mother, and about Jed's mother, Bess, whom both boys had loved unreservedly.

They talked about the farm and the fact that Loran had seen fit to leave it to George alone. Jed said, "Smartest thing he ever did, I guess. I'd have lost it, sure's the world. Probably gambled it away. That is, if I'd lived long enough. Hadn't been for Pepper…"

He let the words trail off. Both men recognized the truth; at the time, George had been ready to take on the responsibility whereas Jed had not. Loran might have loved his two sons equally, but he was too smart a man to risk losing what had been passed on to him by his own father and grandfather.

Jed set out early, as planned, taking time only for a quick breakfast. The sun hadn't yet cleared the far ridge when the family gathered on the front porch to watch him ride out. All but Pepper, who was not an early riser now that he was retired.

Zach stood beside his father, feet and hands positioned

in exactly the same way. He said, "He didn't look mean to me."

"He bites, though. He'll kick when you aren't expecting it, too," said Eleanor, knowing the little boy had been begging to be allowed to ride his uncle Jed's horse.

Once the dust had settled behind horse and rider, George said, "I think I'll go bring those saddlebags inside the house. Wouldn't want a twister to blow up all of a sudden and scatter the money all the way back to Asheville. Happens now and then this time of year."

"Ha," Lorly crowed. "I know you, you want to count it, see if it's all there. Jed said there's more than enough to pay the interest, even after he spent some of it buying himself a new saddle and some clothes and things."

Eleanor said, "There was even more, but it was stolen along with McGee and his saddle. He got the horse back, but there was no way we could recover the rest. We told you all that, though, didn't we?"

"No more'n a dozen times," George told her, but he was grinning. They were all keyed up, waiting for the coming confrontation. All but the children, who started a game of hopscotch. Zach lifted his baby sister under the arms and swung her over the lines. Eleanor thought it was the sweetest thing she'd ever seen a child do.

Nine months, she promised herself. Nine months to the day after she was married, she would be in the same shape Lorly was in now, and that would be only the beginning. She could hardly wait!

They trooped back inside, but no one could concentrate on anything but the coming meeting. First one, then another would wonder aloud whether or not Jed had got there yet. Whether or not he'd met with Stanfield.

It was Eleanor who said, "What if he's not there? Mr.

Stanfield, I mean. Jed didn't exactly have an appointment with him, did he?''

Which engendered yet another round of speculation.

Jed had been riding for perhaps three-quarters of an hour when he spotted someone headed his way. There was only one road down the center of the valley, leading from the Dulah farm past Scotts', the Stanfields' and on to the Gillikins', all the land but the Dulahs' now owned by Sam Stanfield. The Scott and Gillikin families had left the valley more than a year ago, according to George. Which meant that whoever was barreling this way in a two-wheeler had probably come from Stanfield's place.

If it was Pete Marshall, Stanfield's foreman, Jed had his own debt to pay. It wasn't exactly the way he wanted to start off the day, beating the crap out of a man, but the opportunity might not come again.

It wasn't Pete. Pete's hair was the color of dry grass. Besides, he'd always worn a black, curl-brimmed Stetson. Drove standing up, too, not sitting on a bench seat.

Jed reined McGee to a walk and narrowed his eyes against the harsh morning sun. A woman?

Damned if it wasn't. With her back to the sun, he couldn't see her face, but she was wearing a shiny blue dress, a flowered bonnet and yellow gloves.

He came to a halt and waited. Where the devil could she be going in such a hurry? To see Lorly? Might be a midwife…it was about that time. But George hadn't said anything about expecting one.

"Vera?" he muttered as the distance closed. The face was the same…sort of. But—

"Jed? I heard you were back."

He nodded slowly. "How do, Vera. You're looking…fit.''

It was the best he could do, caught off guard. She'd put on some pounds since the last time he'd seen her. Squeezed up inside that shiny blue dress, she looked red-faced and fit to bust wide-open. The one thing she didn't look was happy to see him.

"Did George tell you about me?" she demanded. Had her voice always been that shrill? Funny, he didn't remember her voice at all.

"About you?" Move out of the way, lady, I'm in a hurry here. He thought it, but was too polite to say it. Marginally.

"About me marrying Pete Marshall. I reckon you wondered about that, seeing's I wrote you. You did get my letter, didn't you? I never heard back, but George said you were moving around a lot."

"Yeah, I was." What the devil was she up to? The Vera he remembered wouldn't have gotten up this early if her bed was on fire. Stay out all night and sleep till noon, that was more her style.

"Yes, well...I had to."

She had to. Had to what? Get up early this morning? "Were you on your way to see Lorly?"

She blew out her cheeks like a puff adder. "I told you, didn't you hear me? Jed, can we go somewhere and talk? It's warm out here in the sun and this bench is miserable. I told Daddy I wanted a padded seat, but you know Daddy."

He did indeed. "Vera, this isn't a good time for me. I'm on the way right now to see your father, and I'm already running late."

"About the money," she said, and his eyes narrowed further. "Oh, I know all about the money. Everybody's heard how you went off and got filthy rich and now you're back to lord it all over everybody in the valley. Jed, there's something you don't understand.''

There was a lot he didn't understand, he'd be the first to admit that, ''Vera, s'far's I know, there's not that many people left in the valley.''

''Well, there's me. And our son.'' She waited. Jed was starting to sweat. He'd had a bad feeling from the moment he'd recognized her. It wasn't getting any better.

''Your son. Yeah, I think George mentioned you and Pete had a son. Is that the only one?'' Maybe that explained the added weight. She might be breeding right now. She didn't look anything like Lorly, but then, Lorly was tall and skinny—used to be skinny. Vera was built more like one of George's part-Angus heifers, low to the ground and blocky.

She teared up, and he thought, God alive, not now! ''Look, Vera, maybe we can get together before I leave the valley, but right now—''

''He's yours! Little Petey is *your* son, not Pete's. I found out I was expecting right after you ran away, and Daddy made me marry Pete, but I hate him! Now that you're back, we can—''

Oh, Jesus. Oh, Jesus. ''Look, Vera, I can't talk about that right now. I need to think. But first I need to see your father before he gets away.''

She beamed, her damp eyes miraculously clear again. ''Fine, you talk to Daddy, tell him you're willing to take over your rightful responsibilities. I'm sure we can work something out.''

Chapter Twenty-Three

Jed's head was still spinning when he pulled up before Stanfield's square, yellow house. It was the only painted house in the valley. Biggest one, too. You'd think the man had a whole herd of young'uns instead of one daughter and one grandson.

A grandson.

Was it possible? Could Vera be telling the truth?

He had no idea whether or not he could trust her, as they'd both been young back when they'd known each other. Neither of them had done a whole lot of talking. He didn't know...he just didn't know.

Hitching McGee to the rail, he strode up the front walk and banged a fist on the door. While he waited, he reminded himself that she'd lied to her father about slipping out all those nights when she'd met him at the lineshack. But that didn't mean she was lying now.

Someone was home, he could hear footsteps. Hear the sound of a door slamming somewhere inside, and then a querulous voice muttering, "Awright, awright, I'm coming, dammit, I'm coming!"

No maid to answer the door? "How the mighty have fallen," Jed muttered. He remembered reading it somewhere. Couldn't recall just where or when, much less who'd said it.

Sam Stanfield had changed. The same eight years that had broadened Jed, both physically and mentally, turning him into—well, at least not the same ignorant fool he'd been at age seventeen—had had another effect on the old man. The last time he'd seen Stanfield, he'd had to look up. Way up. Jed had been lying on the ground with a ring of grim-faced men surrounding him; one holding a buggy whip, two others rubbing raw knuckles and another one, Pete Marshall, coming at him with a red-hot iron.

"Heard you were back. Whatya want?" Never tall, the old man was now stooped, his lined skin a sickly shade of yellow that hinted at liverishness.

"Business," Jed said, surprised at the lack of emotion he felt. He would have his revenge, all right, but it wouldn't be physical. "Can we set up a meeting in a couple of hours? George and a friend of ours will be waiting at the property line."

"Heard you went off and robbed a bank or something. You want to pay off Dulah's loan, bring the money to me here. I ain't riding out nowhere."

Jed could think of a dozen things he'd like to say. He said none of them. Some scars remained forever, others faded. At least his was in a place where he didn't have to look at it. This poor shell of a man faced his own scars each time he looked in a mirror to shave.

The smell of burning bacon drifted into the front hall. Stanfield yelled over his shoulder, "Take the damned pan off the stove, you idiot!" And then he mumbled something about not trusting anyone to do a damned thing. "Where's Vera?" he yelled.

"Out," someone—a man, Jed thought—called back.

"I passed her on the road," he said. "I think she was headed over to see George's wife."

Stanfield eyed him as if he'd turned into a jackass. "Why'n hell she do that? Got no call to go running all over the neighborhood."

"She said something about having a son. I didn't realize you had grandchildren." What ailed him, Jed wondered. He was almost feeling sorry for the old bastard.

"Boy's all right, I guess. No worse'n most young'uns. Girl sent him off yesterday to stay with Pete's folk, like the plague was coming or something. Plumb dotty." The old man twisted his neck to glare up at Jed. "Well? You gonna go get the money or stand here wasting my time?"

Just then Vera wheeled into the yard. Glancing over his shoulder, Jed said quickly, "I'll be back with George, a witness and the money," and then he hurried out to where he'd left McGee while Vera was handing the trap over to a hired hand.

She called out for him to wait. He tipped his hat—his new hat, bought along with new boots, new Levi's, two new shirts and a bolt of the very finest dress goods—and kept on going.

From the open doorway he heard Stanfield yell after him, "What witness? We don't need no goddamned witness, just bring me the damned money!"

The sun was blazing down with a vengeance by the time Jed reached the post that marked the line between the two properties. In past years the thing had had a habit of moving farther onto the Dulah side until Loran had caught Stanfield's men in the act of digging up the post to move it yet again. He'd held a gun on them and forced them to plant it back in its original position, then sent his own hired man out to pour a slab of cement around it.

So far as Jed knew, the marker hadn't moved since.

Hard to tell, though. Eight years was a long time. Bushes grew into trees, trees blew down or broke under a coating of ice. Winters weren't always easy this deep into the mountains, but the valley was sheltered from the worst winds. Up on Mount Mitchell, it was nothing to have winds of over a hundred miles an hour.

Jed wondered idly how anyone could tell how fast the wind was blowing. Something else to look up once he got close to another set of encyclopedias.

And then he wondered what the devil Vera had been talking about. Could it possibly be true that he'd fathered a son with her? What the hell was he supposed to do about it now?

Thank God she was already married, he thought, swallowing a feeling of guilt.

"What took you so long?" George met him halfway between the house and the property line.

Jed reined in. "He won't come. We'll have to go there."

"When?"

"Sooner, the better, I guess. Is Pepper up and around yet?"

"Oh, yeah. Him and your lady are talking about starting up a school. Lorly's ragging 'em on."

George wheeled his mount around, but Jed called him back. "Wait up a minute, will you? Listen, I heard something that's got me worried. You know anything about this kid of Vera's? I met her on the way there and she said— she claimed—" Dragging out a handkerchief, he lifted his hat, mopped his forehead and then shook his head. "You happen to know when the kid was born?"

George looked thoughtful. "It was a long time ago, I know that much. She was already married by then, else I reckon there'd have been talk. Why?"

Jed was too worried to keep it to himself. At any other

time, he might have tried to work things out alone, figuring times and ages. Come to that, he wasn't even certain of the date when he'd left the valley. Early August, he seemed to remember, but he sure as hell hadn't been in any shape to look at a calendar.

"She claims he's mine. Said her pa made her marry Pete before the baby started showing, but he's not Pete's, he's…mine."

He had a son? Sweet Jesus, no—not this way, he thought, seeing all his dreams collapsing like a house of cards. Like that burned out tool shed.

After a silence that lasted several minutes—lasted until McGee grew impatient and tried to take a bite of Jed's new boot—George said, "Let's get this other thing over with first. Then I'll go with you to talk to Pete."

"What the hell good will that do? Who do you think used a red-hot iron on my ass?" Jed rode on ahead, his shoulders hunched as if he were in pain.

George pulled up beside him. "What are you talking about?"

"Guess I forgot to tell you that part. Stanfield not only had his men hold me while they beat the shit out of me, the old man himself planted his foot on my neck and held me down while Pete—I'm pretty sure it was him—burned a Bar Double S on my sitting part."

"Pity he didn't think to bring a pattern, but we can cut it from one of my old dresses and pin it on you to fit the bodice. The hem'll be easy. I can lay it out on the parlor floor if you'll keep the young'uns out."

"Lorly, you're not going to crawl around on the floor," Eleanor scolded. "Don't you dare even think of doing such a thing. I've cut down and made over more dresses than I

can remember. Schoolteachers don't earn enough to keep
body and soul together.''

The women talked of practical matters like thread and
buttons—Jed hadn't thought to bring any—and shoes. He
had brought her a pair of lovely shoes that fit perfectly.
They were red kid.

"White cotton thread'll be close enough, and I've got
aplenty of that. We'll use the lace overskirt from my dress.
I can soak it out and put it in the sun, either that or use it
like it is. If we cut off a few medallions and sew them on
the bodice, the different color won't look out of place at
all.''

And on it went, all morning, while the three men dealt
with Sam Stanfield. They had left more than two hours
earlier. Jed hadn't even come inside, sending George in to
get Pepper while he hitched up the buggy.

From time to time Lorly would pause, her gaze drifting
to the window. "Nothing can go wrong, can it? I don't
see how it can when they have the money and a witness
to see that Stanfield doesn't get up to any shenanigans.''

"Jed can take care of it. Stop worrying.''

"What if I start having my baby just as Pepper's getting
ready to perform the ceremony?''

"Why then, he'll just do a christening first. We'll celebrate that and get on with the wedding later. Another
day's not going to matter.''

"Ha,'' Lorly said, and Eleanor blushed. The house was
large for a country farmhouse, but there was little privacy
to be found, not even out in the barn.

On her hands and knees, Eleanor crawled around on the
floor, measuring and cutting first the bodice, then the
sleeves, a band to double over for a collar and another,
narrower one for piping. The rest of the material, a rich
ivory sateen, would be used for a simple gathered skirt,

which would be much quicker to make than a paneled skirt.

From time to time, Lorly struggled up and went to the door to look out. "It shouldn't be taking this long. Something's gone wrong, I just know it has."

"It takes as long as it takes. They're probably talking, that's all. Maybe Jed's explaining that the railroad's not coming here anyway, that they've already bought land from him on the other side of the ridge. I know he's been looking forward to telling Mr. Stanfield that."

"You know about Jed and Vera, I suppose?"

With a mouthful of straight pins, Eleanor nodded. "His old sweetheart. He showed me her letter. It was…sweet."

"She came here looking for him."

Eleanor glanced up at that. "I know. I was here, remember?"

"Wits gone begging, as usual." Lorly shrugged. "I told her Jed was gone. She said she'd see him when he got back, but she hasn't showed up yet. Maybe we'll get lucky."

"She's married now, isn't she?"

Lorly nodded. "Married her father's foreman. I reckon he'll take over the place until the boy's old enough. Little Petey takes after his father, thank goodness. Vera's not got the brains of a hat pin. Spiteful female, I never did like her, even when we were children. Papa used to hold services at Stanfield's place for his hired hands and their families once a month when we came through the valley. I remember once when the cook made rice pudding for dessert and Vera spit in my bowl when no one was looking. She couldn't have been more than five years old."

Eleanor laughed. "What did you do, tell her mama?"

"Her mama died when she was born. I was scared of

her daddy, he had mean eyes, so I waited until we went out to play again and put a caterpillar down her back.''

The two women fed the children and settled them for a nap. Eleanor urged Lorly to go to join them. "You need to get off your feet. Just look at those ankles."

From her place on the sofa, Lorly peered over the swell of her belly to her bare feet. "I know, it's disgraceful. They look like sausages. I couldn't sleep, though, even if I went to bed. I'd just lie there wondering what was going on. Go look out the front door again, will you?"

From the doorway, Eleanor searched for a cloud of dust. The air smelled faintly of manure, faintly of sweet shrub and mountain ash. Several dozen steers grazed peacefully in a pasture bordered on the far side by a narrow creek. How could one valley be so different from another, she wondered, when they were scarcely more than a hundred miles apart? Less than that, as the crow flew.

She straightened, squinting against the sun. "They're coming," she called softly so as not to wake the children.

"Oh, glory be, how do they look? Can you see their faces yet?"

"Jed's riding, George and Pepper are in the buggy, and no, I can't see their faces."

By the time the men pulled into the clearing between house and barn, both women were standing on the front porch. George waved, and Lorly whispered, "It's all right, thank God. What did I tell you?"

"You told me Stanfield was going to claim you owed him twice that much, and he wouldn't take Jed's money. You told me the buggy was going to throw a wheel and they'd be late, and—"

"Oh, hush, I had my fingers crossed."

Everyone talked at once. Everyone except Jed.

Pepper said, "My, my, that's a thirsty ride, isn't it?"

Eleanor said, "I'll pour cold tea…unless you'd rather have water. Or coffee?"

George said, "Honey, you need to get off those feet. Come on in the front room and…what the devil is that all over the floor?"

So then they laughed and Lorly explained about the wedding gown they were cutting out, and Jed still didn't say a word. Looking at him, Eleanor felt herself grow cold. He looked as if he were coming down with something.

She busied herself gathering up the dress parts while Lorly set out tumblers for the cold sweetened tea she favored. "If you want coffee, George, you'll have to stoke up the fire again. I let it go out, it's just so blessed warm in here."

Eleanor's gaze followed Jed as he went outside and stood, his back to her, staring out in the direction they had just come from. She joined him there. "Jed? Is something wrong? Did you get the deed, or whatever papers were necessary?"

He drew in a deep breath and let it out. "Cancelled note. Signed by both parties and duly witnessed. Once I told him—Stanfield, that is—where the railroad had bought land, all the fight seemed to drain right out of him."

"Then…is everything all right?"

It took forever, but finally he replied. Without looking at her, he said, "I don't know. We might have to postpone our wedding for a while, or even…"

Or even call it off. The words echoed as if he'd spoken them aloud.

He turned to her then, and she was reminded of the wounded man she had dragged up the hill and into her home again. This time there were no obvious wounds, but his tormented eyes told their own story. Something bad had happened.

"Jed, tell me," she whispered.

He shook his head. "Not yet." He clasped her face in his hands and said, "Tell George I'll be back by nightfall. One way or another, we'll work this out, I promise."

Chapter Twenty-Four

There were several men working in the area, two loading hay into the loft, two more running cattle through a chute. Jed found the man he sought in the equipment shed. To be sure he had the right man, he called him by name. "Marshall?"

Pete Marshall had aged more than eight years would account for. "Heard you were back," he said by way of greeting. He'd been sharpening a disc harrow. Laying aside his file, he straightened, his eyes watchful.

Jed stood, feet braced apart, sizing up his opponent...if it came to that. "I'm back," he allowed.

"Heard you went off and got rich."

He hadn't exactly gotten rich, but he wasn't about to say so. "Heard you and Vera got married after I left." *After I was beaten, branded and run the hell out of the valley. I hope she was worth it.*

The other man nodded. His hair was still thick, but more gray than blond now. He couldn't be much older than George. Late twenties, early thirties. He looked older. Bitter. "You come to pay me back for what I did?"

"I'll fight you, one on one, but that's not what I came for."

Pete nodded toward the personnel door. "Come on out back where we can talk private. There's things I've wanted to say to you for a long time. Might as well get 'em off my chest before you beat the shit out of me."

Outside, Pete led the way over to a five-rail fence. Hooking a boot heel over the bottom rung, he leaned his elbows on the top rail and commenced to talk. "I live to be a hundred, I'll never quit thinking about it. Man, I was so sick after that, I puked up my guts, that's the flat-out truth. I quit that same day, but I ended up coming back when Vera…" He broke off and shook his head.

Jed waited. He knew what he was going to hear and it tore him up worse than a knife in his belly. "Vera. Oh, yeah. I guess I owe you for that, too. You want to call it a draw, we'll work out the finances."

Pete shot him a wary. "Finances?"

"For the kid's upkeep."

"Why the devil you want to do a thing like that? Did she mean that much to you?"

Jed knew in his heart she hadn't, not even back when they were going at it hot and heavy most every night, but he felt like a dog admitting it. Whatever had happened all those years ago, it was Pete's wife they were talking about now. "She was…well, hell, you knew her," he said lamely.

"Me and half the men in the valley. The Gillikin boys, that I know for sure, and I'm pretty certain Amos Scott's foreman was getting into her bloomers that same summer. You just happened to be the one she got caught out with."

Jed stiffened away from the fence. "Whoa, back up. You telling me she—Vera—she was messing around with somebody else? When the hell did she have time? She was with me three nights a week all that summer. Up until we got caught, at least."

"She was with me at least two of those other nights. That's why I felt so damned bad when you were the one got caught when the old man saw her climbing out her window and had her followed. Maybe it even had something to do with…ah, hell, you know what I mean. What happened—guilt can make a man do crazy things.'' He took a deep breath, raked his hand through his hair and said, "Look, Blackstone, I needed that job. All my folks had was what I sent 'em, else they'd have ended up in the poorhouse, sure's the world.''

"You just said you quit.''

"Yeah, I quit. Got drunk, stayed that way until Stanfield tracked me down a couple of weeks later with a proposition. Offered me a big bonus and said I could bring my folks back here with me if I'd marry Vera and come back to work.'' He spread his callused hands in a gesture of helplessness. "What would you have done?''

It was an hour or so after dark when Jed got back. Eleanor had spent more time at the front door watching for him than she had in the kitchen helping put supper on the table. Zach stood beside her, looking, too, for a while. He asked if she was looking for a shooting star.

"I suppose I am,'' she said, forcing a smile.

He nodded, looking more than ever like his father. "Mama says if you see one, it don't mean God's shootin' at us. She says it means good luck. Do you believe that?''

"Zach-y, come finish your supper and quit bothering Miss Eleanor.''

Standing beside her, arms crossed, feet planted apart, the little boy looked up at Eleanor. His face was in shadow. Fortunately, hers was, too, else he'd have seen the tears in her eyes and wondered why she was crying when everyone else was celebrating. "You coming to supper?''

"I'm not hungry tonight."

"Good thing. Pa cooked, and he can't cook worth a damn."

"Worth shucks, you mean," Eleanor admonished gently.

"'S what I meant. I'll save you a potato. They're okay."

Eleanor had gathered up the scattered parts of her wedding gown, folding them away out of sight. The light wasn't good enough to work at night, and besides, with all the talking and celebrating, work of any kind was the last thing on their minds.

"You stay downstairs," she told her hostess. "I'll get the children settled and then I think I'll go to bed, too. All that crawling around on the floor today..."

She managed to escape before the tears fell again. She even managed to fall asleep after hours of lying awake and wondering what had happened to destroy her shiny new dream.

They were having breakfast the next morning, the two women and the children, when two people rode up to the house. Leaning back in her chair, Eleanor reported, "It's a man and...a little boy."

Zach slid down from his chair and raced to the door, with Lorly calling after him to come and finish his oatmeal.

"There's no more children left in the valley, if you don't count Vera and Pete's boy."

"Why not count them?" She was coming to be more and more curious about everything pertaining to the woman Jed had once loved.

"Well, for one thing, we're not on visiting terms with any of the Stanfields, not even the children."

"Didn't Vera come just the other day?"

"Looking for Jed."

"Well, this is a man, not a woman."

By that time, Lorly had dragged herself to a standing position and was staring out the kitchen window. "That's Pete Marshall," she murmured. "Now what in the world do you think he wants here? I reckon that's his boy with him, I haven't seen him but once in his life when the Gillikins were leaving. George and I went to say goodbye and he was hanging off his granddaddy's gate, looking lonesome."

"They're out in front of the barn talking. George and Jed and Mr. Marshall. The boy's over near the paddock fence where…"

Suddenly, she let out a shout and ran out of the house, waving her arms. "Get away from there! Jed, for Lord's sake, do something!"

The three men turned to gawk at her. The towheaded boy looked from the horse to her and back again. Eleanor yelled, "McGee, you bite that child and I'll rip your ears off! Now behave yourself!"

And then the stranger swooped up his son and Jed headed for the small paddock. By that time, a breathless Eleanor had joined them. "You shouldn't have left him where the children could reach through the fence."

"Sorry about that. Zach knows he bites, and the girls don't come out here that much, but you're right." He was grinning as if it were a great big joke. She felt like swatting him, and not just for breaking her heart. Insensitive clod.

"Honey, I want you to meet some people," Jed said, slipping an arm around her waist. "This is Pete Marshall and this is his son, Petey."

Pete Marshall? But wasn't he Stanfield's foreman as well as his son-in-law? Puzzled, Eleanor nevertheless extended her hand to the man and smiled at the boy, who seemed more interested in McGee than in her. "I hope I didn't scare you, but you see, that horse is rather infamous.''

Jed, with a fatuous grin, said, "Infamous. You can tell right off she's a schoolteacher, can't you? Even talking about starting a school right here in the valley, once we're married. Her and the Reverend Pepperdine.''

It never even occurred to her to correct his grammar. Once they were *married?* Then the wedding was on again? Since when?

"Where'd you get him? How long you had him? He ever bite you?'' the boy asked. He was a smaller edition of his father, with the same pale hair, the same widow's peak. Blue eyes instead of gray, like his father's, and with a look of bright expectation instead of one of defeat, but definitely a chip off the old block, as the saying went.

Jed said, "I met McGee about eight years ago. We had a lot in common about that time and decided to team up.''

"I got a pony, but he's already too little. Pop says I can have me a real horse for my next birthday. I'll be seven years old then. How old is he?'' He looked toward Zach, who was showing off by poking hay through the fence at McGee.

"'Bout the same age you are,'' George reported.

"I'm bigger,'' Petey boasted.

"You're not, neither, I am,'' Zach shot back, and the two boys squared off, glowering at each other until Pete Marshall called a halt. "'Mon, son, time to go home.''

"Can I come back and play sometime?''

"We'll see,'' his father promised, meeting Jed's eyes in silent understanding.

All debts were canceled, the future still to be written.

By the next morning, the front parlor was off-limits again, the floor spread with ivory sateen and ecru lace. On her knees pinning together various parts, Eleanor was entertaining the two little girls with a story while Zach and the three men, Pepper included, were outside surveying the ruins of the tool shed and discussing whether to build it back on the same location or farther away from the house.

Lorly, propped up with bed pillows on the sofa, said, "I hate to tell you this, but I'm afraid you're going to have to set your sewing aside again. Call George in to help me to the bedroom and then get the children out of the house, it frightens them when I yell."

Three days later, the wedding between Jedediah Blackstone and Eleanor Scarborough Miller took place in front of the fireplace in the Dulahs' parlor. Guests had not been invited, and so it wasn't important that the flowers that had been gathered by the three Dulah children—weeds, for the most part—were wilted now. They'd been lovingly arranged in various jars and tumblers.

It wasn't important that the groom wore Levi's and a borrowed necktie, nor that the bride wore a gown that was partly basted and partly pinned together. With red shoes.

Nor that her two-inch-long curls were covered by a lace overskirt that doubled as a veil.

The three eldest Dulah children were suitably solemn, the youngest, Laura Eleanor, belched noisily once or twice, but for the most part, behaved with suitable decorum.

"Dearly beloved," Pepper intoned, and Eleanor squeezed Jed's hand tightly.

"Finally," he mouthed.

And before they quite realized it, he was instructed to kiss the bride. Which he did, with rather indecorous enthusiasm. The girls threw handfuls of rice; Zach threw a handful of cracked corn. Lorly scolded, "I told you to wait until they were outside,'' but it didn't matter. It would be swept out anyway, for the yard chickens to scratch in.

While the men toasted the occasion in white liquor that could have come all the way from Alaska's still, for all anyone knew, Eleanor took the baby up in her arms. ''I'll miss you, you precious thing. Don't do too much growing before I get back, will you?''

''Not likely,'' Lorly said dryly. ''You'll be gone what— three days?''

''As long as it takes. Probably no more than that.''

The plan was to borrow money, from a legitimate bank this time, against the forty or so acres left over from the railroad purchase, and use it to build a house at the far end of the Dulah farm. George needed help; Jed needed a place to settle. Where better than where both his parents were buried—where he had grown up, made any number of mistakes, and learned from each one.

Jed came up from behind her, slipped his arms around her waist and said, ''Trap's ready. If we leave now, we can be in Asheville by suppertime.''

Looking from Eleanor to Jed and back and seeing the melting look of love on their faces, Lorly sighed. ''Don't forget what you're going to town to accomplish. Have you got your shopping list, El? Don't forget the books.''

''I won't. We won't. Tell Pepper to remember to take his medicine before he goes to bed, and tell Zach—''

''Go,'' Lorly said, laughing. ''Just go, will you?''

And they went. Hands clinging, touches lingering, eyes speaking without words of a lifetime commitment to family and friends, to a future filled with riches more valuable than gold.

* * * * *

ITCHIN' FOR SOME ROLLICKING ROMANCES SET ON THE AMERICAN FRONTIER? THEN TAKE A GANDER AT THESE TANTALIZING TALES FROM HARLEQUIN HISTORICALS

On sale September 2003

WINTER WOMAN by Jenna Kernan
(Colorado, 1835)

After braving the winter alone in the Rockies, a defiant woman is entrusted to the care of a gruff trapper!

THE MATCHMAKER by Lisa Plumley
(Arizona territory, 1882)

Will a confirmed bachelor be bitten by the love bug when he woos a young woman in order to flush out the mysterious Morrow Creek matchmaker?

On sale October 2003

WYOMING WILDCAT by Elizabeth Lane
(Wyoming, 1866)

A blizzard ignites hot-blooded passions between a white medicine woman and an amnesiac man, but an ominous secret looms on the horizon....

THE OTHER GROOM by Lisa Bingham
(Boston and New York, 1870)

When a penniless woman masquerades as the daughter of a powerful marquis, her intended groom risks it all to protect her from harm!

Visit us at www.eHarlequin.com

HARLEQUIN HISTORICALS®

Want to be swept away by electrifying romance and heart-pounding adventure? Then experience it all within the pages of these Harlequin Historical tales

On sale September 2003

THE GOLDEN LORD by Miranda Jarrett

Book #2 in *The Lordly Claremonts* series

The best-laid plans go awry when a woman faking amnesia falls for the dashing duke she's supposed to be conning!

THE KNIGHT'S CONQUEST by Juliet Landon

When a proud noblewoman is offered as the prize at a jousting tournament, can she count on a bold-hearted knight to grant her the freedom— and the love—she ardently desires?

On sale October 2003

IN THE KING'S SERVICE by Margaret Moore

Look for this exciting installment of the *Warrior* series!

A handsome knight on a mission for the king becomes enamored with the "plain" sister of a famous beauty!

THE KNIGHT AND THE SEER by Ruth Langan

In order to exact his revenge, a tortured military man enters the Mystical Kingdom and enlists a bewitching psychic to summon the spirit of his murdered father....

Visit us at www.eHarlequin.com

HARLEQUIN HISTORICALS®

HHMED32